D0889532

The text of this book is composed in Garamond with the display set in RB No2.

Author photograph © Greg Levin

Library of Congress Cataloging-in-Publication Data

Levin, Greg

The Exit Man / Greg Levin.

Published by White Rock Press First Printing, 2014

ISBN 978-0-9904029-1-6

the exit man

Greg Levin

To my brother Jeff.
(4/11/63 - 1/1/07)

CHAPTER 1

My client smiles calmly at me as I slip the clear plastic bag over his head. After fastening the bag around his neck using the attached Velcro straps, I take the tube that extends from the controlled-release nozzle of the helium tank that sits beside his armchair and place the end of the tube into the small hole in the bag. I use a couple of pieces of duct tape to make sure that where the tube enters the bag is airtight.

"Comfortable?" I ask.

Two thumbs up and another smile.

I place one of my gloved hands on his knee and smile back. "I'm ready if you are."

Another thumbs up and a nod.

I give the valve atop the helium tank nozzle a quarter turn counterclockwise to start the release of gas.

"*Ave atque vale,*" I say. Latin for "hail and farewell." It's my standard closing.

My client clasps his hands in front of him, smiles again, and mouths "Thank you" through the plastic bag before closing his eyes.

I pick up the copy of *Arthur Rimbaud: The Complete Works* that's lying on the end table near my client, sit down on the folded chair next to him, and begin reading aloud from page 219, as previously instructed. Rimbaud has never been my cup of tea, but this reading isn't about me. Besides, I won't be reading for very long. My client will be sound asleep in less than a minute. Dead within five.

Four pages into the prose poem "A Season in Hell," my client's right arm twitches and his head falls forward. He could still just be sleeping, though it's unlikely – I'm a slow reader. Not only that; about one minute in I couldn't resist giving the valve another quarter turn.

It's always a bit difficult to get a clear read on a pulse while wearing surgical gloves, yet it's far too risky to remove them in these situations. I check my client's left wrist and detect nothing. I give it another couple of minutes, which is about all the Rimbaud I can take. After another pulse check reveals no sign of life, I start to undo the Velcro straps of the plastic bag. I turn off the gas valve, remove the tape and rubber tube from the bag and slowly remove the bag from my client's head. Just to be sure, I check the carotid artery. Not a single blip on the radar screen as far as I can tell.

Delivery complete.

After executing my client's exit strategy, it's time to execute mine. First, I place Rimbaud in my client's lap, wondering if the latter's death will be attributed to poetic asphyxiation. I then stuff the helium tank, the plastic bag and the tube into my army surplus duffel bag, which I zip up and leave over by my client's front door. I go back to the den to retrieve the folded chair and return it to the closet from which it came, and then conduct one final inspection to ensure that I've covered all my tracks. All looks good – at least from my perspective. Ask my client's wife what she thinks when she returns home from work in about three hours, and you'll likely get an entirely different answer.

I snap off my surgical gloves and Lycra skull cap and place them in the duffel bag by the door. I then pull out a pair of regular leather gloves and a Yankees cap from one of the side pockets and put them on. I hoist the duffel bag up onto my shoulder, pull my cap down low over my eyes, and open the front door. Not a neighbor in sight.

I step out into the crisp October afternoon and start walking toward my car, which is parked three streets away. I'm now just a harmless guy taking a nice slow stroll, toting a bag, stopping every so often to admire the squirrels, smiling the friendliest smile I can muster at any automobile that happens to drive by. Sure, some overly suspicious neighborhood snoop might be eying me through her kitchen window and wondering who I am, but I look inconspicuous enough. By the time any neighbor gets word of my client, I'll be nothing but a ghost, a fuzzy figment – if remembered at all.

Suicide should come with a warning label: *Don't try this alone.*

If you truly need out and want the job done right, you should seriously consider using an outside expert.

Like me.

Nobody *sets out* to become a euthanasia specialist. It's the sort of profession one might fall into after years of failure or apathy in more traditional fields. Or after reading too much Nietzsche. Or after carefully evaluating the global parking situation.

Or after witnessing an ailing loved one endure lasting physical and emotional suffering.

Or, as in my case, all of the above.

Though it's not exactly accurate to say I fell into the profession. More precisely, it found me.

Prior to my job that centers on cessation, I had one that centered on celebration. Fact is, I've never left the latter. I own a party supply store called Jubilee in Blackport, Oregon. We offer everything from tissue balls and bunting to rentable clowns and bouncy houses. I'll spare you the full list of products and services; just know that if you ever need anything to help celebrate or commemorate a birthday, anniversary, graduation, homecoming, hiring, promotion, pregnancy, parole, bat mitzvah, bar mitzvah, bar exam, engagement, divorce, or Irish death, then you will almost certainly find it in our shop or catalog.

I wasn't the original owner. Jubilee was my father's shop. I had intentionally spent the majority of my post-collegiate life far enough away from Blackport, such as to never be pressured into peddling plastic plates and Mylar balloons. It's not that I was ashamed of my father's line of work; I was merely ashamed of *me* doing it. I was an artist, after all, living free of any bourgeois nine to five shackles and well on my way to making it as an assistant glass blower's apprentice in my late twenties.

But biopsies have a way of changing plans.

Four years ago, when I was 29 and my father 56, he was diagnosed with stage III non-Hodgkin's lymphoma. The chemo quickly wreaked havoc on the man, whose seemingly indefatigable vigor soon succumbed to daily bouts of diarrhea, nausea, and exhaustion. Pain seemed to emanate from his fingers and toes. His hair fell out in clumps. Radiation therapy left him with minor burns across his body. After just a few weeks of treatment, he looked like an angry, elderly skinhead who had fallen asleep in a tanning bed. Not a good look for a man who earned a good portion of his living persuading people with surnames like Goldberg and Horowitz to spring for the jumbo tent at their upcoming event.

Thus I had been called on to lend a temporary hand at the shop while my father completed his initial treatment. Six to eight weeks I was told. My parents viewed the whole arrangement as a win-win: They needed somebody familiar with the inner workings of the enterprise (I had worked there as a teenager and during college breaks) and I, in their eyes, needed something to do that didn't involve me experimenting with molten sand while blitzed on whiskey.

Not that I had to be strongly persuaded into helping out at the store. I am Jewish by blood, thus had enough hereditary guilt already coursing through my veins to eliminate the need for any coercive words from external sources. My father was gravely ill and in need of support – end of story. I had no choice but to step up and make some sacrifices. Besides, it wasn't as if there was much to the life I was being asked to temporarily place on hold. I had been slowly spiraling downward socially and professionally for a few years, with no real prospects for money, love or self-respect on the horizon. I had nothing resembling a career; everything resembling a drinking problem; and a string of short relationships that had each ended in something resembling an Amtrak collision.

Who better to run a shop called Jubilee.

Things ran surprisingly smoothly at the shop during the first few weeks of my father's cancer-fighting sabbatical. I quickly got back up to speed on the various party products and services available, and was able to mimic enough enthusiasm to keep customers happy and engaged.

Actually, the enthusiasm was real – albeit artificially induced. I had gotten a hold of some Adderall after my third day on the job. It was the only way to reduce the number of naps I needed to take during operating hours and to keep up with the frenetic pace of discourse during conversations with heavily caffeinated soccer moms. One little blue pill in the morning and one after lunch gave me just the jolt of functional euphoria required to carry out my daily duties and keep my father's business afloat.

Where amphetamines lifted me through the days, whiskey got me through the nights. The few friends I had back in high school had all long since moved away from Blackport, so I didn't have many social options. Not that it mattered. I was busy consoling my mother while the two of us watched my father wilt. I'd sip my Maker's Mark or my Buffalo Trace before and after dinner and lie to Mom about how everything was going to be okay, how Dad was tough enough to take whatever the gang of angry cells inside him could dish out, how he'd soon be back in the shop selling the hell out of Sweet 16 and Deluxe Pirate Theme party packages.

Whatever hope I was able to raise during that first month or so soon plummeted. The head oncologist pushed it off the ledge. The letters and Roman numerals in his file on my father now spelled out:

STAGE IV.

A.k.a., terminal.

Words and phrases such as "untreatable" and "incurable" and the more direct "fatal" soon followed, spoken to my father and us by clean, clinical faces awash in fluorescent light. Not long thereafter came "maybe six months, maybe more" and "hospice care" and the very bold – though behind Dad's back – "proactive funeral arrangements."

The entire oncology team was shocked at how quickly my father's condition had deteriorated. To go from Stage III to Stage IV so rapidly was completamente loco according to one Nicaraguan doctor, who told me that he and his colleagues were thinking of petitioning the AMA to see if it would consider adding a Stage V to the lymphoma spectrum based solely on my father's unfortunate case.

Naturally, my initial reaction was to point a finger at the professionals. I asked if perhaps some first-year doc had inadvertently given Dad placebos at one point rather than the proper cancer cocktails. I questioned if the team had checked to make sure the radiation machine was actually plugged in for each treatment. (It turns out there was no electricity or actual machine involved in the type of radiation my dad received, but I feel I got my point across to the presumed quacks.)

Quite frankly, I'd rather not relive the weight loss and the chest fluid and the agony and the defeat of my father. If you simply can't control your curiosity, there exist countless websites that elaborate on the progression of Stage IV to Stage Funeral for non-Hodgkin's lymphoma patients.

Suffice it to say that six months turned out to be two, my

mother turned out to be tough, and my father's final words (or more precisely, *word*) turned out to be, "Eli."

The first name of his only son.

Dad's passing cemented my permanent employment status at the store. Worse, it made me seriously question my devout Existentialism, as I was left asking myself over and over, "What choice do I have?" like some spineless fatalist or game show contestant.

But even Sartre himself would have agreed that I couldn't in good conscience make my freshly widowed mother (to whom Jubilee had been left in the will) run the place. The poor woman was in mourning for the man with whom she had spent the past 31 years. And as if that weren't enough, the shop's daily 10 a.m. to 9 p.m. schedule conflicted badly with her early afternoon water aerobics class.

I did consider suggesting that we find a new manager to replace me so that I could return to my basement efficiency apartment in Portland and continue my glass-blowing lessons, but I scoffed at my own shamelessness the way you just did and in the end decided to keep quiet.

Besides, I needed the steady income from the Jubilee job to support my growing speed habit.

As it turns out, my substance abuse was great for business. I was up to six little blue pills a day, fueling me with a level of pep that many customers found infectious. A client would come in with plans for a private garden soiree and leave with enough products to stage a bash of ancient Roman proportions.

It's not that the drugs had turned me into an invasive and aggressive up-seller; rather they stripped me of my negative ions, and the resultant positive charge, with little actual effort from me, inspired clientele to seize the celebration. *Party diem.*

Not *all* customers, however, were so drawn to my newfound frenetic demeanor. Several of the regulars – folks who had known my family and been patrons of Jubilee for years – were confused if not put off by the inexplicable mania I exhibited in the days just leading up to and following my father's death. Evidently, a few close friends had asked my mother why I had suddenly started whistling and skipping in public when I should have been sitting Shiva and sobbing. When my mother confronted me about such concerns, I told her it was all just my odd little way of coping with the tragic loss – and then I apologized for unintentionally disrupting everybody's misery.

But there was one old family friend who was neither bothered nor inspired by my peculiar kinetic spike.

William Rush.

He had far too much on his mind to even notice my abnormal excitation when he came to see me in the shop about a month after Dad's passing.

"Hello Eli, how are you and your mother holding up?" asked the tall and gaunt retired police sergeant, hacking and coughing afterward to remind the world of his advancing emphysema.

"We're doing okay, thanks. And thanks again for the lovely card and your kind sentiments at Dad's memorial service."

"Oh Christ, it was the least I could do." He shook his

head and frowned. "Fucking cancer. Took a damn good man in your father... and a damn fine woman in Mrs. Rush before that."

Sgt. Rush, a widower of three years, was one of my dad's closest friends and the first person I ever heard say "fuck" when I was a kid. He was also the first person I ever heard say "motherfucker" and "cocksucker." Needless to say, I idolized him throughout my formative years.

"Yup, cancer certainly could have chosen two far more deserving people than Dad and Mrs. Rush," I said, anxiously reviewing my awkward phrasing afterward to confirm that I hadn't unwittingly insulted our respective loved ones.

"You could say that again, goddamn it," he responded, before letting out another loud cough and expectorating into his ever-present handkerchief.

"Is there anything I can help you with today, Sgt. Rush?"

He momentarily surveyed the shop, looking uneasy.

"Yes, I think there is. But I just wanted to let you know that it's not a typical request." He looked at me and winked, as if I was supposed to be privy to something.

"Okay, we do atypical here."

"Atypical is putting it lightly, actually." Again with the wink.

"We get all kinds of strange orders and requests here. You can tell me what you need and I'll hook you up."

"Yes. Exactly. That's just what I need – you to *hook* me up."

My initial thought was that Sgt. Rush was on to my amphetamine use and wanted in. Perhaps Adderall helped with emphysema.

"I don't follow, sir."

"Damn it. I was hoping maybe your father had let you in on our arrangement."

"Arrangement? Look, if Dad used to offer you special pricing or services, I would be more than happy to do the–"

"No, Eli, that's not what I'm talking about. Shit, this is not going to be easy."

I was getting anxious. Sgt. Rush had never been one to beat around the bush. Maybe he had a thing for mannequins or ladies' unlaundered costumes and relied on my father for such supplies. I dared to delve further.

"Listen, whatever you used to get from Dad you can get from me."

"It's not something I got from him, it's just something we had been discussing before he got sick."

"Okay, well, all you have to do is tell me what–"

"He was going to help me out in a big way."

"I see, just tell me–"

"And receive twenty thousand dollars for his services."

"Twenty grand?"

"Yup, for about an hour of his time."

"Twenty grand for an hour's work? And just who was he going to have to kill?" I asked with a laugh.

"Me," he said without one.

CHAPTER 2

I had never been as impressed by my father as I was during those fleeting seconds when I posthumously suspected him of being a hitman.

Not that I condone murder or lethal violence – quite the contrary – but when you bring "assassin" into the equation and preface it with "professional," things quickly switch from off-putting to engrossing. Add in the fact that the assassin in question is your dead dad whom you had never known to be anything other than a humble merchant, and the intrigue increases exponentially.

Until the conversation continues.

"You asked my father to *kill* you?" I spoke in a hushed voice with my hand partially covering my mouth, even though we were alone in the shop.

"Sorry Eli – I should have handled that last part more subtly," said Sgt. Rush. "'Kill' is not the word. 'Assist' is much more accurate."

"Assist? You were going to pay my father twenty grand to 'assist' you. With what, exactly?

"Stopping my cough."

"What the... why?"

"C'mon Eli, *look* at me," Sgt. Rush said just before unloading some more dust and dry phlegm into his handkerchief.

"What? You're still a strong man... barely in your sixties. You used to get shot at by junkies and gang-bangers – surely you can hack a little emphysema?"

I was aware that I was severely understating his health condition, and that I had inadvertently issued a bad pun, but it was a very emotionally charged moment with little room for stronger arguments or better diction.

"Aw, Christ, will you spare me the obligatory 'You have everything to live for' bullshit and just hear me out?"

"And why would you want to involve my father in this?"

"I'm getting to that, if you'd just close your mouth and open your ears for a second."

"Sorry. I'm listening."

Sgt. Rush cleared what was left of his throat, walked around to my side of the shop counter and sat down in the seat next to mine.

"First off, I've heard it all – hell I even used to say it all myself when on the force: 'Suicide is a cowardly act.' 'Suicide is selfish.' Oh, and my favorite old chestnut, 'Suicide is a permanent solution to a temporary problem' – well, *not* when you're chronically ill with *two* diseases, one of which eats your mind."

"Wait, what else do you have?"

"Alzheimer's. Goddamn early-onset 'SDAT' – Senile Dementia of the Alzheimer Type, to be more specific."

"Oh shit. I'm sorry, Sgt. Rush, I had no idea."

"Yeah, apparently neither will I within the next few months. And as for being 'cowardly' and 'selfish', that's just people getting angry and tossing out insults because they're too afraid to admit that sometimes taking one's own life makes sense."

"Okay, but what are we *supposed* to say when a friend mentions suicide? 'Hey, good idea, Bill – let me know how I can help.'"

"No, but people do need to try to see things from the perspective of those in anguish. Especially when a degenerative disease – or two – is involved. To NOT do so, *that's* selfish."

"I agree. But it's one thing to respect one's decision to die, it's quite another to *help* them carry it out. It's gruesome and, uh, highly illegal. Why wouldn't you just do it yourself, like normal suicidal people do – not that I'm condoning it."

"Okay, at least we're moving past the platitudes now and into the more pressing questions."

"Yes, pressing indeed. Why did you ask my father to help you kill yourself?"

"I came to your father for three reasons: First, it's really fucking hard to follow through with the act of suicide if you aren't insane, no matter how badly you want out. Secondly, I knew your father was the kind of man who would do almost anything for a friend. And finally, he had easy access to the type of equipment needed for the job."

"What equipment?"

"Helium."

"Helium? That's just going to give you a squeaky voice."

"I'm not talking about inhaling a few small balloons' worth. I'm talking about inhaling a steady flow of the stuff, which is highly lethal and, when done right, one of the most painless ways to die."

Sgt. Rush was grinning – actually grinning – as he delivered his macabre chemistry lesson.

"And best of all, helium is nearly undetectable in toxicology reports."

"Who cares? What, do they take away your pension for inert gas infractions? You'll be *dead*."

"You're missing the point. If nobody finds any evidence of the helium – or anything else – in my system, it won't be ruled a suicide. Remember, I'm a sick man – they'll assume I died of 'natural' causes... with pride intact, and no life insurance coverage issues for my daughter to deal with."

"What about the helium tank and whatever you plan on using to breathe the gas into your body? Won't they find those items when..."

Cue the clicking sound in my head. It was at this moment that I came to fully understand what my father's role was to be in the aforementioned arrangement.

"Ohhhh," I said, nodding my head slowly and, for whatever reason, smiling.

"You're a smart guy, Eli. I knew you'd catch on."

"Okay, so I get the plan... sort of," I replied, trying to picture in my head how it would all go down. "I must say, though, you were asking for an *awfully* big favor from my father."

"You think I don't know that? It took me months to work up the goddamn nerve to even broach the subject with him."

Realizing that I still hadn't asked Sgt. Rush a rather key question, I leaned in and placed my hand on the arm of his chair.

"What was my father's response?"

"The first night he and I talked about all this I stumbled around quite a bit trying to get to the point. When I finally did, well, he reacted much the way you did today – he was confused, then angry… and he threw a lot of the same shit at me about how much I had to live for. But when he simmered down and really started to listen to what I had to say, he grew increasingly empathetic."

"Did he say he'd do it?"

"Not that night. He wanted time to think about it, and for me to do the same. I said my mind was made up, and that I'd be ready if and whenever he was. I told him about the money – the twenty grand – but that just pissed him off."

"He refused it?"

"He said that *if* he decided to help me, there was no way he could take my money. But I insisted – no, I fucking *demanded* – that he take it if he helped me out. As you said, I was asking for an immense favor, one that involved no small amount of risk for your dad. He wanted me to give all the cash to my daughter, but I assured him that she would be more than taken care of."

"And he eventually said yes to the plan?"

"Yes… reluctantly, a couple of days later. But he said that he still wanted a little more time – a few weeks – to get his head around the whole shebang, and to do the necessary preparations. But before we could really start to iron out the details and pick a date, he got sick. I never mentioned the plan to him again, and the couple of times he tried to bring it up, I lied and told him that I had changed my mind. I wanted him to focus on beating his disease."

"Holy shit."

"I know, it's a lot to take in."

"My father came *this* close to being a murderer."

"Hey, what your father agreed to do was a very selfless and courageous thing."

After a few seconds of silence and shock, I voiced another question. "Do you think my father considered the same helium strategy for himself after his sudden tailspin?"

"I asked myself the same question when I heard he had taken a major turn for the worse. But you know, I honestly don't think he ever considered going down that path."

"Why not?"

"David Edelmann was an unwavering optimist... almost to a fault."

"And you?"

"I'm a man who's spent a lifetime in law enforcement and has repeatedly seen humanity at its worst. I keep a slightly looser grip on hope than a man who helps people plan parties."

Sgt. Rush looked at me with a slightly sad grin, acknowledging that he had uttered something teetering between poetic and pathetic. After a few moments of comfortable silence, he inhaled as if about to speak, then stopped. The million-dollar question was lodged in his throat. I decided that it was my job to release it.

"You want to know if I would be willing to pick up where my father left off, I presume?"

"Well, I don't expect you to decide right now, Eli. Hell, I don't *want* you to decide right now. Take some time to let this all sink in. If after a few days your answer isn't a strong 'no fucking way,' then we can take things from there. How does that sound?"

I shook my head – not in disagreement but rather in disbelief. I couldn't understand why my answer wasn't *already* a strong "no fucking way."

"Write down your phone number and I'll call you within

the next couple of days," I said. "Just don't get your hopes up."

The shop's electronic bell announced the entrance of a customer – one who *wasn't* looking for me to kill him.

I once caught a glimpse of my 10th grade humanities teacher being felated by a freshman.

I once found myself staring down the barrel of a body-guard's .357 after accidentally toppling the Reverend Jesse Jackson with an airport luggage cart.

I once walked in and saw the woman I had been dating exclusively for seven months watching *Fox News*.

The Sgt. Rush encounter instantly stripped each of these incidents of their "shocking" status. Back in the day I would recount the aforementioned true tales at parties to get attention and leave a small crowd of acquaintances slack-jawed. But now I merely viewed these events as marginally amusing anecdotes.

Forget about drawing small crowds; I had a new story that would fill stadiums. Trouble was I couldn't tell anybody.

A story. That's all it was to me initially – something too fantastic to seem anything but fictional. But amphetamines have a way of helping one to focus. A few hours and three Adderall tablets after the dark discussion at Jubilee, I was lucid – ready to confront reality and weigh my options.

My parents and teachers had always taught me to never murder anybody – *especially* not friends, and especially not policemen. So one would think I wouldn't have had to spend much time self-deliberating over Sgt. Rush's request.

But while logic may be a product of gray matter, it tends to get tangled in gray *areas*. Here we had plenty of the latter. There I was, trying to untie the knots.

Cue the angel and the demon dancing on opposite shoulders.

Angel: "Euthanasia, even when the victim volunteers – is homicide."

Demon: "Homicide loses its teeth when the victim is begging for it. It morphs into an entirely different animal, shedding its 'hom' and growing a lighter and less hairy 'sui' in its place."

Angel: Suicide is a permanent solution to a tempor…

Demon: "Try to keep up, Angel – we've already tackled that one."

Angel: "Then I'm going back to what I opened with… the act in question is homicide, regardless of your personal interpretation. You can interpret it all you want in prison."

Demon: "Not if you don't get caught."

Angel: "So murder is okay if you don't get caught? Oh, boy… off comes the lid from the worm can and Pandora's box."

Demon: "I really don't think that helping out an old family friend who is suffering greatly is a gateway to serial killing."

Angel: "A real friend would never ask you to assume so much risk and responsibility."

Demon: "Hence the cash. A lot of cash."

Angel: "Twenty grand won't even come close to covering the legal fees."

Demon: "But if… when you don't get caught, it will cover food and rent for quite a while."

This went on for some time, with both the halo and the horns each making cogent points. But in the end, it was the demon who broke the equilibrium, leaving the angel beaten and bleeding by reiterating the following point:

"Remember, Eli, your own father – a good and just man by all accounts – was going to do *exactly* what you are now being asked to do. So, I ask you, how evil an act can it *really* be?"

The angel, now staggering, countered with a final, predictable swing. "Evil enough to get locked up for life."

The lazy punch failed to land.

It was a brilliant ploy executed by the demon, reminding me of my father's benevolence like that. It pushed me past plain vanilla questions of morality and personal repercussions, temporarily at least, and freed me to focus squarely on the dire circumstances surrounding a dying friend.

Sgt. Rush was going to take his own life – or at least try to – with or without my assistance. This I knew. He had admitted the difficulty in doing so, but he wanted out and clearly had no intentions of sticking around until his body and mind became any more decrepit. He'd either find somebody else to help him, or he'd give it a go himself. And, if he went the latter route, he could very well muff the kick and wind up even more disabled and despondent than he already was. It wouldn't be pretty either; he had easier access to (and much more experience with) guns than he did noble gases, thus I assumed any solo attempt would involve pulling a trigger, not turning a valve. If botched, I couldn't bear the thought of this wonderfully profane and once powerful man spending the remainder of his days sitting slumped and speechless in a wheelchair, hacking away while a psych ward orderly mopped the spittle off what was left of his chin.

Despite what you may see on *The Real Housewives of Wherever* or at NASCAR events, humans are innately good and decent. We want to do no harm to others nor watch others being harmed. We are conditioned since birth to be the sworn enemy of death. Nobody must die on our watch, not without a fight at least.

But what about situations where fighting death ends up causing even *more* harm?

That semi-rhetorical question, along with the knowledge of my father's pact, was pushing me closer to an affirmative answer for Sgt. Rush. However, each time the words "I'll do it" came rolling up in my mind that night, they got caught on a lever that unleashed an army of reactionary platitudes:

"Sgt. Rush, have hope."

"Stay strong."

"Keep faith."

"Fight."

Natural defenses, yes, but nauseating nonetheless. So unoriginal and pedestrian. So artless and recalcitrant. So egocentric and void of any real empathy.

I knew I could do better than that.

I knew that Sgt. Rush needed me to.

CHAPTER 3

Helium.

Atomic number: 2. Atomic weight: 4.002602. The second lightest element in the observable universe – conceding the gold medal to hydrogen.

Helium.

Colorless.

Odorless.

Tasteless.

It's easy to see why helium goes so unnoticed, is so uncelebrated. Unless you are a blimp or a hot air balloon, it's nothing, really.

Except that it accounts for nearly one whole quarter of the elemental mass of our entire galaxy. It's the second most abundant element around (losing to only hydrogen again). It's all over the place. The universe simply wouldn't be the same without it.

And very soon, neither would my life.

About a day and a half had passed since Sgt. Rush had approached me. During that time I twice had his phone number locked and loaded – ready to make his day with the news that I would end his life – only to abort the call at the last second each time. Despite having already spent hours upon hours pondering his proposition and battling platitudes, I had yet to absorb the enormity of what I was about to agree to, if such absorption was even possible.

It wasn't until I started researching helium and uncovering some of the aforementioned facts about this odd gas that my decision started to exhibit the properties of a solid.

Why this occurred is difficult to explain. Learning about helium's chemical properties and common applications in science certainly didn't make the act in question any less absurd or illegal. I mean, knowing that this element is non-flammable and thus safer than hydrogen isn't what had me inching closer and closer to assisting a suicide. Neither did finding out that helium, under normal atmospheric conditions, doesn't freeze into a solid at ANY temperature but instead remains a rare "superfluid."

All very interesting information, but by no means the basis of a solid alibi or closing argument.

No, immersing myself in such facts wasn't changing any laws. It was, however, starting to make me feel more impermeable to them. Helium, in my developing view, was far too graceful and stable to be associated with anything criminal or repugnant.

And to think, I experienced all that just from reading a handful of paragraphs on Wikipedia. You can imagine the utter intrigue – something I hadn't felt about *anything* in years – that I experienced once I moved on to some websites offering info on helium's darker side.

I found web pages upon web pages hailing helium as the go-to-gas for those who've had it with oxygen. Apparently when right-to-die proponents aren't busy lobbying Congress they are building online societies and blogging. In about an hour, I learned all one would need to know to build and effectively administer what the hippest among the suicide set were calling a "helium hood." (Some referred to it as a "suicide bag"; to me that sounded like something Sylvia Plath might have carried around at cocktail parties.)

Of course, all of this information was intended for people looking to fit *themselves* for a hood and do the switch-flicking on their own. None of the sites encouraged nor even mentioned doing what Sgt. Rush had asked me to do. The experts were implying that providing a "victim" with the list of helium hood materials and instructions was okay, as was assisting the victim with the actual assembly of the instrument. But hooking somebody up to the helium hood and releasing the goods... that, evidently, was going rogue.

But I didn't care. My entire life I had been playing by the rules and yet I had amounted to nothing more than an aspiring glassblower who, rather than blowing glass, was working an artless job I had previously vowed to avoid. I had no woman, little savings and an ever-expanding liver. Amphetamines were the only things keeping me from drowning in a sea of ennui and party place cards.

And now there was helium – a noble and enigmatic gas offering me at least a *sense* of opportunity, intrigue, importance. The chance to do something that was as beautiful as it was abominable.

As I read on about the helium hood approach, I became increasingly captivated by the exact science and the serenity of it all. The softness of the deadly procedure. I had always hated chemistry in high school and college, because it lacked any relevance or utility for me. I had failed to see what was buried beneath the dead chapters, charts and formulas. However, now I was seeing it. Helium had just leapt majestically from the periodic table to reveal to me its grandeur, and to provide me with a sense of purpose. By wielding this element in the proper way, I could – for the first time in my life – be useful.

I was fully aware that I was embarking on something that, in society's view (and, up until that day, *my* view), was so wrong. Yet I couldn't stop my research. The deeper I went, the less devious I felt.

I awoke two days after Sgt. Rush's visit feeling transformed, and nauseated. This is a common response when one mixes whiskey and speed with a conscious decision to kill a man for the first time.

I had given myself the night to sleep on it, hoping that a healthy rest from the fascinating facts about helium and homemade hoods would help me come to my senses. No such luck. If anything, I was even more eager to assist Sgt. Rush than I had been hours earlier, when I had to force myself away from my computer and into bed.

I wish I could say "eager" was the wrong word, that "willingness" is what I had meant, but the truth is I was far beyond the self-convincing stage. I was struggling much less with the "if" than with the "when." I was ready to do what Sgt. Rush needed me to do – certainly not that day or even that week, as there were logistics to discuss and an apparatus to build. But I was ready. I had an important job to do. I had a worthwhile role to play.

The zeal and fervor I felt was both liberating and disconcerting. I knew that I should have been drowning in deliberation and doubt, but there I was eating a hearty bacon and eggs breakfast in my mother's kitchen, devouring what was in front of me and wishing the clock would hit double-digit a.m. hours so that I could make a certain phone call without fear of disturbing the sleep of a dying man.

After showering, it was time.

"Hello?" answered a ruined voice. I knew I had dialed right.

"Good morning, Sgt. Rush. It's Eli."

"Ah, Eli. I was wondering if and when you'd call."

"Well, here I am. And I've made my decision."

"And what is it?"

"I'll do it," I said with conviction. I felt powerful if a tad incredulous upon hearing myself utter the words.

"Don't tease an old, decrepit man now, Eli."

"I'm serious."

"I'm very glad to hear that. Are you certain?"

"Yes, I am."

"I can't tell you how much this means to me."

He spoke as if he had just been awarded a big prize or a dream job, not a death certificate.

"No need to thank me," I said. "I guess now we need to get together again to talk specifics in person." Phone lines are no place to discuss assisted suicides. I knew that much for sure.

"Sounds like a plan," Sgt. Rush responded.

"How about this afternoon at Gibbons Park? On one of the benches over by the statue of General what's his face."

"That works for me. What time."

"Say, half past four?"

"Okay, I'll see you then."

Considering the nature of the task we were planning, the ease and comfort of the conversation was surreal. There was no tension or anxiety in either of our voices. It was no different than two men scheduling a squash match. It all seemed so quiet, so rote, so innocuous. Like helium.

I arrived at the park a half hour early. This was intentional, and twofold: 1) I wanted to secure one of the three benches before Sgt. Rush arrived and thus avoid wandering around with an invalid man in search of an alternative spot; and 2) I didn't want Sgt. Rush to beat me to the bench and be forced to sit and wonder if I was going to show. As excited as he was that I had decided to participate in his plan, I'm sure he was concerned about me having second thoughts. And while he would have understood had I opted to back out, it would have been a kick to the gut. His lungs gave him enough trouble as it was. I wasn't about to contribute to the torment by wavering or by being tardy.

Two of the three benches were vacant when I arrived – the middle and third one from the statue. I sat down on the latter. Soon thereafter a man and a woman took the middle bench. While waiting for Sgt. Rush, I kept my ears open to see if I could overhear any of the conversation taking place over there or among passersby. There was a constant drone of human voices, but I couldn't make out what anyone was saying. Plenty of din but no details. I had picked a decent spot.

Sgt. Rush arrived right on time, not surprising for a former soldier and life-long officer of the law. There was a lot more color in his cheeks than there had been during our previous encounter. Apparently my decision to asphyxiate him had made his day.

I stood as he approached the bench.

"Good afternoon, Sgt. Rush."

"Yes, one of the best in a long while," he responded as we each took a seat. "I'd forgotten how much I like this park. And I must say, it's a hell of lot better sitting in it and soaking up some sun than it is chasing some cracked-out punk through it in the dark."

"I don't know, nothing wrong with a little night-time exercise."

"Are you kidding me? You try keeping pace with a crackhead. Fuck me. Whenever they're being tailed by a cop, they instantly transform into a combination Olympic sprinter/ marathon runner. Of course it didn't help that I smoked two packs a day and was always in full uniform, including a gunbelt that weighed more than the person I was after."

"I have a new respect for the police."

"Well, that may be bad timing, my friend."

Sgt. Rush chuckled before succumbing to one of his customary coughing fits. My throat and chest burned just watching. I couldn't imagine what it had been like enduring such a condition for years. Sgt. Rush couldn't imagine what it would be like enduring it for several more.

I sat there and waited for the attack to subside, frustrated over my inability to provide any relief. That would change soon enough.

"So, are you ready to talk business?" I asked. The question seemed much more callous upon leaving my mouth than it had in my head.

"I am if you are," Sgt. Rush responded, wiping his mouth with a blue handkerchief. He leaned in. "But we'd better keep it down. Not exactly a conversation that's meant for public consumption."

"Don't worry, I've already done a sound check. We're good."

"Nice work."

"By the way, I would have come to your house, but I don't want to become a familiar face to any of your neighbors. And I would have had you over to mine, but I don't have one. I'm still crashing at my parents' – er, my mother's – house, and there's no need for her to see us together so soon before you... well, you know."

"I'm glad to see you are covering bases, Eli. Smart. If this plan of ours ends up getting you into any serious trouble, I'll come back to life and kill myself... slowly and painfully."

"That's sweet."

"I'm a sweet fucking guy."

"Okay, well I don't want you worrying about what may or may not happen to me. Trust me, I gave this whole thing very careful consideration, and I'm in.

I was careful not to be overly sensitive. Sgt. Rush was no longer seeking empathy, not now that I had already agreed to participate. And he certainly wasn't seeking sympathy. What he wanted now – what he needed now – was for me to take charge, or at least to show that I was firmly prepared to do so. No stammering. No apologizing. No second-guessing my own semantics. It was time to talk strategy. Logistics. Execution. It was okay to be friendly, but not warm or fuzzy, and definitely not tentative. I had read books and seen films featuring fearless protagonists defying conventional morality for a greater good. I just couldn't think of any of their lines.

"So, I've been doing a lot of research these past two days... on the, uh, method you mentioned to me in the shop."

"I imagined you would be. Pretty fascinating stuff, huh?"

"Indeed. I should be able to obtain all the supplies for the hood rather easily. And of course I already have plenty of the 'main ingredient' in stock at Jubilee."

"And you're sure you'll be able to piece everything together to make a hood that actually works? I don't want to come out of this thing a vegetable."

"Installation and application seemed pretty straightforward from what I read and saw online. What you and I now need to discuss in more detail is 'the where' and 'the when' – as well as how to make sure the coast is clear as far as my entrance and exit."

"'The where' is my house. I have a long driveway and the house sits on an acre of land, so there are no neighbors living close enough to cause an issue. And I wouldn't worry about any unannounced guests. I don't get visitors very often these days – I've assured that by becoming a cranky son of a bitch in my old age."

"Don't be insulted by this question, but don't you have some type of nurse or medical specialist who helps you out with your oxygen and stuff?"

"Hell no. But I will need somebody like that if I don't take the bull by the horns relatively soon."

"And what do you consider 'relatively soon'? I mean, do

you have a specific day in mind?"

"That really depends on you and when you can be ready to do this. Hell, if you told me you already had the hood and all the 'whats' and 'hows' covered, I'd say let's do this tomorrow."

"Yeah, that's not going to happen, Sgt. Rush."

"I realize that. Point is, I'm locked and loaded. Don't forget, I was all set to go on this months ago, before your father got sick."

"Can you wait another week or so?"

"A week? How about three days?"

"Five days."

"Deal."

CHAPTER 4

List of Supplies

Small/medium helium tank - have
Controlled-release nozzle - have
Medium/large clear poly bag(s) - need
4-5 ft of thin plastic tubing - need
Medium/large Velcro strap - need
Hole-puncher - have
Duct tape - have
Duffel bag - have
Latex gloves - need

While pushing the oversized shopping cart through the oversized home and garden supplies store, I wondered if the video surveillance cameras used by store security could read minds. Certainly the telepathic messages emanating from mine would have raised more than a few red flags.

The peculiar grin on my face wouldn't have helped. I couldn't seem to remove it. As I coasted from aisle to aisle filling my cart with pieces of the suicide hood (or, as sticklers of the law would say, "homicide" hood), I felt oddly empowered and altruistic. You see similar grins on the faces of people new to volunteering with the homeless and the hungry. Evidently, when overcome with the typical emotions that accompany doing something that makes a difference in the lives of others, it's difficult not to smile like an idiot. Most people would argue that helping to feed, clothe and house the less fortunate is good reason to smile so and to pat one-self on the back. Few, however, would say the same about helping to bring about a precipitous drop in the levels of oxygen to the brain of a fellow human being.

I was grinning not only because I felt I was doing some good, but also because of the sheer sense of adventure that comes with choosing a precarious path.

I easily found all the items I needed for the hood in that single store, except for one: the Velcro strap. This didn't surprise me. Many things in this world *have* Velcro straps, but a Velcro strap in and of itself, acting independently, is hard to come by. It's like trying to buy snaps or zippers à la carte. I could have settled for an alternative fastening device – a large elastic band or a belt, or maybe even some rope. But a Velcro strap was what the leading experts seemed to be calling for, and with me being a rookie, I wasn't about to start straying from established best practices.

I ambled about for a few minutes more in search of the missing item before my big box-store agoraphobia (BBSA) set in. I have always suffered tolerable bouts of anxiety and shortness of breath inside any commercial establishment exceeding 40,000 square feet. But this was the first time I had entered such an establishment since befriending amphetamines – a drug that I quickly discovered exacerbates BBSA considerably.

Rather than seek assistance from one of the store's friendly blue-vested employees who, according to the giant sign at the entrance, were "dedicated to delivering customer delight," I hurried to the least crowded checkout counter one supply short.

There was another customer ahead of me, a man in his fifties buying a couple gallons of paint and primer along with a paint roller and tray. I could only assume that his project was a tad more routine than mine. While eyeing the items in my cart, I was startled by the cashier.

"Suicide's what's needed," I heard her say.

"Excuse me?"

"So d'ya find whatcha needed?" she repeated while ringing up my items.

"Oh, yes, thank you," I responded. "Actually, there was one item I wasn't able to find – a Velcro strap?"

"Do you mean, like, just a strap on its own?"

"Yes. One that's, say, yay long," I answered, holding my hands about two feet apart.

"Not sure if I've ever seen anything like that here. What do you need it for?"

Since when did "delivering customer delight" entail prying into personal matters, I thought to myself while scrambling for a fitting response. Part of me wanted to blurt out the truth to the cashier just for the shock value of it all – to witness the look on her face upon hearing, "I need the strap to fasten one of these industrial-sized plastic bags I just purchased over the head and around the neck of a decorated police sergeant who wants to die."

What I actually uttered was far less bold and incisive.

"I'll be transporting a sculpture and need a strap to keep the protective plastic bag in place."

"You might find it's hard to die, sure."
"What?"
"You might try an art supply store."
"Ah, yes. That's not a bad idea. Thanks."

The basement in my parents' house had never been used for anything other than extra storage for Jubilee, though often doubled as an exhibit space for artful spiders. The intricate webs that spanned the rafters and occasionally ran from one cardboard box to another were a sight to behold.

My mother – a helpless arachnophobe – would disagree. She never once descended the cellar steps in all the years I had lived in that house, not after listening to my father's tales of wolf spiders as big as his fist. And now that his ghost joined those creepy crawly creatures of yore, there was little chance of my mother ever dipping beneath the kitchen.

This, of course, worked out well for me. I needed a private place to work on my new project. Ideally, I would have already moved into my own apartment in town where I would have all the seclusion I needed, but I didn't have the funds for such a move, and wouldn't until I got paid for my assignment.

I didn't see this as a big issue; after all, my mother had only been a widow for a short while. It was only right that I stick around a little longer to make sure she didn't suffer an attack of delayed grief and spend my entire inheritance on water aerobics classes and golf. Thus, in my eyes, our living arrangement was financially advantageous for me, and emotionally advantageous for her. Though, admittedly, I was benefitting far more from the arrangement than was my mother, who had spent much more time since Dad's death socializing in swimming pools and sand traps than she had crying on my shoulder. But I was there for her if she needed me.

So I set up shop in the forsaken basement. I started off by laying each of the supplies I had just purchased out on one of the foldable metal card tables my parents used to break out for bridge nights. All I needed to commence hood construction was to retrieve the helium tank and the release nozzle from Jubilee. I still had to find a Velcro strap, too, but since its purpose was solely to fasten the bag over a human head once the hood was built, its absence would not delay the construction phase.

That night after eating dinner and chatting with my mother about nothing of importance, I told her I had to run to the shop to take care of a couple of inventory issues. I left the house around 10:30 p.m. to ensure I wouldn't run into Carl, the sales clerk who ran things on my days off. The shop closed at 9 p.m. on weekdays, and I knew that Carl would have already locked up and vacated the premises by no later than 9:45.

I entered the shop from the seldom-used back door, which opened into the cluttered stock room. Neither I nor Carl were as dedicated as Dad was at keeping supplies stacked and straight. Righting wrong angles had always been one of his favorite pastimes.

I flicked a switch to turn on the stockroom lights even though I could have found what I had come for without such illumination. I knew exactly where the helium tanks and release nozzles were even in the pitch black, as I had spent the better part of my last few workdays transfixed on said items, continually getting lost in a very real and dangerous daydream.

There were 11 tanks and nozzles in stock. However, thanks to my intentionally inaccurate record-keeping the day before, there were *officially* only 10. I placed the phantom tank and nozzle in the duffel bag I had brought with me, turned off the lights, and slipped out the back door before locking it behind me.

During the short walk to my car, the duffel bag – despite its ample heft – became strangely lighter with each step I took.

All the lights were off in the house upon my return, meaning my mother was out cold in her room upstairs or in her bed on the brink of sleep. Either way, the coast was clear for a quick entrance and descent. Of course, even if my mother had seen me lugging the duffel bag, I would have just told her we had received a surplus of helium and that space was tight at Jubilee. Getting caught in the hallway with a tank was entirely explainable. Less so was getting caught in the basement with a tank connected to a large plastic bag while I was holding instructions printed out from www.deathhood.com.

I made it to the basement and introduced the helium tank and release nozzle to the other supplies. I stood back to look at the collective elements of euthanasia laid out on the card table, each piece looking innocuous enough. Soon they would be fused together and lose their innocence. Soon I would be doing the fusing and lose mine.

It looked less like an instrument used to end a life and more like an apparatus used to start a party. An industrial-strength whip-it or new-fangled power bong created by some misguided college chemistry major.

The construction was a piece of cake; took me all of three minutes to put together, thanks to the no-frills and highly user-friendly instructions composed by the good folks of Deathhood. Excellent technical writers, the lot of them. I, along with my client, would be forever indebted to them and their incomparable ability to communicate the perfect death step-by-step.

The instructions extended beyond set-up into actual implementation, and were careful to eschew any untidy terms. No "toxic" or "deadly" or "victim" or "suicide." Not a single "no turning back now" disclaimer. The authors, while certainly not aggressive or overzealous, made no attempts to talk readers down. There was no moral judgment made or motherly concerns regarding clean underwear. Their function was simply to disseminate uncommon knowledge and ensure success should the decision be made to apply said knowledge.

As simple as the hood assembly was, one rather glaring red flag began waving. The instructions mentioned that, for best results, it was important that the person donning the hood breathe deeply and calmly for a good 30 seconds. The authors noted that this might be a challenge for somebody with a respiratory condition, such as lung cancer. Or pneumonia.

Or emphysema.

It was the first legitimate snag I had foreseen since giving serious consideration to and accepting Sgt. Rush's proposal. The first hiccup in the helium scheme. While not grounds for cancellation, news of the potential inhalation problem left me somewhat deflated. How big of an issue was it? Hard to tell. I'd certainly seen Sgt. Rush breathe relatively freely for more than 30 seconds without hacking and coughing, but that was while hooked up to an oxygen tank, not a hood pumped full of helium.

This was not the type of health concern you could call and ask a doctor about. Dr. Kevorkian, perhaps, yet he had made his own final exit a few months earlier. Besides, even when he was alive his phone number was most likely unlisted.

The only other person to call was the "subject" himself. Sgt. Rush had presumably done extensive research on the method he was so gung-ho on using, thus maybe he knew of a viable way to hurdle the obstacle that his emphysema presented.

While another face-to-face meeting would have been wiser, I was eager for answers. I took out my cell phone and accessed my "last called" list. Sgt. Rush answered, and after the obligatory greetings and small talk, I got down to business.

"According to the experts, emphysema can really interfere with 'the hike' we are planning – you aware of that?" The cryptic language was intentional, in the event the call was being recorded for invasive government purposes.

"I am, but I've got it covered, Eli."

"Yeah? How so?"

"Muscle relaxants."

"You have some?"

"Hell yes. Every respectable chronic emphysema patient

has a valid prescription. Relaxes the diaphragm during severe episodes. Can use them as a preemptive strike prior to a known stressful event, too. Enables free and easy breathing for a short period. Long enough to get my fill."

"Are you sure? We'll have to cancel the hike if you start coughing, and it could leave you with serious—

"Hey, let's chat about this when I see you next. Sound *good*?" Sgt. Rush's interruption and emphatic tone served as a swift reminder: Anything you carelessly blurt out over phone lines can and will be used to ruin you in a court of law.

So Sgt. Rush already knew that coughing can really get in the way of a good suicide. It's not just that failure to breathe steadily renders the hood method ineffective; it could render the subject severely stupid. Helium, remember, is toxic in moderate to high doses. Inhaling enough of it to kill yourself but not gracefully enough will, in all likelihood, result in your brain taking on the functional properties of porridge. I would much sooner want to see Sgt. Rush dead and buried than dumb and drooling.

And what, I thought, if the resulting brain damage turned out to be slightly less severe than usual, leaving Sgt. Rush with enough sense and spite to alert the authorities to my involvement in the exit strategy? The real Sgt. Rush would never even *think* of such a selfish or incriminating act, but I had no idea how the good sergeant would behave with a fried frontal lobe.

That's when the first wave of panic and doubt washed over me. The thought of Sgt. Rush turning into a feeble-minded fraction of himself quickly escalated into more serious concerns – the sort of things that folks far more practical than I would have started worrying about much earlier in the euthanasia planning process: How to fend off passes from prison cellmates if caught; how to keep twenty grand off any ledgers if *not* caught; and how to avoid the claws and fangs of a feral conscience.

Up until that point, I had been so inebriated by the simplicity and intrigue of the plan, so locked into the topical research and the careful construction of the hood, I hadn't allowed myself to get distracted by any potential snags or repercussions. I had been above it all.

After a few minutes of premature dread and regret, I realized the harsh reality that had suddenly begun caving in on me in the eleventh hour was a mere symptom of complete sobriety. I hadn't taken any Adderall in over six hours, nor downed a single drink in nearly a day. Fortunately, this was easy to remedy.

A whiskey shot and two amphetamines later, I was flying above the radar once again. As invincible as I needed to be.

CHAPTER 5

"How are you, Eli? Any trouble finding the place?"

The nonchalant greeting – more fitting for a friend who had come to watch a ballgame or play poker – made me think that Sgt. Rush's recently diagnosed dementia was rearing its head. That concern was quickly laid to rest with his next utterance.

"Let's get that bag off your shoulder. I imagine the tank isn't exactly light."

He was right. I found it quite paradoxical that a container holding a relatively small amount of the second lightest element in the universe could compromise my spinal alignment. I politely refused Sgt. Rush's assistance with the duffel bag and set it on the floor by my feet.

"Where had you planned on, uh... doing this?" I asked.

"I was thinking the bedroom."

I hoisted the duffel bag back up onto my shoulder and followed Sgt. Rush to the master bedroom, located down a long hallway in the single-level home.

"Do you even remember this place?" he asked en route.

"You mean I've been here before?"

"Yup. You couldn't have been much older than four or

five. Mrs. Rush and I used to have cookouts here all the time, and your folks were always at them. We stopped in 1982 after a drunken guest accidentally fired one of my handguns he had found while snooping around in the basement."

"Whoa. Anybody hurt?"

"Yeah, him – I slapped the shit out of him for shooting a hole through my hot water tank." Sgt. Rushed smiled. "But I didn't invite you here to talk about that."

Thankfully, this marked the end of the small talk. Engaging in such trivial discourse with a man I was preparing to euthanize made me uncomfortable, and uneasiness is very unbecoming of an executioner.

When we arrived at the bedroom, I asked Sgt. Rush the first of two big questions.

"Are you absolutely sure you want to go through with this?" There was no fear or anxiety in my tone – my intention was not to dissuade him or to express that I was having any second thoughts. I simply wanted a solid confirmation. I needed to ensure there wasn't a trace of doubt in his decision. A wise tactic, I thought, especially considering that licensed medical professionals had recently discovered he was on the precipice of losing his marbles.

"We are doing this, Eli. I'm ready. Please tell me you are, too."

Some acidity seeped through the cracks of Sgt. Rush's typically cool and casual tone. A twinge of anger. Aimed not at me but at the disease that had been steadily destroying his lungs for nearly a decade. Anger at two packs a day since his twenties. Anger at the Marlboro Man. Anger at forced early retirement from the precinct. Anger over his dead wife. Anger over his dying mind. Anger at the oxygen tank on the floor by his king-sized bed – a bed big enough to sleep three but which had become accustomed to cradling just one.

"Don't worry – I'm ready, too," I said. The look of concern on Sgt. Rush's face instantly disappeared.

He sat down on the edge of the bed, and coughed lightly. I was very happy he wasn't hacking. The muscle relaxants must have worked. How many pills this had required I didn't know, and I didn't want to ask for fear of jinxing things. He seemed lucid and coherent, so I'm assuming he didn't pop more than a couple. Good thing, too. A man trying to fake a natural death doesn't want to be found pumped full of Valium.

It was quite the scene: Sgt. Rush dosed with Diazepam to drown out the emphysema; me amped on Adderall to drown out the fear. His drug was ironic – intended to calm a chronic condition long enough to help him die; my drug was kinetic – intended to lift me up and help me feel alive. Our individual states, diametrically opposed. Our relationship, oddly symbiotic.

I sat next to Sgt. Rush on the end of the bed.

"Before we get started, I have just one other question… it's about the finding of your, um, body."

"Okay, what's your question?"

"You told me you don't get many visitors out here, but I know you are still pretty close to your daughter. I was just wondering if you've taken any precautions to ensure that, you know, she doesn't walk in and discover you after you've been lying here for what could turn out to be weeks."

"Ah, I've taken care of that. I invited my old friend Benny to come by for lunch tomorrow."

"Won't he just go home when you don't come to the door?"

"No, Benny would kill for a free meal, and he knows I usually leave my door open. Plus I owe him some money, so he ain't going anywhere until he's searched the entire house for me."

"Aren't you concerned that finding you might be shocking and upsetting for him?"

"Benny? Hell no, that guy has seen it all – he used to be the janitor in a public high school. Shit, he'll probably just calmly call 911 and then go through my pockets for loose change."

"All right, sounds like a good plan. You know, for a man diagnosed with early onset dementia, you certainly seem on the ball."

"Yeah? You wouldn't be saying that if you had seen me put a sponge in the toaster the other day, or buy a 25 lb. bag of kibble for a dog that's been dead for 40 years."

He shook his head and laughed, though I could see he wasn't joking.

Unpacking my duffel bag, I felt how I imagine a brain surgeon feels lining up his or her instruments while a pre-anaesthetized patient lies supine on the operating table watching. The big difference being that neither I nor my "patient" was hoping he'd pull through.

Sgt. Rush watched intently as I removed each item of the hood (including the Velcro strap, which I had found in a fabric shop) and set it on a wooden chest near the foot of the bed.

"Would you be more comfortable in the other room until I finish setting everything up," I asked.

"No, I'm good."

"You sure?"

"Yes. Eli, I'm not in the least bit apprehensive or scared. I want this more than anything. You are doing me an immense favor – you don't know how much I appreciate it. I know how strange and difficult all this has been for you."

Strange, yes. Difficult? Sure, there were butterflies fluttering in my gut, but they wanted to be fed, not released. Ever since my newfound fascination with helium had begun, it had become difficult to tell who was doing whom a favor. Not that I was standing in Sgt. Rush's room like a mad scientist rubbing my hands in wild anticipation of the procedure. However, I knew I was where I needed to be. And, while I was lamenting the demise of an old family friend, I was grateful that he had chosen me to administer the exit he so desired.

Sgt. Rush watched me as I assembled the various pieces of the hood. I breathed deeply through the butterflies, pleased that I was able to keep my hands from shaking.

"I know you are pretty familiar with the procedure, but do you have any questions about the hood or how this is going to work?" I asked.

"Nope. I'm pretty well versed on it."

Sgt. Rush eyeballed the exit instrument, admiring it as if I had just unveiled a marble bust I had made for him.

"Very nice. Just like the ones I've seen on the Internet." He touched the bag and the tubing, inspected the control release valve attached to the top of the helium tank. He looked up at me.

"Eli, why haven't you asked me anything about the money, about my payment? You didn't actually think I'd tolerate you doing this for free, did you?"

"I guess I figured it would all work out somehow, that you had devised a way to get the money to me."

"Well," said Sgt. Rush, "I appreciate you being so low-key about it, but if you don't pick up that large manila envelope over there on the dresser on your way out later, I'll come back from the dead and break your face."

The money – initially the most enticing part of the proposal – had become a secondary or tertiary concern. It was actually the piece of the plan that made me the most uncomfortable. I felt it sort of criminalized an otherwise poetic act. A Picasso painting isn't beautiful because it fetches millions of dollars; it's beautiful *despite* that. Call me delusional, but I had come to see myself as more of an artist during my one week dealing in euthanasia than I had during my years in glassblowing.

It turned out, however, my artistic ideals weren't quite as high as the payment being offered.

"Don't worry, I'll take the envelope – I just hope it will fit in my duffel bag," I said, shaking my head while eyeing the parcel that looked about to burst. "What did you fill it with, one dollar bills only?"

"You're lucky – I had considered paying you with rolls of quarters," said Sgt. Rush, laughing so hard it nearly set off an ill-timed coughing fit. Fortunately, the sight of me pulling on my surgical gloves helped him regain control of his epiglottis.

"Shouldn't you have had those on when you came in?"

"No need. I've been careful not to touch anything other than what I've pulled out of my bag, and that stuff is all leaving with me." I pointed to the black Lycra skull cap I was wearing. "And this will keep any of my hair from falling on the floor."

"Way to keep the forensics team at bay, but I'm telling you there won't be any reason for the police to order any special investigation, so I wouldn't worry about it."

"You can't be too careful."

Sgt. Rush looked around the room, then at the exit hood, then back at me.

"I'm ready."

"Yeah?"

"Yes."

"Is there any music you want to hear, or something you want me to read aloud while you are, you know, going under?"

"No. Let's just keep things simple."

"You're the boss."

"Thank you again, Eli. You have no idea how much this means to me. You just have to promise me you won't let your conscience torture you on this. You are a good man, doing a noble thing."

"I appreciate that, but don't worry about me. I'm honored to assist."

I wanted to say more. I wanted to tell Sgt. Rush how I admired him for having lived a purposeful and honest life. For having raised a happy daughter. For having endured his wife's illness and death with courage and poise. And for having been such a good friend to my father for so many years. I realized, however, that expressing such sentiments would have been more for my benefit than for his. Sgt. Rush didn't need me to deliver a living tribute or eulogy. He didn't need to be reassured that he had been liked and loved and respected by the people he encountered on this planet. He felt no existential despair. He needed no soft words to send him home. He simply wanted to leave.

I checked to see that the long plastic tubing was securely hooked up to the release valve of the tank, and picked up the plastic bag.

"Remember, there won't be any helium in the bag when I first slip it over your head. You will be able to breathe freely. Once I insert the tube into the hole and turn the valve, just continue to breathe slowly and deeply. It will be just like you are breathing oxygen, and you'll drift off before you know it. Is that clear?"

"Perfectly."

"Good. Are you ready to begin?"

"Yes."

Sgt. Rush scooted back in his bed and propped himself up on a couple of pillows. I carried the connected tank and the bag to the side of the bed, close enough for the tubing to reach Sgt. Rush's soon-to-be hooded head.

Here's where I had earlier thought one of us might crumble. This is the point at which I had half-expected to suddenly come to my senses, or for Sgt. Rush to suddenly come to his. But it turned out to be the easiest part of the whole plan. A dream sequence. Distance and detachment, yet each of us locked into our respective role – doubtless that what we were doing was right. Beyond right. Bordering on obligatory.

Me: Focused and methodical as I slipped the bag over his head and attached the straps, tube and tape.

Him: Unwavering in his response to my final "Ready?"

No tension at the turning of the valve. No coughing as oxygen was ousted. No struggle as helium stole the show.

No panic as the number of living people in the room was cut in half.

Sgt. Rush, or, more precisely, the body he had borrowed for 62 years, lay slumped awkwardly on the bed, his head tilted to the left at a sharp angle, his torso leaning heavy in the same direction yet still supported partially by the pillows. After I removed the plastic bag and packed all the hood pieces into my duffel bag, I carefully un-stacked the pillows and guided the body into a position more in line with that of a man who had been napping rather than one who had been sitting up in bed to watch a program on a non-existent TV set.

On my way out of the room I snatched the envelope Sgt. Rush had left on the dresser and slid it into my duffel bag. Just like that, I had been transformed from a rank amateur to a highly paid professional – nearly doubling what I had earned the entire year before in a matter of minutes.

I turned to look once more at the body. I would miss the man who had exited it, yet I felt no remorse. On the contrary – I was overwhelmed by a strong sense of achievement. An impenetrable sense of… there was that simple word again…

Purpose.

Sgt. Rush had just been released.

He wasn't the only one.

CHAPTER 6

Showing up to manage a party supply store after euthanizing a man is anti-climactic. Even with the help of my pills, I struggled to summon the enthusiasm needed to sell instruments of merriment for days after Sgt. Rush's lift off.

I wasn't depressed by or panicked over the act I had committed; I was nostalgic. Sales were suffering not because I was visibly frantic, but because I was figuratively absent. Each time a customer asked a question about a party package, my mind was wrapped around a release valve. Whenever my tongue was busy explaining the advantages of Mylar over latex, my brain was occupied with the kindness of helium.

Fathers desperate to win back the love and respect of their soon-to-be sweet 16 year-old daughters demand your undivided attention.

Husbands hoping that an anniversary celebration for the ages will mask their recent affair won't tolerate a scripted pitch.

Managers looking to dupe employees into thinking the company truly cares need you to act like you do, too.

There's simply no place for distractions in party supply sales.

But distracted I was. I had fallen in love with the sinister sequence of recent events. I repeatedly revisited them, valued them more than anything taking place before me in the present. Where most first-time perpetrators of a highly illegal act would have been consumed by fear or guilt, I was consumed by pride and feelings of self-worth – by an unconquerable sensation that, having defiantly crossed bold lines and risked so much, I had rendered myself untouchable.

Yeah, 50 mgs of amphetamine a day will do that to a man.

It will fire you up far past the point of who you are but keep you calm when it's required, like when a man who might be a detective walks through the shop door looking inquisitive. It will turn you into a god, yet guide you through discourse suitable for mortals, such as when a longtime customer asks if you heard about a certain sergeant.

"No, what happened?" I responded, feigning sincere concern.

"A friend found him a couple of days ago at his home. Such a shame," the customer said.

"Shit, you're kidding me. How did he die?"

"Natural causes. He had a lung condition, as you probably know."

"Yeah, I knew he wasn't in the best of health, but I figured he had plenty of time left. He was one strong S.O.B."

"That he was. I expect there will be info about memorial services in tomorrow's paper."

"Thanks for letting me know. Damn, he will be missed."

And there it was – official confirmation that Sgt. Rush and I had succeeded. No suicide nor foul play suspected, at least not according to my less-than-authoritative source. While it was possible that some form of investigation or lab analysis was taking place, it was highly unlikely. My partner and I had covered all the bases.

So it was back to business as usual at Jubilee, except I had yet to fully return from Sgt. Rush's bedside. The only interactions with customers that fully captured my attention were those in which my new favorite gas wafted into the conversation.

"Do you rent helium tanks for inflating party balloons?"

Yes, and if you suffer from a terminal disease or two, have I got an offer for you.

Such customer requests – I received two or three every week – were a hypnotist's trick: Watch the party supply guy instantaneously transform into a euthanasia agent spotting a possible lead. Of course, once transported, I assumed a very subtle role. Latent really. And understandably so; openly mistaking a happy customer for a suicidal one is bad for business. It ruins rapport.

Besides, there simply weren't any tactful probing questions to apply in the event I did spot an exit sign in a customer's appearance or demeanor:

"Ma'am, I couldn't help noticing those moles on your arm and that you seem a bit defeated. Are you *really* just looking to fill balloons?"

Somebody entering Jubilee because they were ready to exit was about as likely as me entering Jubilee chemical-free. But that didn't matter. What mattered was that I realized how much I *wanted* the former to occur.

It was obvious. I didn't want my fling with helium to simply be a one-night stand.

It's always nice when you discover what you want to be when you grow up, however late it occurs. But it helps to have at least one role model.

I had none.

Your average euthanasia specialist doesn't go around trying to drum up business. Typically, the folks in the field are a passive lot – patiently waiting behind Internet walls for interested parties to come to them, and then just providing information and instructions. There's no canvassing for potential clients. Right-to-die activists engage in very little marketing or self-promotion.

Sure, one might argue that making available some video demonstrating optimum hood construction and use is more active than reactive, but the aim of said video isn't to attract and encourage, rather it's to educate and support those who are already hip to helium.

When the good people behind such websites are called upon to assist, that assistance never entails shopping for supplies or wearing rubber gloves. It doesn't involve attaching any bags or turning any valves. There's no erasing of any evidence. There's no help with 'this never happened.'

Batteries are not included.

Results may vary.

When you go rogue in the euthanasia game, there isn't much in the way of policy or precedent. No established tactics to embrace. No tutorials, research reports or case studies. There's just you alone with what's left of your logic. You bouncing ideas off yourself. Brainstorming in solitary confinement. Those averse to isolation and self-reliance might rethink whether actively helping people kill themselves is even a good idea.

Of course, having one successful exit already under your belt gives you a solid head start. And a pocket full of Adderall gives you the extra speed you need, the acceleration required for lift off. You launch over all the self-doubt and second-guessing. All the internal shouts of "What are you thinking?." All the common sense. You are Evil Knievel up in here.

But no matter how mentally prepared you are for your next life-defying stunt, it won't happen until you find people who want to participate.

That was probably the most frustrating part for me while looking to break into this exciting new career – knowing I had a very viable service to offer but no simple way to spread the word. In my immediate geographic region there were likely hundreds if not thousands of ideal candidates for my business, people who were dead-set on signing off but whose inexperience would end up landing them in the ICU, or leaving their families with a lot of cleaning up and repainting to do.

I couldn't exactly put up posters or advertise on craigslist. A shame, too, as my talent for writing captivating copy – gleaned from a wasted B.A. in Mass Communications – would most certainly have come in handy. My muse had already sent me several catchy terms and titles: Death Peddler. Suicide Merchant. Exits R Us. I didn't mean to devalue the importance and artistry of euthanasia; I simply couldn't stop the onslaught of sound bites.

I had wasted enough time with fantasy branding and patting myself on the back for my creative efforts. It was time for some practical strategy, a workable plan.

I pondered the question for days: How does one go about finding and connecting with the seriously suicidal, and do so discreetly?

The most obvious schemes that came to mind had the biggest holes, at least for my purposes. Sure, I could have volunteered at some crisis hotline that receives hundreds of calls a day from wrecked men and women, but such calls are heavily monitored by supervisory staff gung-ho on thwarting suicide rather than enhancing its execution. All it would take is one conversation in which I talked a caller down from a ledge by offering a better offing option, one discussion in which I expounded upon the benefits of helium over hanging, a hood over a bullet, and I'd instantly be relieved of my headset – and likely reported to the authorities.

I thought about the possibility of frequenting dive bars and lonely lounges, where I could sip a whiskey and quietly size up who among the clientele was drinking to forget vs. drinking to destroy. I could initiate dialogue with members of the latter category and delve a bit in hopes of discerning the severity of and reasons behind their desperation. Those who had merely lost a job or had their heart broken would be eliminated from the running. Those who had lost to chemo or had a heart that literally was broken would qualify for a second interview.

Considering my affinity for ethanol and drunken discourse, I felt this was a workable approach. And thanks to Sgt. Rush as well as steady work at Jubilee, I had ample cash to cover my bar tabs for an extended period. In the end, however, I decided it was too much of a crapshoot. Even if I was lucky enough to uncover a hot lead every now and again, I feared it wouldn't be worth the damage done to my wallet and liver. Of course, I could have chosen to nurse plain club soda or some other non-alcoholic beverage while on such missions, but that went completely against my personal principles of acceptable bar behavior. Some rules just weren't meant to be broken.

Aside from the other issues mentioned, the common snag shared by each of the previously described approaches was the amount of filtering required. Just because a person calls a suicide hotline or appears to be drinking themselves to death doesn't mean they are committed to dying. You have to spend some time digging and assessing to determine that, and it may turn out that only one in one hundred are the real McCoy. Too much work, if you ask me.

Not that I wanted quick and easy scores, either. I wasn't some monster looking to feast on the weaknesses of salvageable souls. I simply wanted to make my services known and available to lucid individuals who were understandably on their way out. I saw myself as a noble purveyor, a humanist catering to the completely vanquished.

And then it came to me. I had an "in."

CHAPTER 7

The Dignity Forum met every Tuesday evening in a small room on the basement level of the Caswell County Public Health & Human Services Center. I've never fully understood why support groups for the terminally ill are always situated in some musty cellar or other location sans a window. I can only assume it's a subtle attempt to prepare participants for their imminent burial.

I had heard about The Dignity Forum from one of my father's nurses months earlier. She had suggested that my mother and I check it out, explaining that the group warmly welcomed not only folks with cancer and other incurable ailments but their friends and family, as well. While we did give it some consideration, my mother and I never attended a meeting – deciding instead to rely collectively on drinking, drugs and golf to cope with my father's looming departure.

There were about 10 people in attendance when I arrived at the meeting room. Most were gathered around a snack table that was seemingly in place to accelerate their demise. Cookies, brownies, cake and fudge, with plenty of coffee from old, poorly cleaned pots to wash it all down. Not quite the macrobiotic diet items prescribed by the leading oncologists of the day. When you hear people speaking about terminal cases and how it's all about creating comfort, they are referring to the food.

I reached for a snickerdoodle at the same time as an older woman standing beside me. Our wrists collided above the plate. She looked like an X-ray image.

"You first. Please," I said, gesturing toward the cookies.

"Thank you." She placed two on a small napkin and looked at me again. "I've not seen you here before – first time?"

"Yes. I'm here on behalf of my father. He's not able to go anywhere."

"I'm sorry to hear that. Well, you came to a good place. Hopefully you can take away some things that help make what you and your father are going through a little less difficult."

"That would be nice. I appreciate it."

It wasn't my finest moment. Lying about a dying father who was already dead and eliciting sympathy from a soon-to-be corpse. But I needed to blend. I didn't possess the acting talent to pull off being sick myself, not that doing so would have been any less reprehensible. So I dragged my dead dad into the fray, giving him a couple ounces of extra life in a less-than-inventive fabrication.

How was I to know it was the surviving relatives who gleaned most of the attention and pity during meetings of the doomed?

"Okay, everybody please find a seat and let's get started," said a man standing by a circle of chairs. He was the only person in the room besides me who appeared all but certain to live through the end of the meeting.

Once everybody was seated, the man continued.

"It looks like we have a new face among us today. Welcome to the Dignity Forum. Do you mind quickly introducing yourself?"

I stood up, a dozen set of dying eyes fixed upon me.

"Hi, I'm Eli. I'm here because my father has Stage IV non-Hodgkin's lymphoma."

A chorus of "awwws" accompanied a flurry of sympathetic smiles.

"We are happy you have joined us, Eli. Is there anything in particular you hope to gain from attending these meetings?"

A couple of new clients.

"I guess just some peace of mind – both for myself and my father. I'm tired of feeling so angry all the time, and seeing him so scared."

Insert more "awwws" from the audience.

"I think we can help with that, Eli. Please feel free to share whatever's on your mind at any time with the group during these meetings."

Thanks, but I'd really rather speak to select attendees in private during bathroom and snack breaks.

Thankfully, the spotlight soon shifted from me to the people who deserved it. Attendees took turns updating the rest of the group on their physical condition and current mood. Statements about fecal blood, pissed pants, and near-death experiences during futile intercourse attempts were bandied about as casually as comments on the weather.

The Dignity members – or "Dignitaries" as they liked to call themselves – were as spirited and snarky as they were sick. Lots of sharp barbs aimed at their own diseases and the medical establishment. Even sharper ones pointed at insurance providers. Pain, rage and self-pity masked by irreverence. Laughter as both elixir and camouflage.

Unlike other health-related support groups, Dignity wasn't dedicated to any one particular ailment, and didn't exist to save lives. Collectively the folks in attendance represented a rainbow of deadly maladies and had no fathomable chance of pulling through. The aim of Dignity wasn't to educate participants about the latest treatment options or to inspire them to hold on with all their might; rather, it was to help them accept their fate with grace and to let go with, well, *dignity* – yet still manage to get a few good jabs in before hitting the canvas.

While these people had no hope for survival, the regional hospices would have to wait. The Dignitaries still had their mobility and most of their wits. They were dead men and women walking.

I found them to be far more interesting than the living.

Among those who stood out to me at that first meeting:

Patrick. Thanks to Wegener's Granulomatosis (WG) – a condition where severe inflammation of blood vessels wreak havoc on the nasal passages, lungs, kidneys and other important organs – Patrick didn't make it to any subsequent meetings. Despite his spontaneous nose-bleeding, difficulty hearing much of what was said to him, and inability to shake hands due to arthritic pain, I think Patrick and I could have become good friends. For one, we resembled one another somewhat, if you overlooked his glaring conjunctivitis, loose teeth and the reddish-purple splotches that covered most of his body. During his turn at the meeting, he mentioned how much he was looking forward to not having to witness the construction of the mega-Starbucks that was to replace the abandoned bookstore by his house. We could have been best friends.

Denise. Although it would soon kill her, Denise's inoperable brain tumor gave her the courage and the freedom to share how much she despised white people, which, oddly enough, made me feel closely connected to her.

Leo. The first thing that I noticed about Leo when he had the floor was his fantastic accent. I could tell he was from either Argentina or Uruguay the moment he spoke. He sounded like a Spaniard who had spent too much time in Little Italy. The second thing I noticed were the tiny white spots on his tongue. Such markings, I was later told, are a common symptom of full-blown AIDS. It turns out that Leo had peaked as a Latin lover at the most inopportune time – the mid 1980s.

And then there was *Christiana.* Not many Stage IV Leukemia victims can get out of bed. This one controlled the room. Throughout her monologue, she playfully referred to her fellow Dignitaries as "deadbeats." Her dark humor shined particularly bright toward the end of her talk, when she expressed concern that her coffin might make her look fat. But it wasn't until the laughter died down that Christiana captured my attention.

"I love you guys and all," she said, her tiny body trembling in her seat, "but I'm ready to go."

And as most of her peers nodded their head in unison, silently expressing empathy, all I could think was, "I'd be more than happy to give you a ride."

Approaching a woman to discuss a death deal is easier than approaching one to buy her a drink. At least for me. My moves in bars and nightclubs have always left a lot to be desired, but I was evidently a natural on the terminally ill circuit.

"Hi, Christiana. I just wanted to tell you that I was both amused and touched by what you said tonight."

"So, like, you laughed, you cried... Was it better than *Cats*?"

"Much better. Had you broken out in song, it would have seemed too forced, less real."

"I could do with a little 'less real' right now. What was your name again?"

"Eli."

"Nice to meet you Eli."

She extended her osseous hand, and as I shook it she smiled and said, "When you're dying, introductions take on a very Groucho Marxian feel – 'Hello, I must be going.'"

"Well, I for one am glad you're still here."

"That makes one of us."

A clever yet sensitive response would have been ideal here, but my tongue was tied. Christiana sensed my struggle.

"I'm sorry," she said. "I guess I'm just more comfortable with death than most people are."

"Please, don't apologize. I love black humor, and I can certainly understand why you would embrace it."

"Yeah, I'm Stage IV funny. If it weren't for the fact that

I'll be dead in a few months, I bet some network would offer me my own sitcom."

I laughed louder and longer than was probably appropriate, but the outburst was authentic. After catching my breath and wiping off my grin, I got down to business.

"Do you have a moment to chat, preferably in private? I'd like to ask you about a rather sensitive matter my father brought up the other day."

"Uh, sure. My brother will be here soon to pick me up, but I have a few minutes."

Christiana and I snuck out the doors and up the five steps to the ground level. We stood beneath the outside atrium of the building with nobody in sight.

"I realize I don't know you, but I wanted to gain the perspective of somebody in a similar position as my father."

"I hope I can help."

"Okay. This isn't easy, but here goes."

I leaned in closer and whispered. "My father wants to kill himself. He wants to go out on his own terms."

"His cancer's that advanced, huh? I'm sorry to hear that."

"He wants me to help him do it."

"Yikes," responded Christiana, but her tone revealed neither shock nor surprise. "Listen, I'm not sure what you want to hear right now, but I will tell you that there isn't a person in that room down there that hasn't had a similar thought."

"Do you guys ever discuss it as a group?"

"Not really. I mean, we joke about it, and I'm sure some have talked it over with the group members they are closest with, but it's not a big topic for open discussion. Ben, the leader, likes to keep things more positive."

"Well, my father, like you, says he's 'ready to go.' He even has a plan."

"What kind of a plan?"

"I'd rather not go into the details of that right now," I said, sounding more abrasive than I had intended. "I'm sorry, I'm not really sure why I'm even telling you all this anyway."

"It's okay, Eli. It's really not all that big a deal. I think about ending it every day, but I've got a bunch of family and friends who would be very upset if I did. It's ridiculous really – they know I'm going to die in a matter of months, but they all demand that I ride it out."

"But they aren't the ones who are suffering the way you are, or the way my father is."

"I know, but they look at suicide as something more horrible than dying 'naturally,' regardless of the circumstances. I admit, it's a little selfish on their part."

"Well, in my father's plan, his death wouldn't look like a suicide – not even an assisted one. It would look like he just passed away peacefully, like his cancer simply got the best of him."

"What you're saying actually sounds pretty good to me – I know that seems creepy. Nevertheless, your father's asking a lot from you. You're his son, and whatever his plan is, if you're helping, you're breaking some serious laws."

"I know, I know. But I want to help him. He's always been there for me, and I want to be there for him."

"So are you going to do it?" Christiana shook her head the second she posed the question. "I'm sorry, don't answer that. It's none of my business. You don't need another person walking around with that info."

"It's okay…"

"But don't worry – everything you've said to me goes with

me to the grave. Fortunately for you, there's not much time for any secrets to leak."

"I'm not worried. *I* came to *you* with this matter, remember? It's me who should feel uncomfortable right now, not you."

"Yeah, but you actually don't seem all that uncomfortable. Something tells me you have already made your decision."

I smiled but said nothing.

"Just be extremely careful."

I so wanted to respond with, "I always am." Delusions of grandeur were setting in. One assisted suicide to my name and suddenly I was the James Bond of euthanasia. I managed to rein myself in.

"Let me ask you, Christiana: If somebody you knew was willing to do what my father is asking me to do, would you go through with it?"

She pondered the question for a moment.

"Honestly, I think I would – if it's as simple and non-incriminating as you mentioned. But I wouldn't let my mother or father or either of my brothers do the deed, not that any of them would ever offer. It's way too emotional a thing to involve them in. It would have to be a friend or, better yet, some Kevorkian-like person."

"Somebody detached but who really knows their stuff."

"Exactly."

"Yeah, I wish my father had somebody like that. It would make my situation a whole lot easier."

"Hell, now that you've got me thinking about all this, I wish *I* had somebody like that."

And there it was. It was like the moment during a date when you realize you are going to get lucky. I had a live one.

She was eager, practically begging for it. Everything I was looking for in a dying woman.

It happened three weeks later. You don't need to know where Christiana lived or the color of her house or what time her brother was expected home from work the day I entered with my equipment in hand.

It's better I don't tell you how long she held a portrait of her aging parents before kissing it and taking a seat on her brown leather sectional for the final time.

It will only make things more difficult if I describe the look on her face when she heard Tom Waits singing, the silk and broken glass of his "Somewhere" mixing with the helium that eased her to sleep.

This glossing over of details is for your own good. The fact that you are still reading this likely means that you understand what drives me and have perhaps even sided with me to some extent. But remember, we are really just getting started here. You won't make it if you get too close, if I let you see and hear and feel each and every one of my clients. Trust me, you aren't built for it. Besides, I don't have a lot of time.

However, there is one particular detail I'd like to share about Christiana's exit before we leave her behind. Just before I turned the nozzle a half-inch toward infinity, she uttered something I didn't understand. I asked her to please repeat it.

"*Ave atque vale*," she said. "It's Latin. Look it up."

CHAPTER 8

Things started to take off from there. I don't mean to imply I was out every night slinging helium and slipping hoods over heads, but my satisfied client list was growing – roughly one a month. It was no coincidence that Dignitaries were dropping off at a similar rate.

Not wanting to draw suspicion or cause the Dignity Forum to disband due to dwindling membership, I started attending a couple other support groups in the area – one designed for late-stage cancer folks, the other aimed at AIDS patients.

I had to sharpen my acting skills a little more for the latter group since I didn't have my dad's experience to draw upon. Fortunately, I did have a friend named Pierce who died of AIDS back in college, giving me something real to go from. So, for the meetings, dead Pierce became my dying boyfriend and I played a gay widower in waiting. Nobody seemed the wiser, though I did get a few disparaging looks from fellow members for what I assume they found to be a slightly forced lisp.

While I was no longer a rookie, I was still learning. My technical skills – hood set-up, utilization and breakdown –

were second to none, but like with any new business in a developing field, strategic tactics needed to constantly be tinkered with and reshaped. For instance, my selection criteria – what I looked for in a candidate prior to approaching them – was initially limited to just three things: 1) The candidate had to indeed be dying; 2) the candidate had to have expressed or at least hinted that they have considered taking their own life; and 3) the candidate had to be easily accessible – i.e., they couldn't be surrounded 24/7 by personal nurses or reside in any kind of assisted-living facility.

Those were the big three; however, I soon found it necessary to add another key stipulation: I had to like the candidate at least a little bit.

I learned that one the hard way.

Bernard Prescott was 51 years old, riddled with colon cancer, and one of the biggest schmucks I have ever shaken hands with. When I first heard Bernard speak at the cancer support group, it wasn't his turn. He had interrupted a fellow member who was explaining gleefully to the group that some herbal supplement she had been taking had relieved much of her discomfort.

"Whatever!" Bernard blasted. "We're supposed to believe that some ground up roots and flowers bottled by a Chinese snake oil salesman are going to miraculously cure what a team of oncology specialists have already given up on with you? Forget that concoction – give me one that makes me disappear, forever."

Allow me to introduce myself.

Just a week later I was inside Bernard's hunting lodge an hour outside the city, enduring his verbal assault against liberals, illegal immigrants, blacks, Jews, Muslims, homosexuals and environmentalists while he smoked one last cigar and sipped two final snifters. I sat anxiously through the racist and reactionary machine gun spray, biting my tongue and counting the seconds until I could silence the shooter.

Therein lay the problem. With each of my previous clients (four in total at that point) I had believed wholeheartedly that I was doing them a favor. With Bernard, though, it felt more like I was treating myself – and most of the free world.

This was not me kindly helping somebody toward the exit. This felt more like murder.

I inadvertently grinned as I started the flow of the gas – not an "I'm here for you" grin, but rather a "Take that!" one. The grin widened when moments later Bernard visibly lost consciousness. Minutes after that, my first thought after checking his pulse wasn't "Goodbye" – it was "Good riddance."

This was unsettling. It's quite one thing to fantasize about a person getting creamed by an 18-wheeler right after they cut you off on the freeway. It's quite another when the fantasy becomes reality, and you're the one driving the truck.

So after Bernard, I tweaked the system. I know it's not right to discriminate against others based on their political or religious beliefs, but if you're a suicide specialist who wants to be able to live with himself, it's essential.

The new policy caused me to disqualify more than a couple otherwise viable clients. There was Jack, a septuagenarian afflicted with Amyotrophic lateral sclerosis (ALS, a.k.a., Lou Gehrig's disease). Jack had helium written all over him, and I was all set to offer my services until I saw him reading *The Way Things Ought to Be* by Rush Limbaugh, with a highlighter in hand.

There was Elizabeth, a woman far too young to have had breast cancer spread to the bones and liver, but far too good a friend of Jack's for me to consider fitting her with a hood.

I came close to relieving Terrence of his highly advanced melanoma, but had to retreat after he spent what remained of his energy trying to get me to embrace Jehovah.

Steven had a swastika tattoo the size of his spinal tumor.

Paul (pancreatic cancer) managed a hedge fund.

Holly (lymphoma) kept up with the Kardashians.

And Edward. There was really nothing wrong with Edward, aside from his untreatable osteosarcoma. However, there was something about his clavicles that reminded me of Ann Coulter, thus Edward was removed from the exit list.

You may say I was being too picky and elitist, but you weren't the one faced with turning the valve. Anybody can shout out plays from the stands; get in the actual game and then come talk to me. Trust me, it was contentious enough extinguishing people I admired or at least felt indifferent toward. Snuffing out people I couldn't stand would have been totally inappropriate.

Additional modifications to the client selection process soon followed. For instance, no matter how much I liked a potential client, or how badly they were dying, or how easily accessible they were, I found I just couldn't seriously consider them if they had young children. Call me a softy, but I didn't want to have any hand in leaving a little kid fatherless or motherless and conscious of that fact. Babies were a different story – I could do a client with a baby. Humans less than two are too busy having their minds blown by their own fingers and toes to fathom tragedy or loss. Infants suffer no permanent psychological scarring just because a nipple gets taken away or because a familiar face and voice disappear. Sure, there will be some crying, but no more so than if an unsafe toy is removed from the room. Babies rebound in minutes if not seconds.

So absolutely no clients with children aged 2 to 10. If the kid hit 11, we could talk. If 12 or 13, no problem. At that age a kid becomes a reason why a parent who isn't even dying might be open to an early exit. Tack a fatal disease on to having a tween daughter in public school, and you'll be looking in the yellow pages for suicide services.

Another disqualifier: Insanity. For me to even think about approaching you regarding my services, you had to be of sound mind. If I sensed any hint of crazy caused by a tumor or a lesion or some potent medication, no exit for you. This meant that all the poor souls battling advanced Alzheimer's and dementia were automatically out of the running. Sgt. Rush had slipped in under the wire, his mind still intact despite a devastating diagnosis.

I guess it's somewhat ironic that insanity precluded a person from becoming my client. After all, it could be said that I – in opting to do this very odd line of work – had lost my own mind. Of course, I hadn't lost mine in the same way that a man who mistakes his wife for a hat loses his. With me, it was more a case of a man misplacing something that, as it turned out, had been weighing him down all his life.

You are wondering about the money.

I, too, pondered the cash question considerably before ever setting foot in the Dignity Forum that first time. The question wasn't "What should I charge?" but rather "*Should I charge?*."

The thought of stripping people of their life *and* their life's savings repulsed me. Each client would have survivors to provide for, funeral services to cover, and an array of everyday bills to be paid. Not everybody had an extra twenty grand tucked away for a tidy departure. Not everybody was Sgt. Rush.

Besides, I was aiming to be a true exit artist, not a soulless suicide merchant. I couldn't allow myself to be driven by financial gain. I couldn't be about price points and payment methods.

Unless, of course, the client brought it up.

Without me saying a single word or dropping even the slightest hint, I found that nearly every exit candidate I approached asked something along the lines of, "How much would that cost?" during our initial discussion.

Each time the question was posed, I'd play it cool; careful not to blurt out a frightening sum that would end the conversation abruptly, but also careful not to brush the question off entirely to imply I worked strictly pro-bono.

"I have no idea," I'd say, "I hadn't really thought about it. I don't want to make this about money."

It was critical that I maintain such a "Gosh, I don't know" naiveté. Remember, I approached every candidate in the same manner as I had Christiana – explaining to them what my dying father was asking of me and letting the conversation develop from there. If after being asked about the cost I were to respond quickly and assuredly with *any* figure, regardless of how low or lofty, my cover would have been blown and the person would have felt played. In a flash I would have gone from compassionate ally to sinister hustler. And once you get labeled as shady, you are done in the suicide business.

If the candidate pressed on and insisted on compensating me to serve as a facilitator, I would timidly ask them, "What would you feel comfortable paying?" This worked wonders.

It was a "name your price" operation, and I was open to all offers. Have helium – will travel. Whenever I decided somebody was worth approaching, it meant the job was worth doing. Dollars had nothing to do with it.

That's not to say that lots of them didn't land in my pocket.

Most clients offered me between $10,000 and $20,000 for my services. Some opted to pay more. Much more. One threw down $50,000 for me to cure his osteosarcoma, insisting that fifty Gs was the going rate for a professional hit. You don't argue with somebody who has intimate knowledge of the earning potential of assassins.

Not every job was a lucrative one. I administered a handful of exits for nothing or next to it, and was fine with that. I never passed judgment on those clients. How could I? Some simply *had* no funds due to months or years of expensive treatments and inadequate insurance. Others just didn't think to offer anything. I certainly couldn't be upset with them – it's not like there is any common protocol or accepted etiquette when dealing with suicide assistants. You can find books and websites that touch on how to tip in Fiji or haggle in Hanoi, but you won't find any that cover how to compensate your friendly neighborhood euthanasia man.

In defense of those who never thought to offer money, there is a fair amount of distraction when you are busy dying. When not consumed by the daily existential angst involved, there are friends and relatives to comfort, bucket list items to scratch off, bosses to verbally eviscerate, and past actions to woefully regret. You are permitted – nay, expected – to become self-absorbed and forgetful at death's doorstep. And if, in the midst of all you're dealing with, a stranger approaches to ask if you might be at all interested in having him help you shuffle off this mortal coil, nobody can judge you as inconsiderate or lecherous if the idea of payment never crosses your mind.

Besides, I was receiving more money than I would ever deserve from my higher-rolling, less distracted clients. I amassed a six-figure stash within my first four months. To complain about doing a few freebies now and again would have been the epitome of avarice.

Regardless of payment amount, each and every one of my clients received the exact same level of service and professionalism. Shelling out twenty or thirty grand didn't get you a premium package featuring a pre-exit massage, a purer form of helium and a gold pendant. It's not like I wore a tuxedo for those who met a minimum payment requirement, and dirty sweatpants for those who didn't. I was an equal opportunity executioner.

Despite the sudden and exponential increase in my net worth, it was easy remaining inconspicuous. I didn't have any expensive hobbies to support or tastes to satiate. I had no friends or women to splurge on, nobody tempting me to show off. I did buy my mother a new set of top-of-the-line golf clubs for her 55th birthday, but all she suspected me of after that purchase was being a closet homosexual.

"You shouldn't be out buying titanium drivers for your mother, you should be taking nice girls out to dinner. Why *haven't* you been on any dates, Eli? You know, it's okay if you don't like women. You can tell me."

I'm not gay, mom – I just pretend to be at a weekly AIDS support group.

"Mother, please."

"Well, you don't seem to be trying very hard to meet any women."

Oh, I've met several. It's just that I usually say goodbye to them forever following my first visit to their bedroom.

I knew I would soon have to move out and find my own place – not just to escape the maternal prying, but also because I was running out of places to hide my money. It had graduated from a manila folder hidden under my mattress to a shoebox hidden in my closet to a large cardboard box buried in the attic. Sticking it in the bank or investing it would have left an egregious paper trail, setting off some loud alarms come tax time. There was always money laundering, but I wasn't street smart or corrupt enough to know anything about it.

Thus, I was stuck having to rely on antiquated ways to conceal a whole lot of green, living like a drug dealer or a state Senator.

My biggest fear wasn't getting caught. Not even close. What really kept me up late at night, besides the speed, was the thought of a client having second thoughts after it was too late, experiencing serious doubts during the dream stage – those few minutes of life that remain after the helium enters and induces sleep. Imagine deciding that you're not quite done yet but being buried too far deep in REM-land to interject. Screams during dreams are often silent. A vigorous twist to escape takes the shape of a minor twitch. Nothing for the exit man to see or hear. Nothing for me to notice. In flows more helium, out go the lights.

Not that an aborted exit is ideal, but it beats the hell out of forcefully shoving somebody into eternity. I'd gladly deal with the mess of returning a client's deposit and convincing them to keep our near-death experience on the down-low if it meant not being party to premature euthanasia.

It's why, if you end up working in this racket, you must get in the habit of asking each client several times during your working relationship, "Are you absolutely certain?" It's why, after hooking them up to the hood, you must look for even the smallest sign of reluctance, any inkling of panic. Widening eyes. Rapid breathing. Fidgeting hands.

Once you turn the valve, you'll know. The sound of the helium entering the bag – that soft, dull whoosh, a sort of exhale – separates the seriously suicidal from the second-guessers. If you see anything resembling a change of heart at this point, do not hesitate to ask, "Are we good?" If you don't receive a clear, positive sign or aren't convinced by the response, quietly shut off the tank, remove the tube from the bag and repeat the question, this time speaking directly through the hole. What you need to see at this point is anger – a look from the client that says, "Why the hell did you stop? Let's do this!" Or actual words to that effect. Then you know they mean business.

Some profanity may be thrown your way in the heat of such moments, but no client will ever seriously fault you for having a strict "beyond the shadow of a doubt" policy in place. Worst comes to worst, you'll find that you misread their apprehension and must endure a few moments of awkward unease as you reconnect them to the hood. No big deal. A couple extra minutes of life won't kill them.

CHAPTER 9

After a year or so of helping people die, I was really starting to reach my full potential as a person. For one, I was drinking much less and popping fewer pills. There was no longer a need to extensively self-medicate now that I had important and engaging work to do.

I didn't even mind my traditional job. I recognized its value. Jubilee no longer represented a dead end, but rather the perfect front end to a burgeoning back business. And I was a good shop manager again. I was much less distracted than I had been back when I first entered the exit game. Where before I was too busy honing my hood strategy and altering my unwritten code, now I was able to focus on my dying *and* my non-dying customers, and cater to the latter's party supply needs.

I had my own apartment, too – much to the chagrin of my mother, who had really begun to enjoy having me around to help carry her golf clubs to and from her car trunk. My new abode was a modest one-bedroom rental in a cookie-cutter condo complex, a five-minute drive from Jubilee. I chose a ground-floor corner unit to avoid having to routinely lug a heavy duffle bag up any stairs, and to keep the number of neighbors to a minimum. I had considered renting a detached house in a more remote location, but proximity to the shop was a priority. Besides, living alone in the woods is more suspicious than huddling with the masses.

So, thanks to helium, I was now healthier, happier, more autonomous, and something rarely used to describe a failed artist-cum-shop manager – philanthropic. It didn't feel right keeping the small fortune I had accrued through suicide all to myself, thus I anonymously donated a hefty amount of cash to a handful of charitable organizations. Choosing these entities wasn't easy. With so much pain, hatred and injustice in the world and so many people foolish enough to think they can stop it, countless seemingly worthy charities exist. In the end, I opted to support three that not only fought hard for people in need but that had at least a snowball's chance of winning at least a fraction of those fights. Thus, the Blackport Food Bank, St. Jude Children's Research Hospital, and Doctors Without Borders each woke up to find themselves $5,000 richer with nobody to thank.

It felt good to give back, but before you commend me on my philanthropy, keep in mind that I could have donated to The American Cancer Society or a large AIDS foundation or some other organization dedicated to curing deadly adult diseases. But I didn't. It wasn't a malicious snubbing or even a conscious one – such charities simply never entered my mind when I was deciding where I'd be sending the first set of cash-stuffed envelopes. It's painful to acknowledge, but perhaps a part of me didn't want to contribute to organizations whose success might have threatened my newly established place in the world.

Apparently I still had room to advance on the self-actualization scale.

Nevertheless, my life had meaning and direction. I had carved out quite a nice little routine: Managing the shop four to five days a week; attending support group meetings one or two evenings a week; and conducting an exit every month or so.

Not that I had become complacent. While I was certainly more a master of the craft a year in, I never got too cocky or took for granted the tact and skill required to pull off a seamless exit and stay out of police precincts. There's no autopilot switch in euthanasia. I experienced plenty of odd incidents and close calls to remind me of that.

Look over there. That's me scurrying beneath a client's bed with my full duffle bag as my client's wife — who has decided to come home for lunch for a change — enters the house. That's me whispering to my client to stay calm while we listen to her heels knick-knock off the hardwood floor of the hallway. That's me beneath the bed trembling yet thankful she arrived before I started unpacking — there's no way there would have been enough time to hide the hood pieces. That's me imagining my client's wife (who's now in the room) discovering the helium tank and suspecting her dying husband of planning a surprise party for her. And that's me imagining the letdown she would have experienced upon coming home later that day to find a cold body rather than a cluster of close friends and colorful balloons.

There I am with another client, sweating bullets upon realizing I forgot to check the helium level of a used tank prior to arriving, wondering how extensive the brain damage will be if there isn't enough gas to finish her off, wondering if I have it in me to do so manually if necessary — questioning if I'm capable of choking her out with my own gloved hands, gently enough to not leave a mark. There goes the gauge down to zero just three minutes in. There I am, coming as close as possible to praying, checking the pulse. There she is, without one. There I am, in the clear.

I'd be lying if I said such harrowing mishaps caused me to consider quitting. Don't get me wrong, I've never been a thrill-seeker or adrenaline junkie. Far from it. I always wear my seatbelt. I never swim immediately after eating. But I welcomed the risk involved in being an exit man. Though I took great care to ensure each transaction went off without a hitch, I respected rather than feared the fact that hiccups were bound to happen. I was not a machine. This was not an exact science. I didn't *want* it to be. Without the risk and the danger, my role would have been diminished. My purpose depreciated. If you take away the possibility of chaos and calamity when trying to end a life cleanly, you turn a beautiful and salient act into the clinical pulling of a plug.

One of the problems that occur when you get your shit together is people start wanting to spend time with you.

Running a semi-successful shop, drinking somewhat responsibly and not living with my mother unfortunately made me more approachable. Likeable even. Customers started freely chatting with me about things other than piñatas and party packages. Some tried to set me up on dates with their daughters. Others hit on me. One did both. Neighbors waved and knew me by name. And perhaps most concerning of all, the couple in unit 108 – Kurt and Taylor – invited me over for a cocktail party.

For most of my adult life people had left me alone and allowed me to simply serve as background scenery, an unnoticeable extra. Now that I was living a life where such social invisibility could come in handy, everybody was getting chummy. It was all very bad timing.

Still, I accepted the cocktail party invite. It would have been rude not to, and rudeness only draws attention. As much as I valued and required privacy, I knew it was important for me to assimilate. Clark Kent and Bruce Wayne wouldn't have been nearly as successful in their secret careers if they hadn't learned to blend.

Besides, it was only a cocktail party. It wasn't as if I had been invited over to a sit-down dinner, where escapes from mind-numbing discourse are more difficult due to your fixed position at a table. A cocktail party I could do in my sleep.

Unit 108. A couple drinks, some superficial banter and I'd be out of there in less than two hours – home in time to plan my next exit.

Knock. Knock.

"Eli! So glad you could make it," said Kurt upon opening the door. "Get on in here, man. You have some catching up to do if you don't want to be the sober guy among a bunch of drunks."

"Don't worry about me – I *may* have had a pinch or two at home beforehand."

"That-a-boy. A man after my own heart... and liver. C'mon in, let me introduce you to the gang."

I followed Kurt into the loud and crowded living room.

"Hey everyone," he shouted over the din, "this is Eli. He recently moved into 106. Eli, this is everyone."

I smiled and waved at Taylor and the dozen or so guests as they each raised their glass to me. A handful shouted "Hey Eli!" in unison. I recognized several of the faces from around the condo complex.

"Let's fill that hand with something – what's your drink?" asked Kurt.

I quickly surveyed the bottle options that were scattered across the kitchen counter. *Stick to the soft stuff tonight. A glass of red will do. Just ignore that bottle of Glenfiddich. A glass of red. A glass of red.*

"I'm pretty much a whiskey man, Kurt."

"Then whiskey it is. Glenfiddich okay with you?"

"I guess I can suffer through it," I said with a wink and a grin.

"Good. My boss gave me that bottle as a gift last year, but it's wasted on me. Never liked any of that whiskey or bourbon stuff, and none of our friends drink it either. We're all just simple beer, wine and vodka folk. I only put that bottle out to show off."

"I, for one, appreciate the ostentatious effort."

"Have as much as you'd like. It's not as if you'll need to drive home later."

While Kurt poured, I glanced around at all the guests. How odd to be at a gathering with so many healthy people. No shaved heads. No visible skeletons. No pallid complexions. Much more hair and fat and color than I had grown accustomed to. It was a little unsettling.

The discomfort dissipated as Kurt handed me my glass and began distracting me with small talk.

"What do you do for work, Eli?"

"I run a party supply shop called Jubilee."

"No shit? The one on Bennick Blvd?"

"That's the one."

"I'll have to keep that in mind if Taylor and I ever decide to throw a *real* shindig."

"Please do. I'll give you a deal."

I almost said, "I'll hook you up," but was trying to cut down on the use of cryptic double entendres.

"How's business these days?

"I'm making a killing" is what I would have said had I not been a man of self-restraint and grace. Instead I responded with a simple, "Not bad."

Within a few minutes I found myself sharing and receiving a surfeit of meaningless information and opinions about careers, the economy, the crime rate, Congress, social media, and Steve Jobs. By the time I poured my second drink, I had learned that Kurt had a nice job managing a bank branch but wouldn't be able to afford a new home alarm system or the latest iPhone until the President got off his ass and did something to stimulate the stock market. I also learned that Kurt was providing live party updates on Twitter.

Time for drink number three, and to talk to somebody other than Kurt.

On my way over to chat with the only two guys in the room not wearing pleated khaki pants, Taylor grabbed me and pulled me into her little circle.

"Eli, I want you to meet a few friends of mine. This is June, Tara and Christine."

"A pleasure to meet you, ladies."

Nods and smiles from all three. Wedding rings visible

only on two. This was a trap. Tara needed feeding. Taylor saw me as suitable food.

"Tara here actually used to live in your condo unit," said Taylor. "That's how we became friends."

"Is that so? Huh." My eloquence shines after two and a half single malted scotches.

"Yeah, I moved out about two years ago," said Tara. "But I like to come back to the neighborhood to cause trouble whenever I get the chance."

"I see. So, are you the ex-tenant responsible for the dent in my refrigerator?"

"Not me. I did most of my damage in other rooms."

Kurt was correct. I *did* have some catching up to do.

"Tara!" interrupted Taylor, laughing. "This is a *classy* get-together."

Tara blushed, realizing she might have overstepped the boundaries with her lascivious comment.

"What? I just meant that I spilled a lot of wine on the carpet in 106," she said, unable to suppress her giggling.

"Nice try," said Taylor, who politely excused herself to get a refill. June and Christine followed her lead, leaving me alone with the lone single wolf in the pack. Not that I minded. Though Tara was too tall for my taste (read: height), she was the kind of woman most men yearn to approach rather than escape at a social gathering. Slim, blonde and buzzed. There was something that set her apart from all the other women I had been interacting with of late: She wasn't dying.

"So, did you, like, just move in?" she asked.

"About three weeks ago."

"How do you like it so far?"

"No complaints – except for all the wine stains on the carpet."

"What? You mean they didn't replace the…"

"I'm kidding."

Tara snorted. "You! Ha! Ya got me!" A playful arm punch accompanied her three exclamations.

Time for drink number four, and to go back to talking to Kurt.

But I couldn't just leave Tara standing there.

"I'm going to go grab another one," I said, pointing to my glass to avoid any miscommunication. "You need anything?"

"Sure! I'll come with you."

Tara followed me over to the alcohol. I took her glass and, though I could easily have guessed, I asked her what she was drinking.

"White zinfandel."

Precious. All I needed was a baby blue rented tux and a back seat to fully relive my prom night.

After a few sips we found ourselves out on the balcony along with the most interesting guests at the party. We were alone. The small talk continued. It was somehow even smaller than before.

"Have you lived in Blackport all your life?" Tara asked.

"Not yet."

"Huh? Oh, ha!"

And now the arm punch. That one was going to leave a mark.

"So, what do you do, Eli?"

I help the chronically ill end their lives, but after what I've seen and heard tonight I'm considering extending my services to the general public.

"I manage the family business – a party supply store here in town."

"Ha! You run a party store and here we are meeting at a party! Isn't that funny?"

"What are the odds?"

"Oh my god, and I almost forgot – I used to live in your apartment! Ha!" Tack on another punch.

Enough. I had to get out of there. I knocked back the rest of my scotch and looked Tara straight in the eyes.

"You want to come over and see the place?"

Maybe she'd stop hitting me if I had sex with her. It was my only defense.

"Sure! Wait, you're not an axe murderer, are you? Ha!"

No, but punch me again and I might be tempted.

"If it makes you feel more comfortable, you could go tell Taylor and your other friends where you're going. That way I'll be deterred me from doing anything evil to you."

"What if I *want* you to? Whoa! I'm so bad!"

Check please.

We weaved through the throng of inebriated people and each poured another drink before slipping out the front door and walking the few feet to my place. I fumbled for the keys as well as for a single good reason why I had brought this woman to my domicile. Fortunately, logic quickly surrenders to Glenfiddich times five.

"Welcome home."

"Oh my god!" said Tara as she looked around the familiar space, the place where she had no doubt spent countless hours reading *Cosmo* with a nice glass of pink in hand. "It's so weird being back in here."

"Feel free to have a look around and reminisce," I said, happy that a female who wasn't my mother was present in my place of residence.

"Oh, I don't want to intrude – you probably weren't expecting any guests."

It's okay, I keep the place spotless and all evidence well hidden in case the police ever pop by.

"C'mon, mi casa es su casa, almost literally."

Tara sauntered around the unit, clutching her candy wine and visiting ghosts of one-night-stands past. She reached out with her empty hand and let her fingers caress the wall where perhaps a movie poster of *Sex and the City* once hung. When she got to the bedroom doorway she looked back at me.

"May I?"

"I insist," I responded, not intending to sound like a date rapist.

She pinged her wine glass with her index finger. "You going to join me?"

Normally a woman has to buy me dinner first. Or at least know how to spell it.

I walked into the bedroom, trying to remember if I had any special moves. None came to mind. No worries, Tara likely had enough for the both of us.

She sat down on the bed and looked out the window.

"That parking lot lamppost used to drive me nuts, even with the blinds down. Still, I loved living here. I really miss it – even that annoying street light."

"Why did you move out?"

"I had to. My mother got very sick. She lives about an hour from here."

Sex slid over momentarily to make room for this intriguing tidbit.

"I'm sorry to hear that. How is she doing?" I asked as I sat down next to her on the bed.

"Not well. Now both me *and* my brother live in her house to care for her." Tara began to sniffle. "We've been trying to put it off, but we are soon going to have to put her in hospice care. She doesn't have much time left and we can't provide everything she needs."

A normal man in this situation would have issued a strategic "We don't have to talk about it if you don't want to" type statement in hopes of restoring the mood, of bringing the focus back to fornication.

"That's very commendable of you and your brother. If you don't mind me asking, what does your mother have?"

Not Alzheimer's. Please don't say Alzheimer's.

"Ovarian cancer."

Beautiful.

"I lost my father over a year ago to cancer, so I know what you're going through."

"I'm so sorry," said Tara, looking more titillated than sympathetic. "Wow, we really do have a lot in common."

Tara placed her hand on my knee. Such awkward timing. After all, there was possible business to discuss.

"How is your mother dealing with it all? Is she suffering a lot?

"She's got plenty of medication for the pain, and has a very positive attitude," she answered hurriedly as she slid her hand up my thigh. "Um, I can think about something more fun to do than talk about my dying mom."

"Yes, yes, of course. So, is she still fighting, or is she just waiting for the end to come."

"What's the matter with you? Why do you want to keep talking about it?"

Admittedly, my approach lacked tact. I was more accus-

tomed to clearing the path for such discussions directly with
the chronically ill – not with their relatives, and certainly not
with a blood-alcohol level in the 0.15% range. Further more,
the hand nearing my groin was throwing me off my game.

"My apologies, Tara. It's just that I've read a lot about the
terminally ill and am very curious about something."

"Well, can it wait? I went out tonight to have fun, not talk
about terminal illness or Mom."

She finished up what was left of what she considered
wine, placed the glass on my nightstand and turned back to
me with the look of a hungry cheetah. I realized the window
for carnal activity would very soon slam shut if I didn't shut
up and make my move.

"Has your mother ever considered suicide?"

The five scotches in my system did little to numb the sting
of the ensuing slap I received. I thought only parochial school
nuns could hit that hard. Turns out Tara – save for the exces-
sive drinking and penchant for amorous acts with strangers
– practically was one.

"How dare you! We are good Christians, you sick fuck!"

"I'm sorry, I'm sorry. I only asked because my father considered it when he was dying, as have others I have known.
It's not all that..."

"Only God can decide when it's your time! People who
kill themselves spit on God – and they rot in hell!"

I had touched a nerve.

Tara had touched many. Mostly in my face.

You don't enter into a debate on euthanasia with a drunk-
en Baptist whose mother is dying. Game over. How was I to
know that a woman who had been engaging in lust and glut-
tony all night would so aggressively play the "sin" card at the

very mention of assisted suicide? I wanted to point out Tara's hypocrisy, to ask her why it was considered acceptable to scratch one's own itches but abominable to relieve another's suffering. But I knew making my point wouldn't have made a dent in Tara's thick Sunday school façade. Besides, I thought I saw a pistol in her purse.

That she hadn't stormed out of my place yet perplexed me. Perhaps she had gotten the godliness out of her system with the slap and the screaming and was once again ready to play. She sat on my bed glaring at me, maybe expecting me to grovel so that we could resume. However, now that I knew I was dealing with a possibly armed zealot, I was no longer game. I had to get her out of my place without making her feel spurned.

"Why don't we both just calm down and watch a little Bill Maher on TV."

And just like that, she was gone.

I awoke the next morning ashamed – not because of the empty and meaningless sex I had come so close to engaging in with an idiot, but rather because of my deplorable attempt to generate business while drunk. I had behaved in a manner very unbecoming of an exit man. I had disrespected the art form.

I cringed when I played back the previous night's events – most notably my sloppy inquiry that led to the slap. I had chosen the wrong time, used the wrong words and uttered them to the wrong person. An epic failure in judgment and tactics. If this had been a movie about a Special Euthanasia Task Force, my character would have been stripped of his badge.

After a few hours of self-reproach, I decided there was no sense in beating myself up about my misstep any longer. More important was to learn from it, to know that if ever I found myself in a similar situation, I would resist the urge to talk shop and instead just settle for an uninhibited sexual encounter. It's the admirable thing to do.

I wondered what, if anything, Tara had told Taylor and the others upon returning to the party. The last thing I needed was for my neighbors to label me a sociopath. Perhaps, I hoped, Tara had kept the incident to herself – something she might well have done to avoid her friends' judgment and scorn for leaving with me so quickly in the first place. Even better, perhaps our altercation had upset her to such an extent that she got in her car directly and drove off. While she was in no shape to drive and I would have strongly advised against it, I'd rather she have a minor collision or receive a DUI than publicly expose me for the creep I had presented myself as.

I thought about knocking on Kurt and Taylor's door and apologizing for leaving the party without thanking them. Doing so would establish me as a man of etiquette and class, and more importantly enable me to get a read on what had transpired after Tara stormed out of my place. Looks of derision would no doubt mean that Tara had shared and perhaps even exaggerated the unsavory details of our evening. Smiles and easy-going acceptance of my apology would likely mean my image as an upstanding neighbor was still intact. In the end, however, I opted not to knock, deciding it was far more convenient to repress my reprehensible behavior and go for a long, slow drive in the mountains.

Ignoring a lingering hangover, I jumped into my old Path-finder and headed for the hills. It was a drive I often took as a teenager and young adult whenever I wanted to clear my mind or abduct a date. The sharp rise in elevation and corresponding drop in oxygen was ideal for washing away worry and inhibition.

The tight curves of the road did little to settle my stomach, tinged with scotch residue, but the fresh mountain air pouring in through the open windows rescued me. In my chariot I ascended, rising above the city and the suburbs and the mindless concerns of mortals. It wasn't long, however, before drops of the previous evening's events began to seep in through the cracks of a mind that was supposed to be temporarily closed for business.

In itself, the mistake I had made with Tara was relatively minor. Nevertheless, it clearly showed I wouldn't be able to pursue the social life of an average man and still be successful in my secret career. It was obvious that, to stay out of trouble, I would have to avoid gatherings and, especially, women. This hadn't been a challenge back when I was living an unremarkable life – party invitations and open flirting don't often come the way of a flailing glassblowing assistant. But now that I was shrouded in an insuppressible aura of strength and confidence, I would need to learn how to subtly eschew people whom such qualities inevitably attract.

I'm not saying women are prying, conniving creatures. Women aren't even the problem here. The problem is men when we are *with* women. We just can't keep our trap shut in the company of an attractive one. I never would have wound up in the situation with Tara had I found her physically unappealing. We wouldn't have ended up alone at my place, and I wouldn't have been so bold in conversation.

I once read that elite hit men – the ones who enjoy long, lucrative, invisible careers – take an unspoken vow of chastity, or at least vow only to sleep with professional escorts. These women understand and appreciate the privacy of wealthy men, and pride themselves on discretion if a client lets slip anything even remotely incriminating.

I would have to go the same route as the hit man, I decided. I would need to show great restraint, to place my profession high above primal desire. Other than as clients, there was no room for women in my life.

Unfortunately, during my drive that day I saw a very beautiful one – standing on the railing of Panther Gorge Bridge.

CHAPTER 10

Overreact at the sight of a person perched on a bridge railing in Oregon and you risk embarrassing yourself. Nine times out of ten it's a bungee or base jumper – somebody seeking thrills rather than oblivion.

Upon closer inspection I saw no cords tied to the petite young woman's feet, no chute strapped to her back. Not a single can of Red Bull in sight. It was safe to intervene.

"Are you okay?" I asked as I rolled by slowly in my Pathfinder.

The woman, whose back was to me, didn't budge. I assumed she couldn't hear me over the high winds that rattled the steel all around us. I pulled over and parked on the narrow median of the bridge, put my hazard lights on and stepped out of the vehicle.

"Please come down from there, Miss," I said loudly without actually shouting, afraid I might startle the woman and set off a premature plummet. She turned around slowly, glaring at me with green eyes through wind-tossed red hair, clutching one of the bridge's thick gray girders with both hands.

"Please just go away."

"I'm afraid I can't do that. What kind of person would I

be if I just left you here like this?"

"Get out of here!"

"Please, just step down from there and let's talk." She was just out of arm's reach.

"Fuck off – and don't come any closer!"

"Okay, okay. I'll stay right here. Just please don't do anything permanent."

"This isn't any of your business."

Actually, it's very closely related.

"It became my business the moment I drove by. C'mon, don't do this."

"Oh, because everything is going to be okay, right?"

"Most likely not, but it *definitely* won't be okay once you hit those rocks down there."

"You're wrong – that's the cure."

Poetic, but this wasn't the time to admire poignancy.

"The cure? What, are you sick?"

"And fucking tired. Now LEAVE, asshole!"

Her fury and insults were a good sign. The fact that she bothered to engage in any discourse – however abrasive – likely meant she wasn't fully committed to the cause. A true player would have just stepped forward into the end of time.

But I wasn't taking any chances.

"Holy shit, is that a condor?" I asked, pointing behind her.

My hands reached her waist just as she turned around to look at the fabricated bird. Obeying physics, she teetered forward, pulling me into the railing and nearly escaping my precarious grip.

I had bested gravity by the smallest of margins.

"What the fuck!" she screamed. I wrestled her from the

Greg Levin

railing and, averting a flurry of elbow jabs, managed to pin her to the concrete walkway.

Had a cop, hunter or any other gun-toting individual arrived on the scene at that moment, I likely would have been shot on the spot. What I was involved in looked much more like sexual assault than suicide prevention.

"Get the hell off me!" she shouted, squirming to escape.

"I'm sorry. Just trying to keep you alive."

"I didn't ask you to do that!"

"You can thank me later."

"There isn't going to be a later."

"There will be if I can help it."

"You can't."

"I'll try my luck.

"Get off!"

"No. Why are you doing this?"

"Don't worry about why. Forget about trying to be a hero here. You can't hold me down forever."

"But I can hold you down until another car comes along. And when it does I'll wave it down and ask the driver to call the police."

"And what do you think the police are going to do?"

"They'll hold you until they feel you are no longer a danger to yourself. Or they'll get you checked into some place that can help you."

"Just delaying the inevitable. At some point I'll make my way back to this bridge."

"Why are you so intent on jumping? It's an awful way to die."

"I'm not asking for your opinion or approval."

"There are much better ways."

"Yeah, well this is my way."

"A pretty damn gruesome one."

"I'm done talking."

"And maybe not even immediately effective. You could end up lying down there all broken but still breathing, and have to suffer through the horror of having a cougar or coyote finish you off. You might even be conscious when the buzzards swoop down and start picking at you."

"Shut the hell up."

"Why put yourself through all that? It's not like you get more points for agony and gore."

The woman turned her head away. I was getting somewhere.

"To jump off a bridge," I continued, "one has to be either completely insane or just temporarily out of one's mind with anger or despair. Pardon my quick assessment, but you don't seem like a lunatic to me, thus I'm thinking yours was a heat-of-the-moment decision. I predict that, given a few hours, rational thought will return and you'll be thankful for what I've done."

"You honestly think you've saved me from killing myself?"

"I hope so, but that's not even what I'm saying. I'm saying that, at the very least, I've saved you from killing yourself the *wrong way*."

"What the hell are you, some kind of suicide consultant?"

"You could say that."

"'Cause you sure as shit aren't a shrink."

Relax. You know the code. I don't work with people who are looking for an end to mere depression or to heartbreak – only to fatal ailments. And while I had no way of knowing for sure that she wasn't on medical death row, few women in the throes of Stage IV possess the strength, curves and complexion of the one I was lying on top of.

I saw nothing wrong with leading her on, though – making her think I might help her find a better route to ruination. It was a stall tactic. All that mattered at this point was that I prolonged the conversation. This woman needed to be brought back to life, but she wasn't about to chew on and swallow the "you have so much to live for" chestnut. Tempting her with the idea of a superior suicide option seemed like the best way to keep her breathing.

"What do you say we get up off this concrete and go chat about all this somewhere over coffee?"

"So that's what you do? You get women to postpone killing themselves long enough to go out with you?"

"I just think you need somebody to talk to right now."

"I don't. Talking isn't going to fix anything. Besides, I don't know who the hell you are. I'm not going anywhere with you."

"Why not? What's the worst that could happen – I turn out to be a psychopath and murder you, a suicidal person? You should be so lucky."

"Get off me, you nut-job."

"I'm not the one who just tried to jump off a 200-foot bridge."

"That's right, you're not. You're the one who stepped in to ruin it."

"Not necessarily. I might end up improving your approach."

"There you go again with your 'suicide consulting' shtick. It's really creepy. Most people would try to convince me *not* to kill myself – *not* sell me on how to do a better job of it."

"Well, you've made it pretty clear that you want to die. I'm simply respecting your wishes. However, I can't stand idly by and let you do it in such a brutal manner."

"It's a fitting end."

"There'd be lot of clean-up involved. And just think of the poor person – your next of kin – who'd have to identify your remains. It's cruel of you, really."

"Yes, shame on me. What does the expert suggest?"

"Talking about it over coffee."

"I'm about to leap off a fucking bridge – sorry if I'm not up for a date."

"Not a date – more of a tutorial."

"Why don't you just share your insight and expertise with me here? Then we can both be on our way."

"I can't think straight without my coffee."

"Whatever, it doesn't matter – there's nothing you can do for me. You think I don't know about less messy methods? About pills or carbon monoxide? What you fail to understand is that I have no interest in going out with a whimper. I WANT messy."

I had finally met somebody stunning with whom I could enjoy spirited, edgy banter, and she wanted to smash her bones against jagged rocks. It figured.

I'm generally an enemy of cliché, but all I could think was if you love somebody, set them free. And while this wasn't love, it was something – enough for me to roll the dice.

"Well," I said as I stood up, "if you're absolutely certain it's what you want, I have no right to stand in your way. If you really want to jump, then jump."

She sat up and rubbed her wrists, picking off the gravel pebbles softly imbedded in her skin. Her perplexed expression soon morphed into one of satisfaction and relief, and as she stood up and looked out over the bridge railing, I began to think I had made a grave mistake. She carefully climbed back up to her original position. I stood there and watched, struggling to keep my word as she clung to the girder. She was taking this farther than I had expected. One step or slip on her part and I'd be a murderer, at least in my eyes – more so than after any hooded exit I had facilitated. *Say something. Grab her!*

Before I could unfold my arms to intervene, she leapt from the railing…

…the wrong way.

Her feet landed on the ground beside mine. Seconds later her face was buried in my chest. Out of her mouth came sounds like those of a wounded wild animal.

But all too human.

Set them free. If they come back, they're yours.

Releasing the trapped. Catching the fallen. I was really developing into quite the unexpected hero. One week I'm helping to end a life, the next I'm stepping in to save one. Seemingly dichotomous acts, but actually one in the same.

I knew exactly what to do after ending a life – just tidy up a bit and walk away. This life-saving thing, however, was very much uncharted territory. I was out of my element.

Some in my situation would celebrate having at least extended somebody's timeline and demand nothing more of themselves. Others would feel somewhat responsible for the life they had saved and commit to further nurturing. Complicating matters was the fact that the soul I had temporarily salvaged had a remarkable body and face. It's hard to leave such a being behind to fend for itself.

"You're coming with me to have that coffee, and maybe a bite to eat," I said to the woman whose head was still nestled against my sweater. Neither of us had spoken during her five-minute catharsis of tears. "I can bring you back to your vehicle later, wherever it is."

"I took a taxi out here."

A one way ticket. She had meant business.

"Well, then I'll drop you off wherever you want afterward."

"I don't really live close."

"Don't worry about it – neither do I."

She didn't protest or resist in any way as I slowly escorted her to my Pathfinder. Good thing – I'm not sure what I would have done had she thrown a fit over my gentle abduction. It would have been perfectly understandable for her to scream and scratch and claw at me – a strange man in a remote place – as I attempted to get her into my passenger seat, especially considering her emotional state. But the physical fight in her was gone, fully spent. I was leading a dazed girl out of a war zone, away from a village that had been leveled.

As defeated as she seemed, I half-expected her to open the car door and make a dash back to the bridge after I had placed her in her seat and walked around to the driver's side. But she stayed put. It didn't stop me from pressing the auto-lock button to seal all exits as I started the ignition, revving the engine and clearing my throat in hopes of masking the *click*.

"After what we've been through together I don't think it's out of place to ask you your name," I said as I put the car in gear and turned off the hazards.

"Zoe," she said softly, looking down at her lap.

"I'm Eli."

She looked at me, forcing a smile and a nod. It was the first time I noticed the tiny freckles on her cheeks and nose. I may have gotten a little lost in them.

"I think I passed a diner about 20 minutes back in Cedar Springs," I said. "Probably our best option."

Zoe looked out the window and said nothing. Restaurant selection wasn't a high priority for somebody who had assumed they had eaten their last meal. How odd the concept of coffee must be so soon after flirting with obliteration. Meeting for coffee is already arbitrary enough under normal social circumstances; add near-death to the equation and the beverage suggestion borders on the absurd.

As much as there was to say, it was a time for silence. Zoe's body language begged for it. She sat leaning hard right, her face pressed up against the car window, one eye watching the trees and the rocks and the mile-markers and everything else she thought she had seen for the final time roll by.

When she fell asleep a few minutes later, I considered skipping the diner and instead driving her to a hospital back in Blackport. She needed a licensed therapist or clinician, not me. She needed a man trained in the prevention rather than the perfection of suicide. But it was over an hour back to the city. Even if she didn't wake up during the drive, she would be none too happy upon realizing I was trying to have her admitted. I could already hear the shrieking and feel the fingernails. I wanted what was best for Zoe, but I didn't want to be disfigured in the process or be responsible for her being force-fed Thorazine by Nurse Ratched in the waiting room. Thus, I decided to go with the original plan.

Zoe awoke as we pulled into the parking lot of The Cedar Springs Diner. She rubbed her eyes and looked over at me, sighing as the disorientation subsided. It was difficult to tell by her expression if she was embarrassed over her earlier dramatics on the bridge or frustrated over continuing to exist. A bit of both was my guess.

"You ready to head in?" I asked, pressing the auto-lock button to unlock her door.

"Yeah, I guess."

We stepped out of the car onto the loose gravel and walked toward the entrance of the nearly empty diner. It was 4:30 – a couple of hours past the lunch rush and a couple of hours before the dinner one.

"I didn't make a reservation, but let's see if we can get a table anyway," I said to Zoe as I held the door open for her.

She almost smiled as she entered.

Zoe started toward the stools at the counter before I tapped her on the shoulder and pointed to a booth in the back corner. No need for the line cook to be distracted by what promised to be an interesting conversation. He had grease fires to avoid.

The lone waitress on duty brought us a couple menus after we were seated. Zoe opened hers and pretended to peruse the items on offer, but I could tell she was lost in the spaces between the pictures and words.

"Order whatever you'd like. It's on me."

"I'm not hungry."

"Well, at least get something to drink."

"I'll just have some coffee. That was the plan, wasn't it?" She closed her menu and looked out the window.

"Yes, that, and chatting about what happened. Tell me, what put you up on that bridge?"

"I don't want to talk about it."

"I can't help if you don't."

"I never said I wanted your help."

"That's true, but that doesn't mean you don't want it. You didn't jump, and you got in my car to come here. I think you *do* want to talk about it – at least a part of you does."

"So you think it was all just a plea for attention, a cry for help?"

"No, I don't think that. I believe you went there with the full intention of... anyway, I'm not trying to belittle your attempt. But now we're here, and I think it could help a lot to talk."

"Just forget it. You wouldn't understand. And there's nothing you can say to help me, to fix what has happened to me."

"I'm not saying I can fix anything. I'm just telling you I'm here to listen."

The waitress returned.

"You two ready to order?"

"Yes, we'll each have a cup of coffee, and I'll have a piece of pie, if you have any."

"Apple, cherry or peach?"

"Peach please."

The waitress collected the menus and left with an even larger scowl than she had arrived with. I turned my attention back to Zoe.

"I have all afternoon and night to listen."

"I need to go to the restroom."

She slid across the vinyl seat and out of the booth, making a beeline for the dingy door marked "Ladies" just a few feet away. Maybe she had a pocket full of pills she was going to down in a locked stall to escape my makeshift intervention. Maybe she was going to shatter the bathroom mirror and use one of the shards to slash a major artery.

Or maybe she simply had to vomit.

I could hear the retching from where I was sitting. I thought to knock on the restroom door and inquire if everything was okay, but decided against it. I didn't want to draw attention to the poor girl. Nobody else in the joint had noticed what was happening, and I aimed to keep it that way. Besides, I wasn't overly concerned about Zoe's health. It was perfectly natural to throw up following a thwarted suicide attempt – the body's way of re-calibrating itself for continued commuting and mortgage payments.

When Zoe returned to the booth, she found her coffee waiting for her, and me halfway through my slice of pie.

"Sure you don't want a bite?" I asked, acting as if I hadn't heard what had transpired in the bathroom.

"I'm sure." She looked at her coffee cup and slid it aside.

"No coffee, either?"

"I really don't want anything."

"A glass of water, maybe?"

"No. Thanks. I'm fine."

I sensed her irritation increasing, and thus finished my pie and coffee in silence while she stared out the window. We looked like a couple that had been married for decades. The hospital idea was starting to look good again.

"Maybe I will take that glass of water," said Zoe moments later, rising from the dead.

I motioned for the waitress, who, after hearing what I wanted, rolled her eyes and muttered, "Big spender," as she walked away.

"Water usually comes without having to ask for it, grumpy," I shouted.

The waitress turned around.

"And customers usually come in here to eat and spend more than their kids' daily allowance," she responded, finishing off the sharp retort with a snap of her chewing gum.

I twisted in my seat to face the waitress, verbal barbs locked and loaded, fully prepared to do battle. Just as I was about to retaliate, I heard gasping behind me. I turned and saw Zoe practically doubled over, laughing as hard as she had cried back at the bridge, struggling for breath. I looked back at the waitress, who gave me a dismissive wave before resuming work.

"It's not *that* funny," I said to Zoe, half-heartedly trying to hide my smile.

She looked at me and continued laughing wildly, eventually downshifting into a giggle. Just as she was about to regain total control, the waitress slammed two giant glasses of ice water down on the table and barked, "Enjoy," before turning and walking off in a huff, causing Zoe to suffer a recurrent attack. This time it was contagious.

It's fascinating how thin the line separating devastation and delight can become.

The two of us sat in the booth holding our stomach, laughing so hard we emitted no sound for several seconds. The waitress, the line cook and the handful of other patrons stared at us as we convulsed. It was time we left.

To avoid any further confrontation with the waitress, I dropped $20 on the table without asking for the bill. It was more than triple the cost of what we had consumed, but the waitress had earned it. Her rancor had saved a life. At the very least, extended it.

We made our way out to the car, trying but not succeeding to stifle our snorts and snickers. Such attempts to silence ourselves ceased once we were out of sight, once we knew that our laughter could flow without making anybody feel ridiculed. We weren't laughing at the waitress. We were laughing at the hilarity of contrast, at the madness of rapidly changing life scenes, at the improbable juxtaposition of self-destruction and deplorable service. As it turns out, rudeness – and the knee-jerk reaction to it – is a riot when laid next to suicide.

As badly as I wanted to pull out of the parking lot and leave the diner in our dust, I was laughing too hard to drive. I made the mistake of announcing this to Zoe, who found my inability to operate a vehicle hilarious. Tears poured from her eyes as she pounded the dashboard and stomped her feet on the floor mat. This only fueled my own amusement. It seemed we would be stuck in an infinite loop of laughter. Fortunately, Zoe managed to push a few audible words through the whoops and howls.

"I killed my ex-fiancé this morning."

CHAPTER 11

Confessing a murder is one way to quell a laughing fit.

Now I was *really* kicking myself for not opting for the hospital drop-off earlier. There was a killer in my car, and it wasn't me.

"Yeah right," I said to Zoe, hoping my skepticism would transform what she had told me into an untruth.

Zoe looked at me, a smile still lingering.

"Zoe?"

"I shot Keith."

"You *shot* him, or you *killed* him?"

"Both."

"This morning?"

"Yes."

"Holy shit. Where? Why? Did anybody see you?"

My barrage of questions floated over Zoe and evaporated. Though her body was strapped into my passenger seat, her mind had returned to the crime scene.

"Hey, Zoe. Zoe!"

"Don't shout at me!"

"I'm sorry, but you're kind of leaving me hanging here. You can't drop an 'I killed my ex-fiancé' on someone and then just disappear."

"I can't believe I told you. I don't even fucking *know* you. Oh shit, are you going to go to the cops?"

"No, no. Relax. Just tell me what happened."

Zoe paused to compose herself, taking deep breaths and wiping the tears and melted mascara from her eyes. As intrigued as I was to hear the details of her confession, I couldn't help wondering if she still had the weapon on her, if it was still loaded, and if she suffered from the kind of chemical imbalance that might urge her to turn a hearsay witness into a second victim. All I knew about this woman was that she was beautiful and had both suicidal and homicidal tendencies. Not so very different from the last couple of women I had dated. A legitimate cause for concern.

"It actually started last night," she said, her voice shaking. "He came over to my house out of the blue, completely trashed. We hadn't seen each other or spoken in a long time – we had a clean break-up over a year ago. But when he showed up last night, he was so angry. I let him in because I didn't want him making a scene and disturbing my neighbors. He kept babbling about how I'd ruined his life by not marrying him, how everything was turning to shit for him. This was ridiculous because we ended the relationship pretty amicably. Both of us had agreed that calling off the engagement and breaking up was the right thing to do.

"Anyway, I made some coffee in hopes of sobering him up, and it seemed to be working. After he stopped being so belligerent and seemed okay to drive, I tried to send him on his way, but he said he wanted to talk some more. I told him I was exhausted and had to get to sleep. He begged to stay for just a little while longer. The last thing I remember before waking up on the sofa four hours later was him taking a sip of coffee and grinning at me after I had returned from the bathroom. When I came to around 3 a.m. he was gone and I was lying on the sofa naked from the waist down, knowing for certain that he… that he had done something despicable."

"Are you saying he *raped* you?"

"I'm not *saying* he raped me – he *raped* me! Motherfucker roofied and raped me!"

Zoe buried her face in her hands and cried as angrily as I've ever seen anyone cry. As much as I would have liked to console her by softy rubbing her back, I was afraid to touch her.

"It's okay," was all I could manage. Pitiful on my part. I pressed on.

"So when, and where, did you shoot him?"

Zoe raised her head and took a deep breath.

"A little after eight this morning at his house. In the basement." She recoiled. "Shit, I can't believe all this is happening."

"Did anybody see or hear anything?"

"I don't think so. I mean, nobody else was in the house, and I didn't see any neighbors when I got the hell out of there."

"How many shots did you fire?"

"Just one, in the chest. Oh, god!"

"And you're sure he's dead?"

"Yes. There was so much blood. I'm pretty sure the bullet hit his heart."

"That'll do it."

"It was like somebody else was holding the gun and pulling the trigger. I was out of my mind."

"You had every right to be. Can I ask where you got the gun?"

"It was his. I knew he kept it under his bed and I went and grabbed it when I walked into his house – I still have a key to his place. He was in the basement doing laundry. He never heard me come in. Didn't know I was there until I came down the stairs."

"What did he say when he saw you?"

"He said 'Whoa, whoa, whoa. Drop the gun, baby.' That's what did it."

"What's what did what?"

"Him calling me 'baby' after what he had done to me the night before. Him standing there thinking he still had control. That's what really made me pull the trigger."

Zoe wringed her hands and chewed her lower lip. Furious and confused and exposed.

"Did you do anything with his body after you shot him?"

"I just left him there in the basement. I didn't try to dispose of it or to clean-up or anything. I wasn't trying to hide what I had done. I figured it wouldn't matter since I was going to be dead soon, too."

"Pardon me for asking, but you already had a gun in your hand – why didn't you just... you know, instead of heading out to the bridge?"

"I don't know. I didn't plan any of this out. I'll tell you what, though, I wish I *had* used the gun on myself."

"Don't say that. It sounds to me like this guy had it coming. Your life isn't over. The police and the courts will most likely side with you once they know the whole story."

"I don't even care about that. Whether I get murder or manslaughter or off scot free, it doesn't mean anything. It doesn't change how ruined everything is."

"I know it feels that way now, but –

"You have no *fucking* idea how it feels."

"You're right. I don't. But I think you need to try to ride this out a little longer."

"Yeah, why's that? And what the hell ever happened to you giving me advice for a better suicide method? All the sudden you're softening into Johnny lifesaver."

Not a moniker that's likely to stick.

"I'm somewhat of an expert on suicidal protocol and appropriateness. You're just going to have to trust me on this."

"What the? So, you're *suicide-blocking* me?"

"You simply aren't what I consider an ideal candidate."

"What the hell gives you the right to decide? It's *my* life."

"Look, it's not like I'm some all-powerful guardian or gatekeeper. I can't stop you from killing yourself. But I *can* decline to assist you. You aren't the right fit."

"I see. And just what, pray tell, would make me the 'right fit'?"

"For one, you would have to be dying of an incurable disease."

"How do you know I'm not?"

"Because I know these things."

"Yeah, well it just so happens that I have, um, I have a malignant brain tumor. Will you help me now?"

"Please, don't. It's insulting."

"How insensitive of you! I'm dying of brain cancer and all you can say is –

"Zoe, just stop. Show some respect. I have keen sensibilities and strict standards. Blatant lies are useless."

"But you promised me back at the bridge."

"I promised nothing. I merely mentioned there were much better methods, and suggested we sit down and chat about your situation. Now that we've done that, I see that you do not qualify for my services. It's nothing personal."

"What are these services you keep mentioning? What are you, some kind of hired killer for the terminally ill?"

Zoe's wording wasn't entirely off the mark, but she made it sound so cold and inhumane. It was hurtful. I wasn't about to appease her with an affirmative response.

"I'm sorry, now that your request has been denied, it prevents me from further discussing the details of my services with you. Just know there's a lot more to it than what you have inferred."

"Whatever, I hit the nail on the head, didn't I? You're a cancer-patient killer. A freak!"

"Fine, if that's what you want to believe."

"That's some sick shit."

"Listen, would you like to continue with the ignorant epithets, or would you like me to help you figure out what to do about your dead ex-fiancé situation?"

"I already know what I want to do about it – I want to kill myself, but you've made it clear you aren't going to help me with that."

"You don't want to kill yourself."

"Yes, I do."

"No, you don't. If you *really* wanted to, you would have done so already. You had two golden opportunities – one with a pistol and one at the bridge – and yet here you are in one piece."

"I told you, I wasn't thinking straight after the shooting. As for the bridge, *you* interrupted the jump."

"Interrupted, yes, but I gave you a second shot at it – one you opted not to take."

"So now you're daring me?"

"No, I'm submitting clear evidence that deep down you want to live. You want to *live*!"

Zoe bristled, then softened. What I had said struck her like a new invention. As my words sunk in, I saw the muscles in her jaw release, the swollen arteries in her neck contract. My statement served as a catalyst. Her subconscious desire to keep breathing cracked the surface. However, she refused to acknowledge this verbally.

"You don't know what you're talking about," she said, almost in a whisper.

"I think I do. And I think you know it."

Admittedly, "Ha! I'm right, you're wrong" is not typically the tack to take with somebody in the midst of a meltdown, but I felt Zoe required tough love more than sympathy.

"Fuck off!"

Okay, maybe a little sympathy.

"I'm sorry. It's just that I look at you and I don't see a hopeless case, a life extinguished. I see a troubled, frightened girl who's dealing with some major shit and who needs some help."

"'Major shit' is a bit of an understatement, wouldn't you say? I murdered a man."

"Shhh. Don't go bandying that word about. From what you've told me, it doesn't sound like murder. More importantly, you might get away with it."

Apparently it wasn't enough sneaking around helping sick people disguise their suicide as natural death. I needed some excitement in my life.

Most people, after hearing about the mess Zoe was involved in, would have urged her to turn herself in, or would have turned her in themselves. I've never cared much for most people. Just those who throw extravagant parties or who don't have very long to live.

Evidently, I was also partial to those who *did* have long to live but who just needed a little more convincing – and a little assistance averting the law.

I was going with my gut on this one. For all I knew, Zoe could have been lying about the whole rape thing. She could have been a psychotically jealous woman who couldn't bear to be without the man she shot, or for him to be with somebody else. She might have killed him in cold blood rather than out of revenge in the heat of the moment. There may have been pre-meditation of a point-blank bullet. But I was giving Zoe the benefit of the doubt. From what I could gather, she was telling the truth.

I just couldn't imagine this woman destroying anybody or anything in a cold and calculated manner. Except maybe herself.

I felt compelled to help. Doing so further fueled my ever-burgeoning sense of purpose. Of course, it didn't hurt that she was gorgeous.

"Where is the gun now?" I asked.

"I threw it off the bridge before you showed up."

"Okay, that's good — assuming it didn't hit anybody walking down along the gorge. That would be most unfortunate. Still, we should hike down there tomorrow, gather up whatever's left of the gun and bury it."

It was odd hearing myself hatch such a plan. I sounded less like a party-supply guy and more like a character from a Tarantino film. All the exit experience had apparently sharpened my "cleaning" skills.

Zoe just nodded, seemingly still in a mild state of shock, but no doubt a little impressed by my take-charge tactics — however improvised and possibly erroneous they were.

"Now I need you to think," I continued. "Did you leave anything at the scene that could incriminate you? Anything at all?"

"I don't think so. I mean, there's always hair and fingerprints that could be found, but I didn't do anything stupid like leave the gun or my purse or some other item of mine behind."

"Good. And you didn't scratch him or spit on him or anything like that?"

"No. Not this time."

"So there was a history of fighting? Violence?"

"Nothing serious, just your typical couple spats. Not physical, and nothing that was public."

"Okay. Now, how long ago did you say you guys ended things?"

"It ended about a year ago and, like I said, without much drama. I mean, he was pretty upset when I called off the wedding and broke up with him, but —"

"So *you* ended the relationship?"

"Well, it ended up being a mutual decision, but yes, I initiated it."

"That's great – pretty much eliminates you as a spurned lover seeking revenge."

Zoe smirked.

"Now, did anybody know anything about what he did to you last night? I mean, would anybody say you had a motive?"

"No. Nobody knows anything. I let him into my house last night before he drew the attention of any neighbors. And I assume he left my place quietly, the son of a bitch."

"Did you tell anybody – a friend or family member – that you were going to see him this morning?"

"Nobody."

"Had you spoken to him via phone recently?"

"Not that recently. Maybe two or three months ago."

"Excellent. Do you have your cell phone with you now?"

"Yeah, why?"

"Because it's important you answer any calls that you receive from this point on, whether you recognize the number or not. In fact, *especially* if you don't recognize the number."

"Why's that?"

"It could be the police calling to inform you what's his name… Keith has been killed. After the body's been found – by whomever – the cops are going to want to talk to you, you being his ex-fiancé and all. You don't want to be dodging such calls. That will only rouse suspicion."

"Okay, but when I speak to the police, do I –"

"You were never there."

"But I thought –"

"Zoe, you were *never* there."

"You said that once my side of the story – the *true* story – was heard, the punishment might not be that severe."

"That's true, but that was before I knew there was nothing putting you at the scene. Completely innocent is a hell of a lot better than three to five, don't you think?"

Zoe winced. It was hard to say if her discomfort was caused by the thought of lying to the police or of being incarcerated. Either way, I took her negative reaction as a positive sign. Those with a serious eye on suicide don't show concern over personal ethics or freedom.

"Even if my claim that I wasn't there sounds plausible, they might still give me a polygraph. I don't know if I can trick one of those machines."

"Don't worry about that. Worry about perfecting your role – about seeming genuinely shocked and saddened by the news about Keith when you receive it. Do that, and a lie detector won't even enter the picture."

Zoe scowled at me.

"This is all nice and easy for *you* – *you're* not the one whose life is fucked. You're not the one who has to put on a convincing show for the police and others. It's like some kind of game for you, but I'm the one with everything to lose."

"You don't think I have anything to lose? The very fact that I'm not turning you in or reporting Keith's death to the police could make me an accessory to murder, or manslaughter, or whatever. And I'm pretty sure my actively trying to help you get away with it all makes me an accomplice or something."

"So then why *aren't* you turning me in? You should. As for your plan, I didn't ask you for help. I certainly didn't ask you to become my partner in crime."

"I guess I just like teetering on the edge of the law at times."

"Yeah, well, you should have left me teetering on the edge of that bridge."

"Now *that* would have been a crime. Against humanity."

Zoe just shook her head – mostly at me for my stubborn persistence and attempt at charm, but perhaps also at herself for liking it a little.

Now that I was no longer laughing uncontrollably or investigating a murder, I was ready to drive. I inserted the key into the ignition and lightly revved the engine.

"So, where to now?"

In asking this I was relinquishing control. Up to that point, I had been calling all the shots. But we had come to the point where me blurting out what I thought was the best next step in the plan might have caused Zoe to feel uneasy. "Let's find a motel so we can get an early jump on finding the gun in the morning" would sound inappropriate. And while I was concerned Zoe might still be a danger to herself if left alone, I couldn't presume to start monitoring her every movement.

"Could you just take me home?" she said.

"That's a bad idea."

Relinquishing control is overrated.

"Why's that? If I 'didn't do anything' then why should I be staying away from my house? Me not being home might actually make me look suspicious."

She had a point. It wouldn't look good if the police discovered she spent the night just outside the city the day her ex-fiancé was killed. If I proposed my motel idea now it would look like I was a sexual predator, or a miser over gas miles, or both.

"Okay, you're right," I said, feeling awkward about my sudden switching of gears. "Where do you live?"

"Just north of Blackport."

"I live *in* Blackport, so that's easy enough. Are you cool with me coming by to pick you up early in the morning to go look for the gun?"

"I guess so, assuming the cops haven't picked me up by then."

There was certainly a chance of that, but the fact Zoe hadn't yet received any calls from the police or any mutual acquaintance of Keith's most likely meant the body had yet to be discovered.

"Does... I mean *did* Keith live alone?" I asked.

"Yes."

"Is... *was* he one to get frequent visitors at home?"

"Um, not really. The occasional friend might pop by now and again, but most of his friends and family live in Seattle."

"Good, then there's probably some time before people notice that something's awry, especially with it being a Sunday. Tomorrow might be a different story. Where did he work?"

"In an office in the city. He's in finance."

"Folks at work will wonder where he is and why he hasn't called in sick. Still, it will be at least a day before the cops get wind, and I doubt you'll be the first person they'll be contacting. Still, we want to get to the gun before anybody else might stumble upon it. How about I pick you up at, say, six tomorrow morning."

"Christ – so early?"

"Sorry, but we need to get cracking as soon as the sun comes up. It could take a while to hike down to the gorge and locate the gun."

"Fine. I'll try to be ready at six."

"Do more than try. And if by chance the police contacts you between now and then and asks you to come in for questioning, I'll hike down to the gorge myself tomorrow."

"You don't have to do that."

"I know, but I will."

Zoe just shrugged.

You're welcome.

The drive from the diner to her house emulated our earlier drive from the bridge to the diner, with Zoe dozing most the way, waking briefly whenever a road bump would lightly rattle her head against the window.

I focused on taking the S-curves slowly and on ignoring the second-guesser inside me. Helping Zoe was like facilitating my first exit; I didn't really know what I was doing, but nothing seemed able to stop me.

As we neared Zoe's area of town, I gently shook her shoulder to wake her so she could give me directions. As we pulled up to the curb outside her house, which was a small ranch-style domicile in a neighborhood strewn with similar modest suburban abodes, I wondered if this would be the last time I'd see her. I knew that once she stepped out of the vehicle, there was nothing to keep her from fleeing town, or from completing what she had set out to do when she shot out of Keith's house that morning. All I could do was let her go and hope for the best.

Before Zoe got out, we exchanged phone numbers.

"Call me if you need anything or if plans change before tomorrow morning."

"Thanks… I appreciate it," she said softly, almost smiling. "But I still don't see how we're going to pull this off."

Gratitude and a "we" statement. A team was forming. And what a pair we were. Collectively we represented multiple consecutive life sentences – me for my illicit side job; her for a single mistake.

CHAPTER 12

Spotting gunmetal beneath a slate dawn sky is no simple task, especially when rocks, shrubs and twigs are crowding the scene.

Fatigue further complicated the search. I had slept fewer than two hours the previous night – anxiety and anticipation getting the best of me – thus my usual 20/20 vision wasn't functioning at full tilt. I would have been better off blindfolded and brandishing a metal detector.

Oh, in case you're wondering, I wasn't alone.

A certain soon-to-be murder suspect was, as per the original plan, busy kicking through sticks and stones about fifty feet from me. Much to my relief she had answered the early morning call of duty. However, like me, she wasn't fully conscious.

Sleep deprivation, in addition to spoiling the scenic drive, had turned what should have been a 15-minute hike down to the gorge into a 30-minute one full of stumbling and swearing. Conditions didn't improve much even after we reached the base of the gorge, where each chunk of sandstone littering the ground represented a sprained ankle waiting to happen.

After close to an hour of us rummaging through the dead riverbed, the hunt finally came to an end.

"Found it!" Zoe shouted gleefully. She sounded more like a little girl reunited with a lost puppy than a woman reunited with a deadly weapon.

She held up the revolver, which appeared to be totally intact. That I had expected us to find it in pieces scattered among the rocks showed how much I knew about gun composition. The only ones I had ever held shot caps or BBs. What Zoe clutched was built for much more than pinging beer cans off fence posts.

"Make sure the chamber, or whatever it's called, didn't pop open upon impact and lose any bullets," I said, walking toward Zoe. "Can't be too careful."

I didn't know much, but I knew a stray slug from a revolver might attract attention in a region where only shotgun shells roamed.

Zoe clicked a latch on the gun, causing what I've since learned is the cylinder to swing open.

"Five bullets in the chamber," she said, showing me. "We're good."

As curious as I was to hold the gun, I saw no need to add any more prints to it. Why complicate matters for the poor forensics specialist in the event the weapon was ever recovered?

"Put it in my backpack," I said.

As I turned to give Zoe direct access, a flash of panic ripped through me. I had just turned my back on an unstable person packing a loaded pistol – the same instrument said person had used 24 hours earlier to kill what may have been an innocent man. And we were standing in the middle of nowhere.

My heart restarted when, in place of a loud bang and a hole in my skull, I sensed a soft zipping sound and a tug on my shoulder. I had never been more attracted to a woman in all my life. The gun was safely in place.

"Let's head back up," I said. "There's a shovel in my trunk."

"Why didn't you just bring the shovel with you on the way down?"

"Because who knows who's watching from up there," I responded, pointing up to the bridge and the road. "Unless you're in your yard or on a construction site, shovels draw stares."

"So where are we going to bury the gun then?"

"In thick woods far from any overlooks."

Our hike up to the Pathfinder was infinitely more graceful than our earlier descent. Being wider-eyed no doubt contributed to our increased coordination, but it was more than that. A weight had been lifted. Holding the deadly piece of steel in my backpack made each of us lighter. We had recovered a key piece of freedom.

And now it was time to get rid of it.

We hopped into the Pathfinder and drove a few miles until I saw the trees squeezing the road on both sides. I pulled off onto a narrow shoulder and cut the engine.

"You stay here," I said. "I think it's better you don't see where I bury this thing."

"What the hell? You think I'm going to come back and dig it up?"

"I just think if you don't know exactly where it is, it'll be easier for you to forget about this whole thing, or at least think about it less."

"I don't see how it makes a difference."

"Good, then you shouldn't mind staying put while I do this."

I got out, popped open the back door, and grabbed the backpack and shovel.

"Slide over into the driver's seat and stay there until I get back," I said. "If anybody slows down or stops, just smile and wave them on."

"Can I at least have the keys so I can listen to the radio?"

I had hoped my taking of the keys had gone unnoticed. Merely a precautionary measure; it would have been absurd for Zoe to steal my vehicle and abandon me – though no less absurd than me digging a hole in the forest to hide a .38 for a near perfect stranger.

That was the problem – she was near perfect.

Before closing the back door, I flipped the keys up to Zoe in the front seat. Secretly I hoped she didn't know how to drive a stick-shift.

"I'll be back in 10 or 15 minutes. Take a map out of the glove compartment and pretend to read it, so you look like a normal person."

I started my foray into the woods, using the shovel to help clear a path through the dense growth. A couple minutes and several sticker-bush scratches later, I stopped at a spot where soft ground outwitted the roots.

The dead leaves and dirt succumbed easily to my spade, and in short time I had a two foot-deep grave ready for a gun. I unzipped the backpack, removed the revolver using my shirtsleeve, and dropped it in what I hoped to hell would be its final resting place. A couple squirrels scampered by as a yellow-headed blackbird switched branches above. As far as I could tell, they could be trusted.

After refilling the hole and saying a silent rallying cry against soil erosion, I headed back to the road. Zoe was right where I'd left her. At least *somebody* was behaving rationally.

Becoming romantically involved with someone who has shot and killed a former lover is generally not recommended. In fact, for many, the shooting part alone – without the killing – is enough to discourage courtship. Others even draw the line at something as innocuous as an attempted stabbing.

Personally, I feel when you encounter somebody new who makes you lose your mind a little, you sometimes just have to overlook the fact they may have, at one point or another, lost theirs completely. It's hard enough meeting someone you find beguiling enough to want their contact information. Start nit-picking about a few past indiscretions or a police record and you'll end up dying sad and alone.

Maybe it was the way Zoe's long red hair had waved in the wind while she stood on the bridge preparing to plummet to her death. Maybe it was the way she had described why and how she put a bullet through her ex-fiancé's breastplate. Or perhaps it was simply that she was the first woman in a long while with whom I could have an intelligent and captivating conversation, and who – physiologically speaking – had more than a few months left to live.

Whatever the reasons, I didn't view Zoe as merely a worthy project. I saw her as much more than the sum of her problems, much more than something to feed my selfish sense of utility. Yes, I was indeed intrigued by her dire straits and my potential to assist, but what had started out innocently enough as a simple desire to help a possible cold-blooded killer was quickly transforming into something more profound and complex.

So much for my exit man vow to avoid women.

My growing affection for Zoe was slowly being reciprocated. I could tell by her decreased number of scowls, tears and angry verbal attacks – as well as by the way she slept only halfway home in the car following the gun burial. It was obvious she no longer *completely* regretted letting me talk her down from the railing the previous day.

"Thanks for driving – again," Zoe said when we arrived at her house. "And for, you know, helping me get rid of the... well, you know."

Yes, I know. Love is never having to say 'lethal weapon.'

"No need to thank me. I'm happy to help." I purposely used the present tense – to let Zoe know I wanted my role as accessory to continue. A sort of subtle, "When can I see you again" statement.

Apparently *too* subtle.

"I gotta run. Take care of yourself," she said, unbuckling her seatbelt.

"Let me know how things go, and if there's anything else I can do."

"You've already done more than enough. There's no need for you to get any more tangled up in my nightmare."

"I really don't mind. I want to help."

"I still don't understand why?"

"You don't need to. Just know that I would like to stay involved, to assist in whatever way I can."

"Is it because you're afraid I'm still going to kill myself, and you feel responsible?"

"No... I don't know. Maybe that's part of it, but –"

"I'm the only person accountable for me, for my actions. Whatever happens to me now – prison, insane asylum, death – you will in no way be to blame."

"I wish you'd aim higher – those are all very bleak outcomes."

"They are all very *likely* outcomes."

"But perhaps *less* likely if you allow me to help you."

"I can't."

"Why the hell not?"

"Because then I will have ruined two lives instead of just one."

You mean "three lives instead of just two" – you killed your ex-fiancé. But who's counting.

The conversation was going well. Zoe's actual words may have suggested that she wanted us to part ways for good, but the subtext showed otherwise – as did the fact she was still sitting in my vehicle despite there being nothing to keep her from just opening the door and running into her house. Save for the auto-lock button.

While it appeared I had Zoe right where I wanted her, I realized I was trying too hard. This was not a woman to be won over through debate or demands. Up until this point with her, loose reins had served me well. I'd set her free twice before – on the bridge and outside her home the previous evening – and neither time had she evaporated.

I needed to try for three-for-three.

"There's nothing more I can say. I want to help – even if that means just being there for you if you need to talk. But if you want to be left alone to deal with all this, I have to respect your wishes."

Zoe sat waiting for me to finish, not immediately realizing I had. After several seconds of silence, she turned her head away and grabbed the car door handle. Before exiting, she looked back at me.

"Thanks again, for everything."

"You take care of yourself. Keep my number in case you want to talk. And stay the hell away from any bridges."

Zoe smirked. She stepped out of the car, closed the door and walked up to her house without turning around again.

I pressed the button to roll down the passenger side window.

"If you prefer face-to-face over phone, I work at a place called Jubilee," I shouted. "Pop in any time."

Zoe paused for a moment, then took her keys out of her purse, opened the door to her house and was gone.

I still had a full day ahead of me, including an afternoon shift at the shop and a weekly meeting for the terminally ill that night. The weekend had been interesting and eventful, but it was time for me to return to my normal life of selling party supplies and lining up suicides.

I drove home to grab a shower and fix a quick sandwich before heading to Jubilee to relieve Carl – all the while pretending not to be thinking about Zoe. When I arrived at the shop, which was devoid of customers, Carl was napping at the counter. A typical Monday.

I tapped him on the shoulder.

"YeshowmayIhelpyou!" he blurted out upon waking, his tongue still asleep, eyes rolling around.

"At ease, Carl."

"Dude, I thought you were a customer."

"Nope, just your boss."

"Man, it's hard to stay awake when it's this slow."

And when you do five bong hits for breakfast.

"I hear you, Carl. Not napping on the job can be challenging, but it is possible. I find that stocking and straightening shelves helps to stave off sleep. Keeps the blood pumping."

"Cool. I'll try that next time."

"Splendid."

Carl, who was born without the ability to process sarcasm, retrieved his green windbreaker from a cubby behind the counter.

"I'm going to take off now, if that's cool."

"Yes, I can handle things from here. Sorry to have disturbed your nap."

"Don't worry about it, man. See you later."

After three attempts to push open the shop door, Carl realized — as he always did — a pull was required to exit the premises. Watching him leave, I made a mental note to review some of the job application forms that had recently been submitted.

A smattering of customers trickled in over the next couple of hours. While there were no big sales or anything exciting to report, one woman did inquire about helium tank rentals. However, she looked far too healthy and vibrant to warrant any serious consideration on my part. What's more, she was pushing a baby stroller, which automatically disqualified her from my services, regardless of her physical condition.

Later that afternoon while helping another customer select items for an office party, I felt my cell phone vibrate in the pocket of my jeans, indicating receipt of a text message. The sudden look of exhilaration on my face confused the man I was assisting. Further confusion ensued when, soon thereafter, I muttered, "Fuck" upon discovering the message was an automated one from a sleazy money lending firm rather than an authentic one from a woman I'd recently rescued.

"My apologies, sir. I just received some bad news," I said to the customer in an attempt to cover for my unprofessionalism.

"Seems to be plenty of that going around today," he responded. "The Dow dropped 300 points."

Tragic. Maybe I can interest you in some helium?

"Also," he continued, "I just heard on the radio that some guy was shot and killed not 10 minutes from here. What's going on? Nobody gets murdered in Blackport."

There's a first for everything.

"Did they catch who did it?"

"I don't know. The local radio guy just mentioned it quickly and then returned to the news about the stock market."

"I see. So, are we all set for your party?" I asked, hoping to get rid of the guy so I could check out the breaking news online.

"I, um, guess so," he said, unsettled by my sudden switch into high gear. "Unless you think I should get some streamers and bunting. That might –"

"Nope. Not a good idea. Minimalism is all the rage these days."

"If you say so."

"I do. Okay, everything will be ready for pick-up in two days. You can pay then. Have a nice evening. Sorry to hear about your stocks."

After rushing him out the door, I ran back behind the counter, sat down at the computer, and typed "Blackport man shot" into the search box.

<Click>

Man found dead of gunshot wound in Northwest Blackport. - Blackport news – 35 minutes ago
<Click>

Police in Blackport are investigating an apparent homicide that has occurred in a home in the Northwest area of the city. The victim, a 35 year-old man whose identity is being withheld until family can be notified, reportedly died of a single gunshot wound to the chest.

The body was discovered early this afternoon by one of the victim's coworkers and close friends, who went to check on the victim when he didn't show up for a lunch meeting or respond to repeated phone calls.

According to police, there was no sign of forced entry or struggle at the scene of the crime, and no suspects have been apprehended or identified yet.

I had known about the shooting for more than a day, but it was all so real now. Anonymous and sterile, but real.

At least I knew the woman I was falling for wasn't a complete liar.

Trust is essential if any relationship is to work.

CHAPTER 13

Any minute now.

Any hour now.

Certainly before the end of the night.

I lay in bed unable to sleep, surprised that Zoe had yet to contact me. It had been roughly 10 hours since the police discovered Keith's body. Either she had not yet heard the official news, was busy being interrogated, or – and this was painful to ponder – had meant business earlier when she said she refused to further involve me in her nightmare.

I knew she meant it when she said it, but I also felt confident she would crack once the cat was out of the bag – or, more precisely, once the body was in one. It's easy to show quiet resolve when all the lights are off, but once the spotlight hits and starts searching the grounds, quiet resolve can quickly dissolve into a quest for a confidant.

I was likely the only person she could talk to about all this without risking arrest. I had her back. She knew this not only because I had shown it through words and deeds, but because she knew my *not* having her back meant exposing my own.

Other plausible explanations bubbled to my brain's surface when I awoke early the next morning to find no messages or missed calls:

- She *wanted* to contact me, but feared leaving a cell phone trail linking me to her in any way. A wise move. A self-less act. But one that was nonetheless causing me undue suffering.
- She wanted to contact me but had incorrectly typed my number into her phone, or had inadvertently deleted it.
- She had killed herself.

The first two of these were frustrating but fully excusable. The last one was excruciating. Zoe bleeding. Broken. Lifeless. I dealt semi-professionally with the dead and the dying but couldn't stomach the notion of Zoe leaving the building.

I checked the local news online, but no notable progress on the case had been reported since it broke. I resisted the urge to call Zoe, realizing the importance of keeping my word. Also, I was now hip to the phone trail pitfall. In the event the police labeled Zoe a prime suspect worthy of an in-depth investigation, they'd be more than a little interested in any inbound or outbound calls, particularly those involving the phone number of any seemingly new acquaintances.

Dating games like "How long to wait before calling" go out the window when the object of your desire may be wanted for a capital offense. Sort of skews the rules surrounding infatuation.

I couldn't very well pop by her house either. Such an unannounced visit would be unwise in case the cops were watching. Moreover, it could be construed as stalking. It was far safer to pursue Zoe in my mind only, at least until she was either completely in the clear or behind bars – assuming she was still alive.

These are not the kinds of thoughts you want to become preoccupied with when you're scheduled to work a full shift selling jubilation. My focus was shot. The good people of Blackport deserved somebody less obsessed with courting a pistol-packing femme fatale and more obsessed with providing fiesta suggestions. I'd had no problem holding down the fort when my only outside distraction was euthanasia; however, now that a woman was involved, I couldn't seem to keep my head on straight. With assisted suicide, I held dominion, had careful control over most elements, considered myself nothing short of a master. With Zoe, on the other hand, everything was anyone's guess, and my guesses were shots in the dark. She was a dangerous new discovery, a beautiful poison.

Fortunately for me, it was another slow day at the shop. The calm before the autumn party storm. Soon high school and college homecomings would be upon us, with plenty of Halloween mischief mixed in. The winds were shifting. A look at the Doppler showed zero mph to Katrina in two weeks flat.

That morning I busied myself with calls to vendors. These were the folks behind the scenes at Jubilee and similar entities, the people who supply the suppliers. They are the ones contracting out the actual whipping and lashing of child laborers in the third world factories where all the gadgets, accessories and costumes found on my shelves are made. I was just the guy who helped sell said paraphernalia so that young Sujatmi from North Sumatra didn't suffer repetitive stress injuries and chemical burns in vain. I used to playfully give my father hell for his role in keeping this vicious wheel of capitalism spinning. My progressive stance had softened considerably since his death.

Rationalization and denial are useful tools for averting accountability.

Following a call in which I ordered several extra boxes of crepe paper pumpkins and giant rubber spiders, I went to the employee toilet to wash the banality off my soul. Over the roar of the hand dryer I heard the shop's bell signify the entrance of a customer, hopefully somebody who could unwittingly help me help the hard-working children of Indonesia. I wiped my hands on my jeans to blot the remaining water droplets and rushed up to the front.

No customer to be seen.

Only Zoe. I was pretty certain she wasn't there to plan a party.

She looked out of place amidst all the festive material and kitsch. Or it looked out of place trying to envelop her. For a moment, I, too, felt as if I were in a strange room.

Not since Sgt. Rush's last visit to Jubilee had the shop and everything in it undergone such a perfect upheaval.

"So, you *did* hear me," I said.

"What do you mean?" asked Zoe, knitting her brow.

"Yesterday morning when I yelled out where I worked, I wasn't sure if you heard me."

"Oh. Yeah, the name stuck with me."

"I'm glad."

As if she couldn't tell this by the width of my grin, the life in my eyes.

She was wearing a short black jacket over a ruffled white blouse that hung neatly over the waist of a dark green leather skirt. Black laced boots – nearly knee high – finished off the ensemble, and almost me. The outfit was very *fugitive chic*. She looked guilty, but not of anything that would have bothered most male homicide detectives.

"Have the police contacted you yet?" I asked, catching a glimpse of a small spider web tattoo on the outside of her lower right thigh.

Zoe nervously looked around for unwanted listeners.

"It's okay, we're alone," I said.

Her jaw unclenched.

"No other employees in the back?" she asked.

"Nope. The coast is clear."

"Okay." She inhaled deeply. "Here's what went down. Two detectives came to my house yesterday evening around six. They told me about Keith, and I just let loose. I gave them shock, utter disbelief, angry questions about who would do such a thing to such a decent man. And sobbing, lots of sobbing."

"Did they seem suspicious of you?"

"If they were, they didn't show it. They were cordial and sympathetic from the moment they arrived 'til the moment they left. Said they just wanted me to think of anybody who might have had it in for Keith, anything he might have been mixed up in. I told them he didn't have any enemies or questionable acquaintances that I knew of back when he and I were together, but explained that we had fallen out of touch since the relationship ended."

"Did they ask you where you were at the estimated time of the shooting?"

"Nope."

"That's a very good sign. Had they even remotely considered you a suspect, I think they would have asked you that."

"Yeah, but it doesn't mean I'm in the clear. Who knows what they'll find over the coming days. On their way out, they thanked me and said they were sorry to have been the bearer of such bad news, then added they hoped they wouldn't have to bother me again. I told them no problem, and that it was not a bother, that I'd be happy to help in any way if it meant catching who did this. Then I started crying uncontrollably again."

"Beautiful. Sounds like you knocked it out of the park."

"It was strange... I started to actually believe it wasn't me who, you know, *did this*."

"That's what needs to happen."

Zoe nodded and let out a sigh of relief. We were having a moment. Like a patient and a psychotherapist following a breakthrough. She seemed weightless. Her words had floated from her rather than fallen out and crumbled as they had during our previous meetings. And what was that, an unbridled smile? Getting away with murder had done wonders for her complexion.

"Now you just need to carry on with your life as if everything was normal. Business as usual – well, maybe not *usual*, as it's not everyday your ex-fiancé gets whacked. You certainly need to grieve. You don't want to draw suspicion by coming off as either too content or too cold over the next couple of weeks. Try to exhibit an appropriate amount of shock and sadness. Like what you did with the cops, only dialed back a bit."

"I didn't come here for acting lessons. I know what I need

to do. And for your information, I won't have to act shocked or saddened, I'll *be* genuinely shocked and saddened – *am* genuinely shocked and saddened. He was my boyfriend for three years and fiancé for one, for chrissakes. The shock and sadness comes naturally. What I'll need to 'dial back' is the anger."

The anger. At first it seemed she was referring to the fury she felt for Keith's murderer, some imaginary man who was likely running loose across assorted state lines as we spoke. I thought perhaps she had convinced herself so thoroughly of her lack of involvement in the shooting that she was now beside herself with rage thinking about the cold-hearted fictional culprit and the senseless act of violence he committed. But then I realized the anger she referenced was aimed at the murdered, not the imagined murderer. It was the very force that had placed her own index finger on the trigger two days earlier and compelled her to pull.

I had been so busy scheming to help save Zoe's delicate neck, so busy being "purposeful," I had all but forgotten what was at the heart of the matter. Keith had done something unspeakable to her. Something awful enough to drive her to perforate his aorta with a shiny metal slug.

"I'm sorry. I didn't mean to seem insensitive. I was out of line," I said.

"It's okay."

"You have plenty to be angry about."

Zoe turned her head away and grunted.

"I can't imagine the complex set of emotions you must be dealing with right now."

"I've been dealing with a complex set of emotions since birth. Badly, I might add."

Ah, a little self-deprecation, a smattering of wit. Levity lightening the room. The swift mood change made me giddy. I've always enjoyed the company of self-possessed bipolar people.

"Amen to that. But seriously, you seem particularly well-grounded considering what you've been through the past few days."

"Well, I guess I have you to thank partially for that. That's why I'm here."

"You mean you're not here to purchase a punchbowl?"

"Not today."

"A piñata?"

Zoe pursed her lips, not amused by my glibness. I quickly reloaded.

"Seriously though, you needn't thank me. I'm just glad you're okay. And like I've said before, I'm available if you need someone to confide in."

"Don't worry, I have my therapist."

"Yeah, but if you share anything about what happened with Keith, your therapist is required by law to report it to the authorities. Me, I'm just a guy with an open ear and every reason to avoid the police."

Zoe shook her head and smirked.

"I should get going. You have work to do and I have a black dress to buy."

"I'd like to see you again."

This shot out almost involuntarily, a verbal burp, a Tourette-like event. Something in her utterance of "black dress" set me off.

"Why, because I'm obviously such a catch?"

"I enjoy talking to you – isn't that good enough?"

"I don't know if I care to spend time with somebody who isn't mortified by me and my recent actions."

"What can I say? I guess I have a thing for mortification."

"Actually, it should be me who's mortified. What kind of person claims to be an expert on suicide methodology? And you mentioned providing 'services' – what the hell was all that about?"

"Just my odd sense of humor."

"I didn't get it."

"But you also didn't kill yourself."

"So it was all just a ploy?"

"Not entirely. I do know a thing or two about suicide, and I felt you needed to know you were going about it all wrong."

"And what about your services?"

"Okay, *that* part I made up."

"It sure sounded like you knew what you were talking about."

"You're not the only one who can act in times of duress."

Zoe took a step closer and stared at me.

"I don't know if I believe you. You seem nervous."

"What, you honestly think I'm like, uh, some kind of euthanasia expert or something? Party supply guy by day, angel of death by night? Shit, I wish my life was that interesting."

"I just don't buy that you were totally winging it the other day. That stuff about how I'd have to be dying to 'qualify.' And your uppity remarks about your 'strict standards.' Sure sounded like you had experience."

"Oh, come on. What was I supposed to do, tell a highly distraught woman that I was just kidding? I had to keep up the guise so you didn't feel totally tricked and become even more upset. But please know I also spoke from the heart – I really didn't see suicide as the right option for you. Too much raw emotion was involved. You ending your life would have been a huge mistake."

"You don't know me well enough to know that."

"Well, now that it looks like you might be in the clear with the police, and now that you've had a chance for your distress to die down, wouldn't you agree it's a good thing you didn't jump?"

"I wouldn't agree or disagree. A lot remains to be seen."

"That's fine. This isn't about me being right. I'm just very glad you're still around, and I hope you soon begin to feel the same way."

Zoe used her hand to wipe off a couple tears trickling down the left side of her cheek. I offered her a tissue from the box on the counter.

"Thank you."

"Don't mention it."

I looked out at the parking lot to make sure no customers were approaching. Crying was bad for business.

"Just make sure I get that back from you," I said, pointing to the now ruined piece of tissue paper in Zoe's hand.

Zoe sniffle-laughed before slapping me on the arm. Physical contact. The first since she had buried her head in my chest out at the bridge. That was her collapsing. This was sparks igniting.

"You don't have to give it back to me right *now*," I said. "Hold onto it until I see you again – maybe when we meet up for a drink or something. Perhaps this weekend?"

"I don't think a girl whose ex-fiancé has just been murdered should be seen out gallivanting."

"We can pick a spot where nobody you know will see us.

Besides, I don't think anybody would fault you for having a drink to help with the grief, or for chatting with a friend for support."

Zoe tapped her index and middle finger on her lips, contemplating my invitation.

"It wouldn't be a date," she said.

"Of course not. So, how about Saturday night?"

"No, too date-like."

"Sunday night?"

"Sunday afternoon. Meet me at Cormac's Pub. Do you know it?"

"No, but I'll find it."

"Let's say around three-ish."

"I'll be there."

I watched Zoe leave the shop and get into an old red Volvo sedan, circa mid-1990s. As she pulled out of the parking lot, I did some basic math: Tuesday + X = Sunday. X = 5. Five days. Five days and two hours, to be precise.

I could handle the anticipation, but not the uncertainty. Five days left a lot of time for the detectives to uncover something substantial. A recently fallen follicle of hair, the fresh print of a finger, a lucid account of a nosy neighbor. Any one of these things, or, worse, some combination of them, could stick a dagger in the coming Sunday.

Not that I didn't have things to keep me busy while waiting. Party supplies to sell. People to release.

CHAPTER 14

After a week in which you manage to single-handedly stop the suicide of and secure a date with a beautiful woman responsible for the biggest unsolved crime in the county, you start to feel there's little you cannot accomplish.

And when you add to this your unparalleled ability to send eager participants on a trip to oblivion without leaving the slightest trace, you start thinking about getting fitted for your very own superhero suit.

I was aware my ego was inflating far beyond what the user's manual recommended. But after years of having watched it lie limp, I figured there was nothing wrong with letting it take up more than its fair share of space for a while. It's not like I was delusional. I still had a relatively strong foothold in reality. It would be hypocritical for an atheist to develop a legitimate God complex.

That's not to say I didn't bring a little extra swagger to my exit work that week.

I walked into my terminal cancer meeting on Thursday evening ready to choose my next client. Only 15 days had passed since I last worked the hood, thus I wasn't due to come out of hover mode for at least another few weeks. However, the rapid deterioration of a group member I particularly admired compelled me to pick up the pace. His name was Harve, and he needed me – whether he knew it yet or not.

More than any other previous or potential client, Harve reminded me of my father. I was able to mentally reconstruct Harve's ruined muscles, jowls and hair to see a man who could easily have passed for the brother my father never had. Same height as Dad. Same heavy eyelids. Same slight hook of the nose. We're not talking identical twins, but certainly fraternal. Even Harve's voice, though weak and raspy from meds and metastasis, was not dissimilar from the one that had instructed, soothed, scolded and joked with me throughout my life. Funny how you can like somebody immensely even before you formally meet. Feel connected based solely on sight and sound, knowing nothing of their character, personality type or political views. Harve could have been a baby seal hunter or a commercial beachfront condo developer and I still would have struggled to dislike him. All because he unwittingly brought me a small gift each time he came into my line of sight. A warm reminder of the man who created me.

That Harve happened to be a kind-hearted and humorous man – one who likely never killed an arctic mammal or spoiled a shoreline – only strengthened my affinity for him, and my hatred for the disease that devoured him.

I had spoken with him directly only twice before, each a brief and informal exchange over snacks. Not a word about exit assistance. Most of what I knew about Harve was derived from his candid and witty comments during group discussions. A retired Botany professor. Married to an elementary school principal for more than three decades. Two sons living in Eugene. Several tumors living in his liver. And outside of it. Welcome to bile duct cancer. Cholangiocarcinoma for those who like to show off at dinner parties. Only pancreatic cancer kills more swiftly.

Harve often laced his commentary with droll or even hilarious quips about his impending expiration. "What I'm most afraid of is seeing the words 'To be continued' at the end of an episode of my favorite TV series." This had me falling out of my seat despite breaking my heart. Harve clearly believed hyperbole and humor had healing qualities. As much as his own dark comic relief assuaged him, I could tell he administered it more for the benefit of his listeners, those who needed a laugh more than he did. Harve was no longer terrified of dying. He had graduated from fear. It's why I knew he was next.

"How's it going?" I asked him soon after arriving at the meeting.

"That's a dangerous question at these shindigs. You could end up getting crushed beneath the weight of all the bad news people can't wait to share."

"Good point. Allow me to rephrase: Hi there."

"That's better."

"I've been meaning to ask you about something. Do you have time to talk after the meeting?"

"Why wait? Who knows if I'll still be around then."

"It's just that the meeting's about to get started, and what I want to talk about might take more than just a few minutes."

"Actually, Kathy just called Randall to say she's running a little late, so we probably have a good 10 minutes or so."

I silently thanked our tardy group leader.

I pointed to two chairs against the wall, just far enough away from the other members filing in. I had long since modified my approach tactics, no longer asking candidates to join me in the hallway or outside the building. I didn't want some astute group member noticing a pattern, picking up on how people who left the room with me tended to leave the planet not long thereafter. I knew, however, such a discovery was unlikely. I was always careful to rotate groups when choosing clients. At that point I was working with four different groups, and hadn't plucked more than three members from any single one in over a year. Still, I thought it smart to play it safe, and playing it safe meant making my private conversations seem less so.

I guided Harve over to the chairs and helped lower him into one before sitting in the other.

"Forgive the morbidity of the question, but what's your take on euthanasia?" I knew I could shoot relatively straight with Harve.

"What, no comments on the weather?"

"Sorry, it's just that something strange recently happened, and I thought you might help me figure out what to do."

"Go on."

"As you know, my father has been very ill." (Yes, I'd managed to keep my dead father alive for quite some time. My plan was to announce his passing to the group soon to keep things authentic. You can only get so much mileage out of a dead dying father.)

"It's really too bad you can't get him down here to one of these meetings."

"I know. He gets quite nauseous whenever he has to travel even short distances. No worries, though – these meetings are for me. I need more help coping with his condition than he does."

"I understand. My sons are having a tough time watching their old man wither away, too."

"It's tough on all involved."

"Eh, they'll be fine."

Back to business.

"As well as my father has coped, he's tired of it all," I said, looking down at my twiddling thumbs. I looked back up at Harve and moved in closer. "He... he has asked me if I will, you know, *help* him."

Harve smiled.

"I was wondering if you'd come to me," he whispered.

"Pardon me?"

"I know what you did a while back for Jerry."

Jerry. Three clients ago. Stomach cancer. Green bedroom.

"Don't worry," said Harve, "the secret's safe with me."

Yes, but apparently it wasn't with Jerry.

"He... he *told* you?" I asked. My blood started to circulate again, bringing with it dizziness.

"Yes, but I assure you he didn't say a word to another soul. You have to understand, Jerry and I were very close friends."

"He told you."

"You okay?"

"I can't believe he told you."

"Relax. I'm telling you, nobody else has even the slightest clue about any of this."

"*You* shouldn't have the slightest clue about any of this,

Harve. Jerry *knew* how vital it was to keep quiet."

"We were like brothers."

"I don't care if you were conjoined twins. There are rules to this. Unbreakable rules. And how do you know for sure Jerry didn't say something to anybody else?"

"Because I know."

Great. My undercover operations were being tightly guarded by a hunch.

"And how do I know *you* haven't told anyone? Or that you won't?"

"Because I give you my word," said Harve, putting his hand on my shoulder. "And by the way... I'm in."

Not even news of acquiring a new euthanasia client was enough to cheer me up about having my cover blown.

"We'll talk about that in a minute. First, I would like to know exactly what you know, what Jerry told you."

Harve looked around the room.

"You sure you want to talk about that now, here?"

"It's fine. Nobody can hear us."

"Okay then. Well, I know you approached Jerry much the same way you just approached me – asking if you could talk to him in private and telling him about what your father had asked you to do."

I felt like a pick-up artist whose best lines had just been revealed to be the scripted passages they were.

"All right. Please continue."

"While naturally he empathized with your father, Jerry didn't think it was something he himself could ask one of his kids to do. Jerry told me he told you this, and that you asked him if he had ever considered killing himself."

"Okay. What else?"

"He told me he said of course he had, but explained he didn't really know how to go about it, and didn't want to shock or shame his family. He said that's when you hinted you might be able to help him out."

"When did he tell you all this?"

"A few days after the two of you had solidified the plan – so, maybe like a week before he passed."

I liked that Harve used "before he passed," as if it had been an entirely natural occurrence, which, in my mind, it was. I was merely a catalyst, an agent used to help speed the process, evaporate the suffering, preserve dignity.

"Did he tell you what the plan was?"

"Yes, the whole thing with the helium."

"What was your reaction? Being his close friend, did you try to talk him out of it?"

"Not at all. I mean, I asked him if he was sure it was what he really wanted. He said yes. He thought what you were offering to do was an ideal solution, and seeing how bad his cancer had become, I understood."

"Thank you for understanding. Some might view what I do as despicable."

"You said 'what I do' rather than 'what I *did*.' I take it Jerry wasn't the first and only person you've helped in this way."

One slip of the tongue – a single syllable, a simple tripping over tenses – and suddenly I had outed myself, inadvertently removed my novice mask, my cloak of inexperience. Too late to backpedal.

"You caught me."

"Is your father actually sick and dying. Did he really ask you to assist him?"

"He really *was* sick and really *is* dead – has been for over a year – but I had nothing to do with it. His actual cancer got him."

"So, if you don't mind me asking, how did you get involved in this?"

"A family friend. I'd like to just leave it at that, if it's okay with you."

"Okay, sorry to pry."

"Don't be. You have every reason to. I just hope your opinion of me, of what I did for your friend, hasn't changed now that you know I work in more of a serial manner."

"Hardly. If anything I'm sort of relieved. It's nice to know you have ample experience. I'd hate to have the job botched."

"So you're serious about doing this?"

"Absolutely. *I* had actually considered approaching *you* before today, but wasn't sure how you'd react. Thought you might get angry, that maybe you'd deny any knowledge of what happened with Jerry."

"I certainly would have been thrown, as I was a few minutes ago when you made it seem like you'd been expecting me."

"I guess I could have tried to play dumb when you approached me, but I'm too tired and weak to act. I hope you aren't too upset with Jerry or me."

"I won't deny that I wish you hadn't found out, or at least that I didn't *know* you'd found out, but I'm not angry. That said, you need to keep this airtight. I can forgive Jerry's indiscretion, but the slips must end there."

"Again, you have my word."

"Good. My apologies for sounding so stern. I can assure you it's not indicative of my bedside manner. I have nothing but the utmost empathy for what you and others like you are dealing with."

"I know. If I thought otherwise, we wouldn't still be having this conversation."

"Good, so we're on the same page. Now, you and I have some details to discuss before anything can happen."

"Of course, but it's going to have to happen later – Kathy just arrived. It's time to start the meeting."

Mercy killing is not an activity for which you want to attract a personal fan base. Once you have a following, you're finished. The only people who should know what you're up to, the only people who you want rooting for you, are those hooked up to your helium tank. And by the time they find out how good you are at what you do, it's too late to spread the word.

However, some people apparently can't contain their enthusiasm even before they see you in action. Yes, this means you, Jerry.

The minor security breach ignited something ugly inside me, woke me up to something I hadn't wanted to see or feel since entering the exit field. Up until my conversation with Harve, I had never worried about a client jeopardizing my freedom. Yes, I knew the moment I approached these people they had the goods on me, but I didn't see them as possible threats or informants. I wasn't some Mafioso: "You know too much, now you have to go away." My clients already *knew* they had to go away. They were happily *agreeing* to go away. That was the whole point of our relationship. There was a trust between us. I knew they knew the importance of keeping my cover intact, how doing so greatly benefitted them. If they broke the seal, they knew it could result in me being apprehended before I was able to send them on their peaceful and painless way. Or, worse for them still, it could result in our agreement being revealed post-mortem, thus ruining their "natural" death – turning it into something very unsettling for their family members, and something very fortunate for the insurance company.

After speaking with Harve, however, I couldn't help feeling I needed to start shortening the time between "signing" a client and delivering my services. I realized the sooner my clients "left," the lesser the chance of them sharing details about our little arrangement. That I would even think this disgusted me. Where before I had always viewed clients as courageous human beings worthy of a dignified departure, I now had glimpses of them as ticking time bombs to be quickly defused.

Goddamnit, Jerry.

See you very soon, Harve.

Harve and I continued our conversation right after the same meeting that had interrupted it. He called his wife, who always picked him up, to tell her to arrive a little later than usual. His wife had attended a couple of meetings a few months earlier, but, according to Harve, she couldn't handle how civil and relaxed everybody was about their respective fatal disease and was thus relegated to transportation duty by her husband.

While ironing out the details of our next and final encounter, I tried to control my desire to speed things up with Harve. I just didn't try hard enough.

"I could do this as early as tomorrow, if you want."

"Tomorrow? Jesus," said Harve. "I figured I'd have at least a week."

"You can have as much time as you want," I replied, "it's just that I'm going out of town next week and won't be back for some time after that."

Not a lie I was proud of. Just a kneejerk reaction to the *tick tick ticking* I now heard.

"I see. Well, I don't want to wait *too* long. Especially considering I don't *have* too long," Harve added with a morose laugh. "I would like a few days, though. When do you leave next week?"

"Monday."

"Could we do it on Sunday?"

"I wish I could, but I have a prior engagement."

This was a convenient truth. Okay, so my rendezvous with Zoe wasn't until 3 p.m. – thus leaving the morning wide open and the night an option – but I didn't think it right to schedule a date on a delivery day.

"Damn, I can't on Saturday," said Harve. "My wife is home with me all day. Maybe Friday. It's kind of soon, but it sounds like I don't have much of a choice."

Too soon. Little choice. These are the sentiments of second guessers. The ticking continued but I couldn't disregard standard policy.

"Harve, I don't want you to go through with this if you aren't entirely certain it's what you want."

"No, no, don't worry. I'm certain. If Friday works for you, it works for me."

"Are you positive?"

"Yes."

"Okay, then Friday it is."

We decided on 10 a.m. I'd have Carl cover the morning shift. Harve's wife would be at work until 6 p.m., and his nurse wouldn't arrive until after lunch. Curious neighbors were a non-issue – the driveway was long and the entire property was enveloped in evergreens and oak trees. If only all my appointments could have been this uncomplicated.

I gave Harve my cell phone number and told him to call me only if he needed to change the arrival time or got cold feet and decided to cancel. Otherwise I would arrive right on time with everything needed for a placid departure.

"Don't worry, you'll be in excellent hands," I said, hoping these words would compensate for the cooler than usual demeanor I'd exhibited up to that point. I didn't much like what this "time is of the essence" phase was doing to me.

Harve nodded and smiled.

"Speaking of your hands, how do I get the money into them?" he asked in a whisper.

The question caught me by surprise, as did the queasy feeling it caused. Never before had a client's offer to pay for my services shamed or repulsed me. It wasn't the way Harve had phrased the inquiry, nor did it have to do with how much he reminded me of my father. No, the mild sickness that had welled up inside me at the mention of money was caused by the realization I didn't deserve it. Not dime one. Not after the way I had manipulated my client, bumped up his demise a few days from his ideal date to assuage my own insecurities. I took his monumental decision to cease breathing – to cease being – and made it more convenient for me. I was letting personal fear and distrust turn my noble profession into something base, almost industrial. I had allowed efficiency and productivity to seep in, to contaminate the art form. There were now undeniable impurities in my sense of purpose. "The sooner the better" was trying to take over.

My submitting to the haste was a natural reaction perhaps, but a natural reaction was no excuse. I had managed to rise above a host of other "natural reactions" over the previous year and half, and, in doing so, had bettered the lives – and deaths – of many.

"You don't owe me anything, Harve."

"What? There's no way I'm going to let–"

"You don't owe me anything at all. And another thing, if next week or the week after is better for you, if that will make you more comfortable, then let's push this back."

"What about your trip."

"It can wait. I wasn't really looking forward to it anyway."

Harve stood before me blinking, befuddled by my sudden fit of flexibility. In trying to be more sensitive and accommodating, it appeared I might have made things more difficult for him. Perhaps Friday had already begun to sink in as his day of serenity and salvation. Maybe two minutes was all it took to accept what was to be his last day on earth. Maybe the hardest part was over, and there I was putting him through it again.

"If it's not too much trouble, next Tuesday at ten would be nice," he said. "A nice even week to work with. You know, to get things in order – without making things too obvious, of course."

"Next Tuesday at ten sounds good," I responded with a calm grin. I was happy not only to see Harve so satisfied with his selection, but also to hear he understood the importance of leaving a few ends loose. Nothing can kill a natural death like a closed account, a cancelled subscription, and a suicide note.

CHAPTER 15

There's something transformative about sitting in a pub devoid of windows and TV sets on a Sunday afternoon. Sipping a pint when the sun is up and most of America is at home watching a game in their church clothes lets you know you've lost. Touch. Control. The way.

It's what everybody really wants. What everybody really needs. To sink out of the world for a while. It's good for the circulation.

So is watching Zoe enter a room.

She arrived at Cormac's Pub half a stout after I had, wearing a blue denim jacket over a black dress. I raised a hand to signal my location – an unnecessary gesture considering the only other people in the place were the bartender and an elderly man having a bourbon-induced siesta three stools down from me.

"Any trouble finding the place?" she asked as I stood to greet her with a generic embrace, making sure nothing resembling erogenous zones touched.

"Not at all, I actually came with *him*," I said, pointing to our unconscious neighbor.

"I hope *he* drove. You're in no condition to get behind a

wheel," she responded with a sly grin.

I'd always wanted to meet a woman with whom I could conceal a murder and exchange witticisms.

"What do you say we get you a drink and grab a booth?" I proposed.

"Sure. What do you have there, just a beer?"

"Yeah. It's a school night."

"I need something a little stronger."

She motioned for the bartender.

"Can I get a Jamesons, two ice cubes?"

"And a Buffalo Trace, neat," I said. "Just put them on my tab."

"I can pay for my own drink, thank you," said Zoe.

"I'm sure you can, just not *that* one."

"Fine, but the next round is on me."

A whiskey-drinking woman willing to go multiple rounds on the day of rest. Thank you, Moses. I silently prayed the judicial system wouldn't take her away from me any time soon.

With drinks in hand we walked over to the booth and sat facing one another, each of us shifting a little until our haunches found a comfortable position on the solid wood beneath us.

"How are you holding up?" I asked.

"I'm hanging in there, I guess."

"Any other contact with the detectives?"

"Nope. And from what I've seen in the news, the police haven't got a clue."

"That's gotta be strange for you – following this case on the news."

"No stranger than standing in a room with Keith's family. Offering my deepest sympathies. Weeping with his mother and sister."

"I can only imagine."

This wasn't entirely true. I had attended Sgt. Rush's funeral just four days after causing it.

"I *wish* I could only imagine," Zoe responded. "It was really too much. In fact, let's talk about something else."

"Certainly. Why don't you tell me what you do for work? I've known you for a week now, and I have no idea what your job is, or if you even have one."

"I teach piano and voice."

"At a high school or something?"

"No. I used to work for a music school, but now I have my own thing going on and give lessons out of my house."

"That's great. Are most of your students kids, or do you also teach adults?"

"It's a pretty mixed bag. I'd say about half are middle school age, and the rest are anywhere from 16 to 70."

I couldn't help thinking about the field day the media would have if Zoe ever got nabbed for the shooting incident. The press loves dichotomous violence. A quiet piano teacher packing a pistol and blasting her ex-lover – that's near perfection.

I guess a party supplier dealing out death would also sell a few papers.

"Do you only teach, or do you perform publicly on occasion?" I asked.

"I used to play out, but haven't done so in a long time. I was in a pretty hot local band for a couple of years. Played keyboards and did back-up vocals."

"Might I have heard of the band?"

"Depends, were you into the local punk scene about five

years ago?"

"Can't say that I was."

"I didn't think so."

"Not because I don't like punk, rather because I wasn't living around here back then. Just moved back to Blackport about a year and a half ago."

"Moved *back*? So you're from here originally?"

"Yes. But left for college and stayed away until…"

"Until what?"

"Until my father got sick"

"Is he okay now?"

"Depends on how you define 'okay.' He died soon after I returned."

"Shit, sorry. How is that 'okay' in *any* way?"

"Because what he was experiencing at the very end, how he looked and felt, was definitely *not* okay."

"It was good of you to come back to help him. Is that how you ended up managing Jubilee?"

"You got it."

"What were you doing before?"

"Trying to become a glassblower."

"Really?"

"Yes. Glass doesn't blow itself. Not good glass, anyway."

"So, were you, like, taking classes in glassblowing?"

"Not exactly, I was a glassblower's apprentice."

"An apprentice? Cool. It's so 19th century."

"What can I say, I'm old school."

"Have you given it up?"

"Pretty much."

"That's too bad."

"Not really. I have other hobbies to occupy my time now.

How about you – what's your back story?"

"Originally from Chicago. My parents got divorced when I was 11, and I moved to Denver with my sister and mother the following year. I came out here a couple years after high school."

"Progressively moving westward."

"I guess so."

"And your mother and sister, where are they?"

"Mom's still in Denver with my stepfather, and my sister is in San Francisco with her boyfriend."

"And she doesn't know anything about, you know, what happened with you and Keith?"

"No."

"I thought sisters told each other everything."

"We're not all that close."

"But she knows about him dying, right?"

"Yes. I called her two days after, but didn't reveal what really happened. She was going to come up for the funeral, but said she couldn't get off work. I told her not to worry about it."

"How did she take the news of the death of her almost brother-in-law?"

"How do you think she took it? She was shocked and saddened."

"But not at all suspicious?"

"Why the hell would she be suspicious? I already told you, Keith's drunken visit to my place was out of the blue, and shit got chaotic real fast. Everything happened in a blur." Zoe took a sip or her drink and dabbed the corner of her mouth with a cocktail napkin. "Do you mind if we talk about something else?"

"Do you play any Brahms?" I asked, tickling imaginary ivories with the fingers of both my hands.

Zoe smiled, appreciative of my cooperation, of my willingness to take a hard right turn into an entirely different and less emotionally taxing topic.

"I do, actually," she said. "His Piano Concerto Number 2 in B-flat major is one of my favorite pieces."

"I'd like to hear you play it sometime."

We talked and drank for another two hours — heavy on the former, light on the latter. After having knocked back my beer and starting in on the whisky, I slowed the pace of our imbibing. I had learned my lesson the previous weekend, experienced the dangers of excess booze when in the company of a woman.

I needed to stay particularly alert with Zoe, to be ready to coolly deflect any questions she might try to sneak in regarding my involvement in suicide assistance. Moreover, I had to stay sober enough to ensure I didn't carelessly bring up the subject myself. She was already onto me. She hadn't bought my spiel, my claim that everything I had said about "better options" during our initial encounter on the bridge was merely an off-the-cuff ploy to distract her.

But she didn't delve any further that afternoon at Cormacs. There were no interrogations, no attempts to expose me. I returned the favor by staying clear of anything related to Keith. From Brahms on out there was just comfortable conversation, even a few playful exchanges that could have been construed as mildly flirtatious. Anybody listening in would have assumed we were two regular people leading normal enough lives. Just a man and a woman sharing a few laughs and getting to know one another.

Not a speck of blood to be seen. The air free of helium.

If I ignore all the stop signs and get lucky with the traffic lights and pass any vehicle ahead of me, I'll still have a chance. I could be there by 10:30 a.m. Only half an hour late.

How could this have happened?

I hadn't slept past nine – let alone ten – since college. I'd weaned myself off morning alarms years ago. No need for them when you're up at dawn every day.

But that Tuesday morning I awoke to sunlight, to the world flying off its axis. I hadn't stayed up late the previous night or drunk a drop or popped anything into my mouth to sedate me. Forget it. There wasn't time to question or curse my circadian rhythm for its sinister prank. I had to break land-speed records. I wondered when the fuck someone was finally going to invent the jetpack.

10:08. I was eight minutes late the second I had opened my eyes. As if Harve hadn't suffered enough.

This is when you start thinking about early retirement.

I couldn't call or text Harve to let him know I was on my way – not on the day I was to send him on *his* way. Too risky. And finding a payphone would have taken me just as long as the drive to his house.

I tried my best not to think of poor Harve while committing half a dozen moving violations en route to him. I was surprised yet relieved he hadn't tried to contact me regarding my tardiness. Perhaps he was thinking, "What's a few extra minutes of life among friends?"

Fortunately the second half of the drive took place in a rural region – a bucolic township where most of the men in blue were too busy cracking down on hunting infractions and domestic violence calls to bother with pulling over a Path-finder for speeding or aggressively passing a tractor.

It was 10:32 when I turned onto Harve's driveway, which looked more like a nature path. My body bounced and lurched as I made my way up the primitive passage, gripping the steer-ing wheel with both hands and cringing each time I heard a loose rock ricochet off the bottom of the chassis. A reddish brown two-story house soon came into view around a curve.

Along with four parked vehicles.

Not the exterior scene I had envisioned.

Harve had never mentioned anything about being a car collector. And car collectors generally aren't interested in Honda Accords, Chevy Tahoes or Ford F-150s. I considered turning back, but I had to find out what was happening. I'm all about closure.

If somebody besides Harve was in the house, I'd just play it cool. I could cover pretty easily. Would hardly even have to lie – I was just a guy from the terminal cancer group popping in on a friend.

I pulled up behind the Tahoe and parked. This is the point where normally I would pop the trunk and retrieve my duffle bag, but I wasn't about to carry exit equipment up to a possibly crowded house. After a quick mental rehearsal in case I had to change roles on the spot, I got out of the car and started walking toward Harve's front door.

Who could be in there with him? Why hadn't he con-tacted me to report the change of plans? Closed curtains or blinds in every window kept me from gaining any clues as I approached the house. My mind darted in various directions. Maybe Harve had hired a film crew to capture his final moments. (Heavy treatment over the course of months can wreak havoc on one's judgment.) Or, and this one filled me with genuine fear, perhaps he had told other terminal cases about my services and secretly organized a group departure. An unapproved four-for-one deal. I'd have no choice but to oblige, leaving behind not a scene pointing to natural causes but rather something resembling what police might uncover at a cult compound.

I'd never forgive you, Harve.

I pressed the doorbell and heard it echo through the interior of the house, followed by a muffled voice and footsteps. Seconds later a stocky man stood in the doorway.

"Hi, is Harve around?" I asked the man, who was a younger and thicker version of the person I'd come to see.

"And you are...?"

"I'm a friend from his cancer group. Just thought I'd stop by to say hi and see how he was doing."

"I'm sorry, but my father passed away last night."

My first thought was, absurdly enough, the man at the door had made a mistake. *Your father didn't pass away last night, he's passing away today.* My synapses quickly adjusted.

"Oh my god, I'm so sorry. My deepest condolences."

"Thank you. We all knew it was coming, but we thought he had a little more time."

At least another 10 to 12 hours.

"Yeah, me too. As sick as he was, he always brought so much humor and energy to our group."

"That's nice to hear. It's how we all want to remember

him – funny and energetic."

"He'll certainly be missed," I said, looking over my shoulder at my car. "Well, I'll not take another second of your time. Forgive me for coming by like this unannounced. I really should have called beforehand."

"Don't be silly. Dad would have greatly appreciated the visit."

"Would you please extend my sympathy to your mother and your brother?"

"I'll be sure to do that. What was your name?"

"Eli. I've never met the family, but Harve talked about you guys a lot."

"Nice to meet you Eli, I'm Kenneth. By the way, Dad's wake will be at Ingram's Funeral Home at 7 p.m. on Thursday, with the funeral to follow on Saturday at Oakmont Cemetery. We hope you can attend one or both."

"Thank you. I'll see you Thursday. And if it's okay with you, I'll let the group know."

"I think my mother already plans to do that, but thanks anyway."

I extended my hand. "Once again, I'm truly sorry for your loss."

As I walked back to my car, I noticed the Ford and the Honda had Washington state plates.

"Should have caught that before," I muttered to myself. Not that it would have made much of a difference. Sure, it would have tipped me off that Harve's sons were down from Seattle and that something unfortunate had likely happened to Harve, but I still would have rung the doorbell and played the part of a friend paying an impromptu visit. Peeling out and taking off only would have drawn unwanted attention and suspicion.

I climbed into the Pathfinder and, after a precarious three-point turn, I rattled slowly over the stones and other natural debris littering the thin winding driveway. Making my way out to the road was made all the more challenging by the tears hindering my vision.

It was the first time I had cried since my father died. The emotional outburst caught me off guard. I had arrived at Harve's house with the sole intention of ending his life – the same as I had for over a dozen others before him. Never before had I left a client's home crying. Solemn and reflective, yes, but never sobbing. Yet there I was weeping for a client whose death I had nothing to do with.

I then realized I was weeping *because* I had nothing to do with it.

Death is dreadful and dark and morbid when it's out of my hands. Even when expected any day, death can strike at any second with little concern for its victim. It can be positively maddening – and painful – when nobody's around to rein it in.

It killed me to watch my father succumb with such discomfort and uncertainty. Powerlessness. And it saddened me to know Harve had just suffered a similar fate. If only I had stuck with the exit date I had initially suggested to Harve, he would have neutralized death's callous specter and gone out on his own terms.

It would have been better that way.

CHAPTER 16

Oversleeping. Premature expiration. Unexpected interactions with next of kin.

It was only a matter of time before I *really* stepped in it.

I mentally lambasted myself for having lost focus, for having gotten sloppy. This was no time for me to be going through the motions and letting things slip, not with word of my services having already leaked. Who knew if the leak had truly been contained, as Harve had assured me.

I needed to be extra vigilant. It was time to raise my game, to elevate my level of concentration. Zoe sure looked pretty in that black dress the other night.

I picked the wrong time to quit abusing amphetamines.

Zoe and I hadn't even had a proper date yet, a first kiss, and already she posed a serious threat to my secondary career – not to mention my spotless police record. If I didn't get nabbed for being in cahoots with her on the Keith cover-up, I'd probably get put away after some bonehead move I'd make while fantasizing about her during an exit mission. The former offense was more out of my hands, but also less likely than the latter. There was little I could do to keep from being tied to the shooting. If Zoe got caught, she'd either sell me out or not. Simple as that. But the good money was on the "not." I was nearly certain she'd keep me a secret if pressed by the police to name accomplices.

While I was nearly certain Zoe would have my back, I couldn't be sure I'd have my own. As long as the possibility of Zoe and I gelling into something of a "we" existed, I remained a danger to the exit man in me. I had a lifelong history of letting distractions of the heart adversely affect my quality of work. Coloring outside the lines while suffering through a primary school crush. Dropping from an A to a C while infatuated with an Alpha Phi. Ruining a molten glass vase following a lover's row. All relatively minor incidents compared to what could happen if I got distracted while working the hood. Let a woman occupy your mind on this job and you'll leave a tidy little trail for the cops to follow. Might as well tattoo your name on each client's forehead. Or maybe your lapse in concentration will result in your client surviving – and pressing charges. Not only will you face serious jail time, you'll be the first person ever to be sued for "wrongful *life*." Not a precedent likely to be respected by peers in a maximum security prison.

I made a mental note to later conduct some research, to look into whether any renowned serial killers had been able to sustain a romantic relationship during their prime without having it interfere with their work.

I saw Zoe the following Sunday. I had convinced her to have dinner with me at my place. Not a *date* date according to my dining companion, but closer to one than our encounter at Cormac's was. For one, not a single word was spoken of Keith or the case. No need. The very fact she had shown up for dinner signified she was still in the clear. The Internet and the local news would be sure to promptly let me know if the police had made any significant strides. Knowing I could rely on such sources to keep me informed enabled me to proceed with more charming dialogue.

"Sorry about the shrimp being so rubbery."

"I think it's delicious," said Zoe.

"You're just being nice. I always seem to go overboard with the heat when preparing this dish."

"What are you talking about – it's great. I'd usually be at home right now eating a frozen pizza."

"You don't cook?"

"Nothing like this. I can make a decent salad and heat up soup." She placed her napkin on the table and stood up. "Could you tell me where your bathroom is?"

Red flag. The mid-meal, mid-conversation rush to the restroom. I'd dated bulimics before.

"It's right around the corner, first door on your right."

I was relieved when moments later I heard only a faint trickle through the door. No gagging or coughing. No faucets being used to mask any sounds. Some have been known to synchronize their sickness with the flushing of the toilet, but doing so necessitates a second flush – something most women are ashamed to do when mixed company is within earshot. I waited. No double flush. If Zoe was bulimic, she had mastered the art of stealth regurgitation.

She returned to the table, no longer a suspect. I refilled each of our glasses with wine – a Malbec the guy at the wine shop assured me paired nicely with prawns. I bought only one bottle for the meal. Back when I had a single identity and nothing to conceal but my self-loathing I would have purchased three.

After dessert, Zoe shot my attempt at temperance straight to hell.

"You got any whiskey?"

The judges would have accepted the following responses:

-"No."

-"I just ran out."

-"I forgot to pick some up."

-"I do, but I've been sipping straight from the bottle and just got over a terrible cold."

Actual response submitted:

"What kind of man would I be if I didn't have whiskey?"

The judges grumble.

It's easier to be a commercial success than a critical one.

Two whiskeys later we are sitting on the couch.

Laughing. Flirting. Forgetting.

Three whiskeys later we are lying on the bed.

Falling.

Man down. Man down.

I haven't really talked about the funerals.

Before I started packing helium, I had only been to four of them my whole life: My father's, my paternal grandmother's, my maternal grandfather's, and a college friend's.

That number had nearly quadrupled since Sgt. Rush's fateful visit. In just over a year and a half I had gone from being a funereal neophyte to a somewhat recognizable figure among the Blackport cemetery set. Morticians, ministers and burial crews did double takes upon seeing me for the third or fourth time over a relatively short period. I got used to – even started reveling in – the looks of, "Don't I know you?" from people who lived and breathed death every day. Wakes, memorial services, funerals, burials, entombment – this was their collective work. Meanwhile, I was just a repeat traveler passing through, racking up the frequent mourner miles.

I wasn't worried my attendance at so many of these solemn events might cause suspicion of any kind. The truth is, *not* attending was more likely to raise eyebrows. I was, after all, in the same terminal illness group as each of the deceased people in question. There was an inherent bond, a connection. You can't listen to a person laugh, cry and share harrowing accounts about their condition week in and week out and *not* publicly pay your respects once their number is up. And me being one of the few group members healthy and strong enough to make it to the funerals and other death rituals, my attendance was almost expected.

You get used to offering condolences and shaking hands with family members of the person you helped put in the casket or urn before you. You grow accustomed to rubbing shoulders and sharing stories with friends and colleagues of the man or woman to whom you fed a deadly noble gas just days earlier. Naturally, you keep that story to yourself, but you generally manage to come up with another worthy anecdote or two, a quick account to show how you knew and how much you respected the deceased, and how saddened you are by their passing.

Most of the time you don't even have to fake it. Certainly not at Sgt. Rush's funeral, where I wrestled with grief and familial nostalgia while simultaneously experiencing a bewildering sense of accomplishment. While many wakes and funerals have faded or fused into others, Sgt. Rush's remains indelibly etched in my mind. To this day I can recall the exact color and curvature of his steel casket, the tailored fit of his dress blue uniform, the placement of his hands. I can see his face, sporting a touch too much make-up, looking a little less peaceful than it had through my plastic bag. I can see his adult daughter desperately trying to maintain a smile as both active and retired police officers line up to offer her their condolences. I can feel the soft drizzle. I can smell the damp flowers. I can hear the dirt hit the coffin.

You never forget your first time.

You never really forget any of them.

It's just sometimes you forget to remember.

You forget to remember how young everybody at Christiana's funeral was, how even her parents were likely looking at 30 or 40 more years of living without their only daughter. And you get angry. Not at yourself for what you've done, but rather at whatever or whomever is responsible for someone so exuberant ever requiring your services in the first place.

Sometimes you even forget to remember the full name of a client. You'll lay awake at night until you're able to recapture it from the tip of a synapse. The hours of mental struggle and lost sleep is a way of paying respect to the dead. You may not be able to recover intricate details of their exit or their funeral, you may have lost all their friends and relatives in the shuffle, but goddamnit you're not worthy of another wink of rest until the full name of the person whose final breath you took comes back to you.

At funerals, consciousness prevails over conscience. There's no place for guilt in this line of work. Despite all the tears and contorted faces you see at farewell gatherings, despite all the sobbing and words of lament you hear, you remind yourself you've done a good thing. You tell yourself the grief of the people surrounding you can't compare to the pain and suffering you put to an end. You remember it's exactly what your client wanted. You know deep down if those who are grieving were to read a transcript of your private conversations with your client, if they were to watch video coverage of all your interactions with their loved one, if they were to somehow be able to fully enter the mind of the dying, they'd understand what you've done and why. Most would accept it. Many would even give you a hug or pat you on the back or buy you a drink.

During your worst moments, to pick yourself up you remind yourself of all this. The rest of the time, which is most of the time, you simply *know* it. You don't give it a second thought. You embrace your role. You celebrate your purpose.

It's why Harve's wake and funeral were so difficult for me. I hadn't fulfilled my purpose. I'd let the man down, even if he hadn't sensed it. At the church I sat with the others dressed in black, stripped of my badge, no noble secret or sense of power lifting me above the wallowing crowd. I was out of my element.

Adding to my discomfort was the fact that I was mingling with several surviving relatives who had unexpectedly seen my face, who'd come dangerously close to catching me in the act – or at least suspecting me of some ominous involvement. This is why, after taking my place in the procession behind those nearest and dearest to Harve, I felt much more like a criminal than I had at any other client's funeral, despite it being the only time I actually was completely innocent.

CHAPTER 17

Juggling party supplies and suicides is tricky enough without adding a third ball to the act.

Zoe and I had become somewhat of an item since the first dinner at my place, leaving me with little downtime. When I wasn't managing the shop, attending support group meetings, or planning and facilitating exits, I was with Zoe. Not that I was complaining. Yes, I was swamped, but my life was fuller and richer than ever before. Aside from my girlfriend having recently killed a man, I wouldn't have had things any other way.

As fulfilling as my life had become, I was forced to do a lot of finagling. Every week I had to keep some activity a secret from Zoe. On nights when I went to group meetings – which I was doing with a little less frequency now that staying home and having sex was a viable option for me – I would tell Zoe I had to stay late at Jubilee to do inventory or to balance the books. When she found two helium tanks beneath some sloppily folded sheets in my bedroom closet, I told her the shop occasionally receives an extra shipment and that space in the storeroom gets too cramped. My trip to the home supply store to purchase a new plastic bag and tube was a visit to my mother's house for dinner – a safe cover considering Zoe had mentioned on several occasions her aversion to meeting any person who had created any person she was screwing.

And whenever I had an exit scheduled (I had completed only two since we'd started "dating"), I told Zoe I was going to visit my father's grave – something I preferred to do unaccompanied.

Think about what I was up against the next time you start complaining about how difficult it is to meet somebody and maintain a healthy relationship. You may need to tolerate some annoying habits and create some drawer space, but chances are you have never had to lock half your life away from the person with whom you often share a bed.

I wasn't overly concerned about Zoe leaving me or turning me in if she found out about the exit man in the room. I was more worried she'd want to be his next client. Though things were going well with us, my fluttering heart couldn't hypnotize me. I wasn't fool enough to think a couple of months spent with a failed glassblower were enough to enable an unstable musician to rip up her Lithium prescription – a prescription she too seldom had filled.

Zoe had stopped pressing me about the suicide services I had "made up" when we first met, but she knew I hadn't just pulled a rabbit out of a hat. It was fine for her to have her hunches. She just couldn't know the truth. I felt it would be too enticing. She was too volatile, vulnerable. Maybe she didn't seem it on days when we'd sip whiskey and laugh and make love, but every few days I'd see the other side – the vacancy and the torment. She wanted me to believe a hairbrush had just slipped out of her hands while she was untangling a nasty knot, that's why my bathroom mirror shattered one morning. She wanted me to believe mere hormones were behind the crying fits that occasionally woke me up when she'd spend the night.

She wanted me to believe these things, but not as much as *I* wanted me to believe them. On the good days I'd see a talented and beautiful woman who might be able to love me and herself enough to make our every secret acceptable. On the bad days, though, all I'd see was a broken girl trembling on a bridge.

One night when I told Zoe I'd be working late, she showed up at the shop with some Chinese takeout, only to find the door locked, all the lights off, and my Pathfinder nowhere in sight. When she questioned me about it later that night, I told her I'd had to cut out earlier than expected because of a problem with the accounting software. I said I'd gone to the park to get some much needed fresh air and exercise before heading home.

The nice thing about our earlier decision to refrain from using our cell phones until the homicide investigation had ceased was I never had to explain why I didn't call whenever "something came up." The downside, of course, was Zoe never had to call to tell me she was on her way for an impromptu visit.

The day after the Chinese takeout incident, I suggested to Zoe we lift the phone ban. More than two months had passed since Keith's shooting, and the detectives hadn't contacted Zoe since initially questioning her. Even if she still was listed as a possible suspect or accomplice and police were checking phone records, which was unlikely, there would be nothing incriminating about a couple calls taking place between us at that point. Having an occasional phone conversation with a new friend several weeks after your ex-fiancé is mysteriously murdered hardly constitutes a break in the case.

Just to be on the safe side, however, I recommended we communicate via phone only when absolutely necessary. No need for any "Just thinking about you" calls or "Goodnight baby" text messages. Acceptable reasons for contact included letting the other know if you were going to be more than 30 minutes late for a dinner reservation or movie, informing them you were about to be mugged, or alerting them that you were trapped beneath something heavy.

It was also recommended to let the other know if you decided to pay them an impromptu visit. That would give the other a chance to inform you if it wasn't a good time.

Such a shame to have wonton soup go to waste just because you're feeling spontaneous.

Even with the phone ban lifted and the way paved for warning shots, I realized I could no longer keep saying I was working late. While Zoe showed no signs of being a stalker, it would be too easy for her to just drive by the shop to see if my story checked out. I needed a better cover on meeting nights. Easier said than done. I attended far too many group meetings to use the "dinner with Mom" or the "Dad's grave" alibi.

In the end, I told Zoe I had started back with glassblowing – taking an advanced class once a week at a small studio a couple towns over, just to keep my hand in it.

"I think that's great," she said. "Can I come watch you sometime?"

"That's sweet," I replied, "but I don't want anybody besides the instructor and other students seeing me fuck up my shaping and color applications. You need to wait until I get good before I'll let you watch. Besides, the class is closed off to the public."

I was getting better and better at deceit. At least there was some integrity to it, a worthy cause behind it all. I wasn't some typical brute spitting lies to continue some tawdry affair or to get piss-drunk with the guys. My fabrications enabled me to continue helping those in need. And to protect Zoe from herself. And to hold on to her as long as I could.

She had become an integral part of my life — just not the part with all the death.

I'm not so unattractive or so deficient of self-esteem to be incredulous whenever a woman winks at me. However, when the winking woman is manifestly dying of pancreatic cancer, my first thought isn't "she's into me."

Josephine and I had never spoken despite attending the same support group meetings for months. She mostly kept to herself, sitting quietly in her seat while others openly expressed their anger, sadness and acceptance. Though she looked to be in her mid-fifties, she was more likely in her early forties. Cancer age and chronological age are two entirely different animals. Spend enough time in support groups or on oncology wings and you learn how to calculate.

The wink came in the middle of a refreshment break. I was sipping some tea and happened to glance over in the direction of Josephine, who had remained seated while others lined up for snacks. I took her winking and subsequent smile as a signal she wanted me to bring her something from the refreshment table. When I pointed to the various items on the table and back to her, she shook her head. I started to walk over to find out what she wanted from me, but a few steps in she ordered me to stop with the raise of a hand and another shake of the head. I'd been snubbed like this in bars before, but I understood why those women were waving me off. With Josephine, I was at a loss, and showed it by knitting my brow, hunching my shoulders and mouthing "What?" Before I received any clarification, the group leader called everyone back to their seat in the circle. I continued to look over at Josephine throughout the remainder of the meeting, but each time found her looking in another direction.

What a tease.

When the meeting ended, Josephine collected her coat and headed for the door. I kept my eyes on her, hoping she'd give me some signal that it was okay to approach, but she never so much as glanced at me again before disappearing from the room.

I received another wink at the cancer group meeting the following week. But not from Josephine. This one came from a woman named Marta, a 75 year-old-looking 60 year-old losing a battle to ovarian cancer. I just smiled and waited to see if she had anything else for me – some additional signal or hint that she wanted to interact – but no such suggestion came.

I didn't know what was going on.

More precisely, I knew, but didn't know it. Call it denial. Call it dismissal. Call it repression.

It was easier just to think I was giving off pheromones that females in Stage III and IV couldn't resist.

I soon found the Stage II ladies weren't immune to my

scent, either. Lisa (breast) and Claire (rectal) winked at me during the same meeting a couple of weeks after Marta had. Not long thereafter I discovered my allure had crossed groups and gender – this when Christopher from the AIDS group winked at me. Devin did the same a week later.

I could no longer fool myself, however, when Barry from The Dignity Group gave me a wink. Men who manage construction sites, drive Dodge Rams and continue to chew Copenhagen tobacco after getting diagnosed with esophageal cancer don't bat an eye at another man out of sheer attraction, unless the other man is the late Steve McQueen.

My denial was fun while it lasted, but it was time to come to grips with reality.

The winking people weren't *into* me.

They were *on* to me.

That I was still a free man led me to assume all the winking over the previous three weeks was a collective gesture of approval rather than a menacing way to tell me "I know what you did." As I've already mentioned, an exit man can't abide having fans or a following, but it beats the hell out of having informants and makeshift bounty hunters on your tail.

While it seemed those who were privy to my services were on my side, I could ill afford to remain passive as my popularity grew.

The next wink I received was from Fiona (intrahepatic bile duct cancer) at a cancer group meeting about a week later.

It just so happens Fiona was tops on my list of potential clients to approach, thus we were due for a conversation anyway. I won't lie – the fact she was a criminal defense attorney may have helped bump her into pole position.

After I winked back at her, Fiona smiled nervously and fingered the black silk scarf covering her hairless head. I had never seen her prior to her illness but could tell from her blue eyes and bone structure she was a stunner not so long ago. Beauty, brains, status and stocks. All being devoured by microscopic bodies spinning out of control.

The perfect opportunity to approach Fiona occurred later that meeting. Our leader, Kathy, asked everybody in the group to find a partner for an exercise. As I made my way toward Fiona, I ignored a tap on the shoulder from another member looking to pair up.

Nothing personal, Louis. Just business.

Kathy instructed each of us to share with our partner three positive things that have come out of our (or our loved one's) illness. Fiona and I, however, had other matters to discuss.

"Good evening," I said as I sat down in the chair next to Fiona.

"Hello," she responded, struggling to look me in the eye.

"You're about the sixth or seventh person to wink at me during a meeting so far this month. Am I the butt of some practical joke, or is there something more substantial to all this attention I'm receiving?"

Of course I already knew the answer, but I figured I still had to maintain some air of naïveté. Besides, kicking off with "What do you know?" seemed too gruff. Fiona, like everyone else in the room, had suffered more than enough already and deserved a gentle approach.

"I can assure you, nobody is making fun of you," she said, regaining her ability to make eye contact.

"That's nice to know," I said with a smile. "So, then, what are they trying to tell me?"

"If they're like me – and I think they are – they just want you to know they support what you're, um... *you* know ... doing."

"And what *am* I doing?"

Fiona tilted her head to one side, pleading without words for me to cease playing dumb, to meet her halfway.

"Okay," I continued, "who *told* you what I'm doing?"

"I heard it from Randall, who heard it from Jerry, who, well, as you know, was a pretty *reliable* source."

Christ, Jerry, did you put up a billboard I don't know about?

"Okay, so you know about Jerry."

"And Harve," Fiona added softly.

"Hey, I had nothing to do with his passing. That's the truth. Anyway, who told you about Harve?"

"Harve."

You just can't trust the dying anymore.

"He gave me his word," I said, shaking my head and looking up at the ceiling.

"Don't worry, nobody is going to tell on you, or tell anybody who might tell on you."

"No? And how do you know that?"

"Because we want to protect you."

"I'm touched, truly, but who is 'we'? Just how many people *know* about all this?"

"Not that many – only the people who can handle it. Those of us who know are all very careful about who we share information with."

"How many is 'not many'?"

"I don't know, maybe five or six of us."

"You mean in this group?"

"Of course. This is the only group I know of."

"I've been winked at by four or five people in other groups like this one."

"Oh, in that case more than five or six people know."

"Bingo."

"Still, I wouldn't worry. I'm sure they all feel the same way we in this group do about what you're doing. Nobody wants you to get caught. We need you."

That last part. They way Fiona said it. The sincerity of her words, the expression on her face. How her eyes widened at "need" then fixed on me, caressed me. I sensed more external respect and admiration in those few seconds, from those three syllables, than I had in my entire three decades floundering around on this planet.

"Let me ask you something. Do you think each wink I receive is more than just a gesture of support and solidarity – might it also be a personal request for my services?"

"I don't know if everyone who supports what you're doing is totally prepared to become one of your, uh, your –"

"Clients."

"Thank you – clients. But I can tell you with certainty at least one is."

CHAPTER 18

The exit man as minor celebrity. Not at all what I was shooting for. How foolish I was to think I had been pulling the wool over everyone's – or nearly everyone's – eyes all that time. Yes, there was some comfort knowing I had a small army in my corner looking out for me, but where they saw a hero I now saw a hack.

And a cynical one, at that. Rather than take solace in the fact that I remained free despite a dozen or so individuals knowing my secret, I sat and placed silent bets on how long until the blackmail and extortion commenced. When that many people pull the mask off the Lone Ranger, it's only a matter of time before someone tries to cash in.

"Mum's the word, Eli, so long as I get my twenty grand."

I know, a soon-to-be dead man doesn't need a stack of cash. But his family does, and even the most just man's morality is prone to slippage when his wife and kids' welfare is at stake.

I didn't know what bothered me more: The thought of my noble profession being disrupted by a desperate corpse, or the very fact that I'd allowed my mind to create and fixate on such a thought in the first place. After all that Fiona had said, after receiving so much unspoken approval and support from near strangers – all of whom were in far more need of support than I was – I could think of nothing more than which one of them was going to take me for a ride.

Shame on me. So little trust in my minions. The least you can do when you first discover you *have* minions is have some faith in them.

Meetings took on a different air. Instead of walking into the room like a god, I now slunk into them like a cur – looking around nervously to see if anybody appeared to be planning an attack. If somebody looked at me and held their glance for longer than a couple of seconds without winking, they were instantly labeled a potential enemy until proven otherwise. Those who did wink – and there were several more over the following few weeks – were registered as potential clients who likely were working some angle.

The skepticism and paranoia extended beyond meeting room walls. My breathing became labored at the sight of a police cruiser or the sound of a siren. I broke into a sweat whenever driving by a donut shop. If a customer came into Jubilee seeking a helium tank, I couldn't help but think it might be part of an elaborate sting operation.

Time for a sabbatical. Spiderman takes a break when his web isn't working. Superman needs time to recover from Kryptonite. Exit Man is nothing during a nervous breakdown. There was no use in me trying to line up jobs until my head was clear and my hand had steadied. It's hard to build rapport with clients if you stutter and stammer whenever pitching them about putting their death in your hands. It's impossible to create a sense of calm among the hooded if you're thinking any minute the cops might bust in.

My newfound popularity was ruining things.

And then it wasn't.

The more subtle winks and nods and thumbs-up I received, the less vulnerable I started to feel. Roughly one in every five meeting group participants had quietly signaled their support. And nary a hint of anyone anti-exit. The security breach hadn't jeopardized my operation; it had somehow strengthened it. I'd let my guard down, but those to whom I was exposed managed to form a selective force field around my secret. I won't say I was untouchable, but I no longer lost my lunch whenever a state trooper came into view.

The biggest challenge I faced now was managing demand for my services. Gone were the days when I could take my sweet time to carefully select an unsuspecting candidate and formulate a plan at a modest pace. I now had eager individuals approaching *me* and requesting rush jobs. Not a week went by without at least one group member pulling me aside to arrange their way out. "Can you do me Tuesday?" or "What's your schedule like tomorrow?" or "I'd like to be gone before breakfast."

While I understood their enthusiasm, I was forced to temper it. Tactfully, of course. Being turned down for a date with death can be highly demoralizing. I'd politely explain to over-zealous parties that exits had to be spread out and strategically planned. Pleading for a little patience from people forced to spend the lion's share of their days waiting for lab results and for biopsies and for space to open up on top oncologists' schedules was an emotionally trying task. But these poor folks had to understand I was just a one-man operation, not a franchise. They had to accept that assisted suicide couldn't be handed out like Happy Meals, that quality exponentially superseded quantity. As much as I would have liked to dramatically step up production for their sake, I knew – and needed each of them to know – that doing so greatly increased the risk of me landing in prison and them landing on life support. Most saw my point and settled for a spot on the waiting list.

That's not to suggest that everyone who winked at me expressed a desire to go under the hood. Many were merely fans – folks with at least a good year or two of life left who just wanted to show they were down with what I was doing. Quite possibly future clients, but not ready to commit to anything. Completely understandable. After all, death is a big-ticket item.

I was already booked through the following four months, with one exit scheduled every two weeks during that period. That was as fast as I was willing to work, the highest volume I felt I could handle without sacrificing precision. Only once before had I ever released more than a single client in a month, but that was before the figurative phone had started ringing off the hook.

Eight exits over 16 weeks. Fiona was first on the list.

She lived in a gigantic modern loft apartment in the warehouse district of Blackport. I wasn't a fan of working in high occupancy environments for obvious reasons, but wasn't about to deny Fiona my services simply because she cared enough about humans to want to live in such close proximity to so many of them. When planning our rendezvous, I did voice some concern over the security and visibility issue, but Fiona said she had picked a time when all the residents in her building would either be out at art openings or too busy painting, sculpting and/or drinking absinthe to take notice of any visitors in the vestibule or hallways. As for the doorman and front desk attendant, Fiona informed me they were paid a lofty salary not to make eye contact with residents or their visitors.

I parked in a public garage a block away from her building. Carrying a duffle bag drew no suspicion in an area so densely populated by artists schlepping around their supplies. For those of the starving variety, the bags and backpacks contained most of what they owned in the world. Mine, on the other hand, contained instruments to help one leave it behind.

As Fiona had assured me, I gained easy access to the lobby elevator that carried me swiftly up to her fourth floor loft. On my way from the elevator to unit 404, my pocket started vibrating. Without slowing my stride I reached to retrieve it, wanting to make sure it wasn't Fiona calling with a change of plans.

It was Zoe. I pressed ignore, turned the phone off and strongly reconsidered my earlier decision to lift our phone ban. I was crazy about the girl, but I couldn't risk having my pants buzz while bidding adieu to a client.

After returning the disabled phone to the front pocket of my jeans, I knocked on Fiona's door. No footsteps or verbal response could be heard after several seconds, but this was normal. My clients weren't the fleetest of foot. In this racket you become accustomed to waiting on welcome mats for a while when you come calling. It's not just the weakness from disease that causes delays; most people like to savor the act of receiving the last visitor of their life.

After nearly a minute I heard the quiet commotion of someone approaching. Faint footsteps, soft creaks, the sound of locks sliding open. Seconds later I was face to face with Fiona, her frail body lost in a long red silk kimono. An elegant choice for an exit, I thought.

"Right on time," she said before greeting me with a light hug. "Please, come in."

"I'm chronically punctual," I said as I crossed the threshold.

"That's good. Tardiness in your line of work could be torturous for those awaiting your arrival, I imagine."

"Only those who are absolutely certain about what they are doing."

Fiona led me across the open floor plan to a black leather sofa.

"Have you ever had somebody cancel at this stage?" she asked. "Second thoughts in the eleventh hour?"

"I have not. But there is a first time for everything – and of course I'd be fine with it."

Fiona looked nervous. A little anxiety in these situations was natural, but she seemed shakier than I found acceptable.

"Fiona, I will completely understand if you have reconsidered."

"Oh goodness no. I wasn't hinting, just curious."

"Well, if I may say, you seem particularly ill at ease."

"It's not because I don't want to do this, I assure you." Fiona looked at the floor and then back up at me. "It's just… I guess I'm afraid you're going to be upset."

"Upset? What do you mean? About what?"

As Fiona got set to respond, I realized we weren't alone.

When I heard the cough coming from the other room, every muscle in my body locked. The tension left me speechless.

"It's okay," Fiona said calmly, putting her hand on my shoulder. She looked toward the room from which the cough had emanated, leaned forward on the sofa and cupped her hands around her mouth to form a makeshift megaphone.

"Jim, you can come out now."

She turned back to me and, speaking softly again, said, "I'm sorry, I needed my husband here for this."

Oh, no problem. In fact I'll just call my girlfriend and we'll make it a double date.

Down the hallway I heard a knob turn and a door open, followed by the click-clack of hard-soled shoes on Travertine tile. A tall thin man in his mid to late fifties soon emerged from the shadows. He was smiling as he approached, though I could see by his red eyes he'd been crying.

"Jim, this is Eli," said Fiona. "Eli, my husband Jim."

"Hello, Jim," I said as I stood up from the sofa and extended my hand. "Forgive me if I seem a bit thrown. I was unaware you – or anyone – would be joining us."

"I hope it's okay," said Jim while looking at his wife, who was still seated.

Fiona spoke before I could formulate a coherent response.

"I know you were fully unprepared for this, Eli, and that it's not really fair of me to put you in this situation, but I hope you can understand. I just couldn't go through with this without telling Jim about it, and without having him by my side."

What Fiona was asking was completely understandable, yet utterly unacceptable. Nevertheless, I couldn't very well just ask Jim to leave. "Kindly wait outside while I help your wife with her suicide" would have been a mouthful.

I had only two viable options: 1) Refuse to conduct the exit now that Fiona had rewritten the script and broken our trust, or 2) accept their request to turn euthanasia into a spectator sport.

"I'm not sure if I can do this," I said to them. "I mean, you've put me in a very compromising position."

"I know, I know, I'm very sorry about that," Fiona responded. "But you have nothing to worry about. You can trust Jim. He —"

"This will go to my grave with me," Jim interrupted. "Please don't take this away from us... from Fiona. I agree we haven't handled things well here, and I understand if you feel a little deceived, but we really need to go through this together. Fiona considered asking you about this beforehand, but was afraid you wouldn't allow it."

"Can you blame me? And even if I do allow this, it will be very difficult for you to witness it, Jim."

"Not as difficult as witnessing what Fiona has gone through for the past year, and certainly not as difficult as witnessing what she's going to have to go through in the coming months if we don't do this."

"And what happens if the police spot something suspicious, if there's some kind of investigation? You'd be a prime suspect. How prepared are you for that?"

"I'm not worried about that, and I don't want you to be either. If something like that happened, I'd never breathe a word about your involvement. I'd do anything to help stop Fiona's suffering, including taking full accountability and going to prison if it came to that. What you may not know is that, before Fiona heard about you at group, she and I talked about coming up with an 'escape' plan for her. We just didn't know how best to go about it. Then, when she found out what you had done for a couple of the other group members, she came to me, and we decided it was perfect. Well, not *perfect* – perfect would be if you had some kind of machine that could just suck all the FUCKING cancer out of my poor wife's body."

Jim had maintained his composure up until that last line. It was actually that line – an explosion of everything brimming inside him since Fiona's condition became inoperable – that convinced me to willingly accept the offer on the table, to dramatically alter my modus operandi.

It's one thing to preside over a suicide when it's just you and the client. Add a loved one into the fold and an ethereal scene loses all its lightness.

When there are no witnesses, you can almost convince yourself that what is happening is natural. You are merely there to ensure that a fellow human being passes safely through a portal they've been headed toward all their life. You're just helping to light the way and file down some of the jagged edges.

It was difficult to see things that way with Jim in the room – watching me lay out my supplies, watching me test the flow of gas, watching me slip a plastic bag over the love of his life and mother of his two adult daughters. The art and the science and the ease of it all got crushed beneath the weight of tenderness in the room, the density of half a lifetime shared.

"Tell me again, how long will she have once you start the helium?" Jim asked me while caressing the hand of his wife, who was sitting propped up on their bed.

"She'll fall into a peaceful sleep after a minute or so, maybe a little less, then won't feel a thing after that."

"But how long is 'after that' again?"

"About three to five minutes."

Fiona carefully removed the plastic bag from her head and squeezed Jim's hand, pulling him in closer.

"Honey, it's all right," she said. "I'm ready. Just try to remember what we talked about."

"I know, I remember. It's just this is even harder than I thought."

"If you want, we can stop."

"No, you need this. You deserve this. I'm sorry – I thought I could be stronger. I want to be strong for you."

"You are, honey. You always have been."

I excused myself – mainly to give them some privacy, but also to keep them from seeing my tears. I'd yet to cry on a client and fully intended to keep that streak intact. While waiting outside their bedroom, I realized there would be no place for me inside it once the hood was activated.

I knocked on the door a few minutes later. Jim called out, "We're ready." I entered.

"How would you two feel if, after I make sure everything is flowing properly, I left the room again so that you two can be alone for this?"

Fiona and Jim looked at one another nervously.

"You're sure it will be okay?" Jim asked.

"Yes. I wouldn't leave the room if I thought otherwise. And in the unlikely event you need me for something, I'll be right outside that door."

The two looked at each other again, but this time smiled.

"I think we'd like that," said Jim.

"Good. There's no rush, but we can begin whenever you are ready."

Fiona stroked Jim's face.

"I am if you are," she said, her voice breaking a little.

"I am," replied Jim.

I helped Fiona put the plastic bag back over her head, making sure the tubing remained intact.

"Okay, you're all hooked up," I said. "Once I turn this valve it will start the release of helium, and I will leave the room. You just need to breathe normally – you won't feel any pain whatsoever. If you decide to stop, just give Jim a thumbs down. Jim, if that happens, all you need to do is give the valve a little turn to the left, like this."

Jim nodded as he exhaled sharply.

"Do either of you have any questions?" I asked.

Each shook their head.

I placed my hand on Fiona's arm.

"It was an absolute pleasure knowing you. And though Jim's presence caught me off guard tonight, I'm glad the two of you are able to be here together for this. I leave you with a Latin phrase: '*Ave atque vale.*' It means simply, 'Hail and farewell.'"

Fiona smiled and reached out with her free arm to softly squeeze my hand. Moments later my hand gave the valve on the helium tank a quarter turn.

On my way out of the room, hearing Jim's soft sobs behind me, I saw a framed photo of the two daughters, each of them laughing, each completely oblivious to the controlled tragedy that was unfolding right before their Kodak moment eyes.

I was happy to see those girls, happy to be reminded of their existence. They gave Jim something solid to hold on to, something more tangible and less torturous than memories. They were the reason why, when it came time to reenter the bedroom to confirm Fiona was gone and to console Jim, I didn't have to worry about him begging me to do him next – despite the thought having certainly crossed his mind.

CHAPTER 19

Impervious. That's the word. That's what I was. Not untouchable, but impervious.

Incapable of being affected.

I wasn't dodging bullets – the bullets were simply missing me. Curving around me. Turning to dust the second they touched my skin. I escaped harm not because of any skill or strategy on my part. I was Mr. Magoo. A fortuitous blind man who had somehow managed to walk unharmed through a hail of hollow-points.

The trouble with being impervious is the moment you become conscious of it, the properties start to change.

"I'm curious, Eli," Zoe said to me a few nights after the Fiona and Jim episode. "Why is there a package stuffed with $100 bills inside a duffle bag in your closet? And why does the bag also contain a gas tank, a plastic bag and some tubing, among other things?"

"What were you doing rummaging through my stuff?" I asked with a defensive snarl.

"Cleaning."

"That merely requires lifting bags up to vacuum beneath them, and putting them in their proper place – not unzipping them and peeking inside."

"What can I say, I'm thorough. So, do you care to explain?"

"What are you talking about? There's nothing to explain. Those supplies are from work and the money is Jubilee's monthly take. I have to put it in the bank tomorrow."

"Wow. It's one fat wad of cash – business must be picking up. And how odd that all your customers pay you in such crisp large bills."

"What do you care? Why the sudden interest in the family business?"

"Because the family business just got interesting."

"Look, I'm exhausted. When I'm more rested I'll explain how it all works. I'm sure you'll find it riveting."

"Sorry, Eli, you can't sweep thousands of mysterious dollars under the rug. Not to mention the strange assortment of supplies."

"Will you please just... I've already told you about the over-shipment of helium that Jubilee received. It's no big deal."

"You couldn't find space for just one or two more tanks at work? And why keep one hidden in a bag with those other things?"

'It wasn't hidden. If I had something to hide, I wouldn't keep it sitting out in my closet."

"Under a blanket. Tucked in a corner."

"Jesus Christ. This is ridiculous. I'm going to bed, Sherlock."

"No you're not. We're not through here."

"What the hell do you want me to tell you? You apparently are eager to hear some wild tale full of suspense, but I'm sorry – I'm too damn tired to come up with anything creative enough to satisfy you."

"I think the truth will be captivating enough for me."

"Why are you doing this? What do you think I'm up to?"

"You tell me."

"I have no idea what goes on inside that crazy head of yours."

We interrupt this conversation to bring you this important announcement: Never use the "c" word when arguing with a bipolar person off her meds and on the edge.

"Don't call me crazy – you're the one who's fucking crazy around here!"

"Calm down. I don't need the neighbors to be in on this."

"I don't give a shit! They're about to hear a whole lot more 'crazy' if you don't start telling me what the fuck is going on."

How adorable. Our first real fight.

Zoe had me cornered and was bearing fangs. Me acting innocent and offended by her insinuations only elevated her anger. You'd think somebody whom I had saved from a tragic plummet and helped evade a possible murder charge would be more forgiving, more willing to look the other way on this new development. Couldn't we just call it even?

I searched my mind frantically for a trap door, for some spectacular smoke and mirrors, for anything nifty enough to let me escape unscathed. But I found nothing of the sort. Mr. Magoo had taken one right between the eyes.

"Zoe, If I tell you, all I ask is you listen with an open mind. And lest you forget I've been helping you guard a rather dark secret of your own."

"Okay," said Zoe, whose fire had died down considerably. "I'm all ears."

"Let's go to the sofa. This conversation calls for a seated position."

En route to the sofa, I made a last-ditch mental effort to dig up something untrue yet credible, something that would appease Zoe without me having to expose the exit man. But once again my synapses that specialized in deceit were firing nothing but blanks.

"I lied to you about lying to you about being a euthanasia specialist."

Zoe paused to retrace my words, to ensure she'd heard me right and correctly solved the equation. Multiply two negatives and you get a positive.

"Holy sh – I *knew* it," she said, almost giddy over my formal confession. "So, you *actually* help people *kill* themselves?"

"'Kill' is such a strong word. I prefer to substitute it with 'release.'"

"My god. How did you... I mean, why do you–"

"It's not something I ever intended to get involved in. It's a long story."

"Well, I don't have any students until tomorrow afternoon, so I have time."

I proceeded with a long summary of how a relatively sane and law-abiding citizen like myself had fallen into and since remained active in the exit game. How it started out as a magnanimous favor for a dear family friend. How I'd gone from refusal to reluctance to rebirth. How helium had infected and fixed me. How I found clients and how grateful they were that I did. How odd and empowering it was to be thanked by someone before ending their life. How beautiful it was to bear witness to their final breath.

How I hadn't really cared about people until I'd started

getting rid of them.

Zoe sat quietly and listened as I moved through the history and evolution of the exit man. Occasionally her eyes would widen and her mouth would drop open, but she remained silent, save for an occasional exhilarated exhale. Where prior to my confession she was furious, she was now entranced – hanging on each syllable. For her, my honest and intricate explanation was a strange elixir, simultaneously rattling and soothing her.

As typically occurs following any 10-minute summary of a nearly 18-month epoch, the audience had some questions at the end.

"So wait a minute," said Zoe, her eyes rolling upward, exploring a certain blurry element of my account. "Does that mean when you found me on the bridge and talked me down by claiming to have a 'better method,' you truly intended to help me kill… I mean *release* myself? To make me one of your clients?"

"No. As I just explained, I don't assist people who aren't already dying, or who are experiencing severe emotional and psychological distress. If I did, I'd be working around the clock."

"Don't people who know they are dying experience severe emotional and psychological distress?"

"That typically wears off after a few months. I only approach candidates who have more or less come to grips with their condition, people who have known for quite some time they aren't going to survive their illness. These folks are already somewhat prepared."

Zoe started laughing – softly at first, but within seconds she had ramped up to full hysterics.

"What the hell's so funny?" I asked, feeling my frown succumbing to Zoe's infectious cackle.

I waited impatiently for her to control her fit and catch her breath. After finally gathering herself, she replied, "You've dedicated your life to assisting suicides, yet you're sleeping with somebody whose suicide you *prevented*. That's fucking hilarious!"

The irony certainly hadn't escaped me, and I could see why Zoe might find it humorous, but there was a madness to her laughter that I found unsettling – like when The Joker breaks into cacophonous whoops over situations and anecdotes that are more disturbing than amusing.

"It's not *that* funny," I said.

"Yes it is. It's sort of like that famous daredevil who survived a ton of crazy leaps and stunts throughout his lifetime only to die of gangrene from a broken leg he sustained after slipping on an orange rind."

"Where's the similarity? That guy died ironically, where, by your account, my sex life improved ironically."

"I don't know. Your thing just reminded me of his."

"An odd connection."

"Just be happy you're the one with the much more favorable ironic fate. Of course, who knows what lies ahead."

"What does that mean?"

"I'm just saying, you might go down in history like that daredevil guy did if you, say, I don't know, end up dying in a hot air balloon accident or something."

Great. Now I was imagining my own death comically immortalized, serving as a source of giggles and guffaws for future generations.

Me going down in Hindenburg-like horror.

Me getting shredded by shrapnel from a helium tank following a Jubilee stockroom explosion.

Me suffering a myocardial infarction at the sound of a party balloon bursting on my birthday.

"The only way I'd go down in history for an ironic demise would be if my little side-business ever got discovered. And that's not going to happen."

"Confident, aren't we?"

"Not unduly. The stars simply seem to be aligned in such a way as to keep me in the clear."

"Um, some psychiatrists might put that in the category of 'delusions of grandeur.'"

"Perhaps, but I've emerged unscathed from enough fuck-ups and close calls to suggest some unseen force is protecting me."

"So God has got your back on this, huh?

"I didn't say God. I definitely didn't say God."

"All it takes is one slip-up, one person to alert the authorities."

"I know. But here's the thing – several people have found out about my services, people I've never approached or wanted to know anything, yet they all are apparently committed to guarding my secret. I've recently been told I have a small army behind me."

"I can't see how that's a good thing. People are obviously talking – it's only a matter of time before somebody says something to the wrong person."

"That's what I feared when I first found out, but my supporters appear to have developed some sort of communication security system. Things seem to be pretty well locked down."

"If not, prepare to be locked up."

"There's nothing I can do about it now. Word is out. All I can do is have faith in my *followers* and continue on, business as usual."

"Your followers? Sounds like you're leading a cult. And another thing, that's the second time you've referred to what you're doing as a 'business' – are you making *money* off these poor people?"

I despised the question, as there was no way to answer it affirmatively without looking despicable. By merely hesitating a moment to respond I had invoked disgust.

"Holy shit," Zoe snapped. "You *do*! You actually *charge* people to kill them!"

"No. I do not. I never ask for money. However, most insist I take payment."

"And you can't just refuse it?"

"I can, I have. But you don't understand how adamant many are about the money issue. They won't hear of me doing what I do for free."

"I can't believe you would–"

"Hold on a second. You have no idea what it's like to do what I do, what my relationship is like with my clients, what they want or how they feel. I never went into this for financial gain. In fact, when my first client – the old family friend – insisted I accept his money, it made me sick to my stomach. Before you start judging me and thinking I'm a monster, you need to know that I approach each client fully prepared to provide my services for free, and that many times they never bring up the issue of money, so I *do* end up doing it for free. Also know that I only ever accept money if I know for certain the client can easily afford what they want to pay me. And you know what else? I donate a good chunk of the money. I hate even bringing that up because it sounds like I'm patting myself on the back, but you've forced my hand. But regardless of all that, I can look myself in the mirror without cringing because I know that the services I provide are important, that I have relieved more suffering than you can imagine, that I allow my clients to die with some semblance of grace and dignity, and without leaving a trace of anything behind that says 'suicide.'"

I continued.

"Suicide typically upsets loved ones and gives greedy insurance companies a possible loophole to play with. And it's not as if there's no risk for me in doing what I do. You think I'm just taking lives and collecting cash, but I'm putting my own life – my freedom – on the line each time I help a client with a final exit. What I'm saying is, while the money doesn't at all drive what I do, I've earned every penny that has fallen into my hands since starting down this dangerous path. So judge away – I'll still be able to sleep at night."

Zoe sat motionless, speechless on the sofa. My diatribe had sucked all the oxygen out of the room, leaving her with no energy to counter-attack. I'd never neutralized a hostile opponent via monologue before. It was almost as empowering as working the hood.

When the effects of my spirited rant started to wear off, as Zoe started to shift and stir on the sofa, I braced myself for what was certain to be a punishing second round.

But all I had to endure were tears.

Zoe put her elbows on her knees and buried her face in her hands, struggling to catch her breath between sobs. I had merely intended to defend myself, not break her in half.

"Oh come now," I said while rubbing her shoulder. "You can't dig into me like you did and expect me to just lie down and take it."

"I'm… not crying because… you hurt my feelings, you idiot. I'm crying because… listening to you describe what you do sounds… it sounds… almost beautiful. So strange and sad, yet sort of beautiful."

"Strange, sad and beautiful – I'd say that sums it up pretty well."

"I just don't understand how you can do it."

"Is this about the money again?"

"No, no. I mean, I don't really understand that part either, but that's not what I'm saying. What I don't get is how you can sit with these people and orchestrate their death. The emotional toll that must take on you."

"Actually, I get more emotional seeing them at group meetings, witnessing them fighting rapid oxidation and metastasis, trying their best to hang on and to accept their unfortunate, painful fate. They ask for no pity, but you can sense the desperation behind their smiles. All of them just waiting out the day, the hour. When I hook them up to the hood, it's all different. There is a light in their eyes you don't see in anyone other than children. When I turn the valve to release the gas, I'm not taking anything from them. I'm giving something to them. Something transcendent. Something close to what they deserve."

Zoe melted into me, crying even harder than before. I understood why she was overcome. But I also knew if she were ever to witness all that I had just described, if she could see first-hand an exit unfolding, she'd experience something she was unprepared for, something close to joy.

Zoe knowing about my suicidal tendencies was wonderful for
our relationship. No longer did I need to sneak around and lie
or worry about her marring my work with an ill-timed visit or
phone call. Now that everything was out in the open, I could
go about ending lives in peace and come home to a nice relax-
ing dinner with my bipolar girlfriend.

News of my secret profession came as a relief to Zoe,
who admitted she had seriously considered severing ties with
me over trust issues prior to my confession. She hadn't taken
kindly to me ignoring so many of her calls or to my questionable alibis to cover for why I wasn't where she thought I was
or where I should be. Sure, helping her hide a freshly fired
revolver and keeping quiet about it had helped to build trust,
but not the level required to sustain a romantic relationship in
today's highly competitive dating environment. It's one thing
to help somebody conceal a murder or manslaughter; it's quite
another to consistently respond to their text messages in a
timely and honest manner.

I, too, felt relief after letting the cat out of the bag – a bag
I had evidently done a piss-poor job of hiding. A less careless
man would have foreseen the risk of a closet location and instead sought out or created some sort of interior catacomb, a
door in the floor, a flap to the attic. Perhaps a part of me had
wanted Zoe to unearth my secret. If that was in fact the case,
my subconscious was one selfish son of a bitch. It had to have
known that the secret I was unwittingly looking to unburden
myself of was dangerous cargo for someone like Zoe to be

storing. Like asking a pyromaniac to guard your dynamite.

Nevertheless, it was nice no longer having to invent errands and activities to keep Zoe in the dark about my underground operation. Now it was more like, "Can't make brunch on Sunday, baby – I have an exit at 11:00." Or, "I'd love to catch a movie tonight, but I won't be through hooding Mr. Hobson until at least 8:30." Being able to share such honest explanations – statements I had previously only been able to utter internally while concocting some questionable excuse – was good for my circulation and general health. I sensed less tension in my temples and shoulder muscles. My stomach had stopped churning. I was sleeping better. Most importantly, I felt more focused on the job – on *both* jobs. The mental energy I had been expending on fabrications and fibs for months was once again conserved for use during soft up-sells with my living customers and flawless exits with my dying ones. I was on top of my game in both arenas, and without the aid of any pharmacological agents.

It seemed like the best decision I'd ever made, letting Zoe in on my not so little secret.

Until she wanted to *get* in on it.

"I need to see you work," she said to me one morning in bed, before I was even fully awake. "Take me with you this afternoon to your... appointment – or whatever you call it."

"What?" I mumbled, thinking I might still be asleep and dreaming.

"I want to come with you."

"Are you kidding me? Absolutely not."

"Why? Please, I want to see what you do."

"No, Zoe. It's out of the question."

"Give me one good reason why."

"I'll give you *several*. First and foremost, my client would never have it. This is a very private and personal thing. Besides, I need my client to be as comfortable and as relaxed as possible – bringing a complete stranger along would greatly disrupt the process."

"But–"

"Plus having you there would only add to the risk of getting caught. It's one more person to sneak in and out of the home, one more person who might leave some kind of trace. No way."

"Could you at least ask her if it would be okay?"

"Are you even listening to me? Even if she said it was all right, there's still the added risk I just mentioned."

"I would be extra careful – you could train me on everything I'd have to do."

"The answer is no. I'm not discussing this any more. I can't even believe you would ask such a thing."

"Really? You can't understand why I might take interest in the unique and fascinating work you do? You can't fathom why I might want to see something so powerful in person?"

"You can take as much interest as you'd like, but you can't watch."

"I hate that you won't even consider it."

"C'mon, Zoe. There is no 'bring a friend to work' day in this particular profession. Do you think mafia men take their wives or kids along on a hit?"

"Is that how you see yourself – as a mafia hit man? Give yourself some credit."

"You know what I mean. Certain jobs have no place for spectators, and mine is without a question one of those jobs. You should be happy you even *know* about what I do."

"Happy? I'm not happy. It would be easier if I didn't know anything about it. Then I wouldn't be thinking about it all the time. I wouldn't be so damn curious."

"So you'd rather go back to not knowing and having me tell you lies all the time about where I am and what I'm up to?"

"It's probably better than feeling so excluded from this immense thing you do."

"You haven't been excluded. I shared extremely confidential information with you. You are the only person outside of my clients and 'followers' who has a single clue about any of this."

"You only told me because I confronted you with some pretty damning evidence."

"Still, I could have kept my lips sealed. But I didn't because I felt you deserved to know at that point."

"How big of you."

"Yeah, it was big of me. I think other men in my position would have risked losing you to protect the operation."

"Other men in your position? There *are* no other men in your position. Or women, for that matter. That's just it – you are one-of-a-kind. What you do is pretty much unheard of. Sure, some doctors might prescribe a deadly dose of meds out of mercy, and maybe a few regular people have played some part in assisting a sick close friend or loved one, but I seriously doubt anybody has an ongoing operation as impressive and effective as yours. I want to see how it all goes down – not out of mere morbid curiosity, not because I have some sick fixation, but because of the way you described it to me when you first told me about it. I want to experience it the way you do."

I was not unmoved by Zoe's plea, but I knew I had to stand my ground. What she was proposing was preposterous. Rather than continue trying to convince her of this through my words, I attempted to get her to do so using her own.

"And just how would you propose this went down?" I asked her. "What would you have me say to the client so they'd accept your presence, embrace your participation?"

Zoe's eyes widened, surprised I was giving her an opportunity to build a plausible scenario. My sudden shift from "no fucking way" to "let's hear your strategy" had knocked her off balance.

"I don't know," she said, tapping her lower lip while pondering possible options. "You could maybe tell them I'm your, like, assistant or something."

"I'm not a *magician*. 'Ladies and gentleman, assisting me with my next euthanasia trick is the lovely and talented Zoe!'"

"Knock it off. What's so outlandish about you having an apprentice? If everybody in your circle is as supportive of what you're doing as you say they are, wouldn't they be happy to hear that another person was learning the trade, that the operation was expanding?"

I wanted to say it was among the most ridiculous things I'd ever heard, but I couldn't. It wasn't. While there was still no way in hell I was going to allow her to audit an exit, she was dead on regarding how my clients and followers would react to the news of me taking on a protégé. Now it was I who was off balance.

"Even if they might be behind the idea in theory, a client would surely be miffed if I just brought you along to their home for the actual exit appointment without ever having discussed it with them. It's very unprofessional."

"Then, like I suggested before, give them a heads up beforehand and ask them if it's okay."

"And like *I* said before, it doesn't matter if they'd be all right with it, *I'm* not. The whole idea raises the risk exponentially."

"I'm not talking about me actually *becoming* your apprentice or even about me accompanying you numerous times. I just want to sit in and watch once. That's it. All you need to do is feed one client the apprentice line, get permission, let me attend, and I won't bother you about it again."

Zoe had kept her poise and presented frustratingly cogent arguments. But now it was my turn again. It was time to put an end to this discussion once and for all using indefensible persuasive tactics. I was bringing out the big guns.

"I don't want to, and you can't make me!"

"Look at you, being a little bitch about it."

At first I thought the words had come from my own subconscious, but, alas, they had been uttered by my tenacious opponent – an opponent who apparently had no qualms about fighting dirty, hitting below the belt.

I come from a long line of men who overcompensate in the face of emasculation. In fact, had it not been for my mother continuously slapping my father with "You don't have the balls to marry me" back in 1973, I likely never would have sprouted into existence.

"Oh, right, I'm a little bitch. I risk my entire future on a biweekly basis so that others' intense suffering may cease, but I'm a little bitch. I see."

"I agree what you do is bold and risky – much bolder and riskier than letting me watch you in action just one time. That's why I don't know why you're being such a pussy about it."

The last time somebody had called me a "little bitch" and a "pussy" in the same day, I ended up leaping from a 200 ft. steel platform with a bungee cord attached to my ankles and waist.

The thrill is in the utter stupidity of it all.

"Whatever, Zoe. You couldn't *handle* it. If I let you come with me to an exit, you'd either lose it on the spot or sometime soon afterward."

Atta boy. Way to turn the tables and question her fortitude. This woman who shot a man not too far back and hasn't flinched since.

"You're wrong," she said. "I know I could keep it together. It's too important an event – I'd never do anything to mar it. And I wouldn't ask to do this if I thought for a second it would scar me. I'm stronger than you think. You're just too scared to let me prove it."

Whatever you do, don't let her overconfidence and condescension goad you into negotiat–

"Let's just say I did let you come with me sometime... how would your presence help me or the client? What could you do to avoid just being a distraction?"

"I'm not sure I know what–"

"It can't just be, 'I'm here to watch.' That would make everybody involved uncomfortable. You'd have to serve some purpose."

"I could stand lookout, watch the door or whatever."

"Futile. If somebody were to come home during an exit, there'd be no time to hide or clean up. It'd be over."

"I could help you carry supplies and set up."

"No need – everything fits inside my duffle bag, and I can hook up the hood in seconds with my eyes closed."

"I could... um, hmm... I could..."

"Exactly, there's nothing for–"

"I could hold their hand."

It's something I'd always done with my female clientele while they awaited release. But roughly half my clients were men. Hold their hand. Did the men not deserve the same treatment, the same compassion as the ladies taking an identical trip? I had never thought to hold the hand of a male client, nor had any ever made such a request, but that didn't mean such a simple corporeal connection prior to lift-off wouldn't have been appreciated. Why should one's gender determine the level of comfort received while plowing full steam ahead into oblivion? Masculinity, after all, is factored out by the hiss of helium.

"Where'd you go?" asked Zoe, awaiting my response to her most recent proposal. "It's a good idea isn't it? You focus more on the clinical side and I provide the warm bedside manner. Yeah?"

"I'm not exactly an automaton with my clients, you know. I strive to make each person as comfortable and relaxed as possible."

"I'm sure you do, but since holding their hand would be the only thing I do, I could bring a little something extra to it. It would be like having a nurse or hygienist in the room when a doctor or dentist is working on a patient. It just takes some of the cold science and sterility out of it all."

Knocked off my stance once again, I hesitated. Moments later all I could manage was, "This is crazy, Zoe. I just don't want you getting mixed up in–"

"Eli, please," Zoe cut in, looking me straight in the eye, sensing the chink in my armor, moving in to finish me off. "Please let me do this, just once. I won't interfere. I won't distract. I won't crack. I just want to be there with you. I want to see who you are."

CHAPTER 20

Any other man would have been thrilled that his significant other not only accepted his most dangerous secret but was also itching to participate in it.

Not me.

Sure, I was glad my hidden specialty hadn't ruined things with Zoe; however, I found her obsession with it disconcerting – and my disconcertedness dismaying. The whole thing was a sort of strange variation on the old Groucho Marx quip, "I wouldn't want to be in any club that would have me as a member." Mine was more like, "I wouldn't want to be with somebody who'd want to be a member of my club." It was okay for *me* to have become entranced by and entrenched in euthanasia, but anybody else with similar interests and aspirations was sick.

But she was also a natural at it.

I didn't let Zoe accompany me to that first exit after our big discussion – it was too short a notice, and the client in question wasn't male. Instead Zoe joined me two weeks later at the home of Pete Barrett, a wealthy early retiree who had allowed an adenocarcinoma to go untreated for far too long.

Pete had approached me about the hood nearly two

months earlier, not long after I had discovered I had a following. Unbeknownst to several other clients who had requested my services before him, I bumped Pete up in the schedule due in large part to his rapidly deteriorating state – and in small part to the exorbitant amount of money he insisted on paying. $40,000. Not the largest amount I had ever accepted, but up there.

A few days after Zoe had successfully pleaded with me to let her watch me work, I told Pete that I had taken on an apprentice. I explained to him what her minor role would be, and asked if he was open to having her attend his send-off. As Zoe had predicted, Pete was happy to hear I had somebody in training, and he agreed without hesitation for our dyad to become a triad on the big day. I asked if he would like to meet Zoe beforehand, but he said it wouldn't be necessary.

"If you trust her enough to be there, so do I," he said. How lucky I was to have such good people on my suicide list.

Although Zoe would merely be holding a hand when game time rolled around, I ran through every aspect of the exit with her several times in the days leading up to her first and final appearance. I wanted her to be as prepared as possible for what she was going to witness. Admittedly, that was not my only goal. By conducting extensive role-plays and providing vivid descriptions – at times exaggeratedly graphic – I quietly hoped Zoe would lose her nerve, that she'd realize she'd made a big mistake in asking to join in my reindeer games. But the heavier I poured it on, the more intrigued and eager she became. She reminded me of myself when I first started learning the ins and outs of the art form.

What the hell was wrong with her?

When it came time for Pete's exit, Zoe performed impeccably – maintaining the perfect balance of pathos and professionalism. When we stepped through the door of the greenhouse behind Pete's palatial home (Pete wanted to take his final breath alongside his prized azaleas), Zoe slid effortlessly into her role. Her soft smile and delicate handshake upon meeting Pete placed him instantly at ease, brought a level of tranquility to the scene that I had not experienced in my solo career.

She kept quiet and stayed out of the way, yet her presence was eminent. She did everything that was asked of her and nothing that wasn't. It was the least she could do and the most I had hoped for. No overzealous attempts to help me remove or lift or connect any equipment. No kneejerk dramatic displays of sympathy for our client. No panicking under pressure or forgetting her place. She was the perfect assistant for the assist. All she did was offer a gloved hand to hold, but she put her heart into it. She was the subtle star of the show, stealing the scene from the noble gas that swept into Pete's bloodstream and carried him away.

When the show was over and I was busy packing everything up to leave, Zoe remained seated with Pete, still holding his hand. No words. No look of shock on her face. No tears. Just bright eyes and a peaceful grin, as if she had just released a wild animal that had gotten caught in a trap.

When we emerged from the greenhouse and walked toward the car, Zoe stopped and looked back. I couldn't see her face, but I heard a sniffle. *Oh boy, here it comes.*

"Are you okay?" I asked, fully prepared for the floodgates to open.

Zoe turned around, a single tear on her cheek. "I just hope somebody takes care of all those beautiful flowers."

I had a feeling Zoe would get hooked after attending one exit and ask me to tag along for another.

But she didn't.

I asked *her*.

It didn't happen until after my next appointment, which was with a septuagenarian named Teresa who was ready to surrender in the war her ovaries had waged nearly a decade earlier. It was back to business as usual, but while holding Teresa's hand as the helium sang a lullaby, I realized business as usual was no longer enough. Missing was the special touch Zoe had provided back in the greenhouse.

Teresa died peacefully, but I had the feeling I had held something back, had unwittingly blocked the scenery. If I was as committed to and caring of my clients as I claimed to be, as I thought I was, then I had a responsibility to continuously strive to enhance the art form, to embrace every opportunity to expand its boundaries.

Even if that meant going a little Bonnie and Clyde.

"Are you free next Friday morning at 9:30?" I asked Zoe a week before my next scheduled exit.

"I believe so. I don't have any students until the afternoon. Why?"

"I could really use a *hand*."

"Sure. With what?"

I looked her in the eyes without saying anything, hoping she'd pick up on what I thought had been a clever yet transparent enough line.

"Why are you staring at me like that, you goof?" she asked.

"I could really use a HAND."

"Yeah, I heard you the first... ohhhh. You mean... you actually *want* me there?"

"I actually do."

"I don't understand, I thought you–"

"I know, I know. I was adamant about it being only a one-time thing, but your absence was felt at my last gig – at least by me."

Zoe knew I had been impressed by her debut performance, but we hadn't spoken much about it since the drive home from Pete's. Each time she had mentioned or even alluded to his exit, I would just smile and politely change the subject. I appreciated her making it so easy for me to do so. Not once did she become flustered by my deflections or try to persuade me to bend my one-and-done rule. If I had seen she was struggling psychologically in the days following Pete's departure, I would certainly have allowed a conversation to take place for therapeutic purposes. But she hadn't suffered in the slightest, had no emotional wounds that needed closing. She seemed fine with letting whatever happened in the greenhouse stay in the greenhouse. It just made sense to keep everything hidden among the azaleas.

But now I was digging things up.

"So, what do you say?"

"What do you mean my 'absence was felt' – did something go wrong on your last job?"

"No, nothing like that. Everything went according to plan. I just sensed something was missing, something I can't really provide on my own."

"What about everything you said about the increased risk of having another person involved?"

"That was before I knew how naturally you'd take to the task, and how calm and quiet you could be after completing it."

"What did you think, I'd freak out and confess what I'd done – what you do – to friends or the police?"

"I don't know, I guess I was just concerned you'd be a little sloppy at the scene, or inadvertently let something slip to someone."

"And how do you know I haven't told anyone about it?"

"If I had any doubts, I wouldn't be asking you to join me again. I've seen how composed you've been since the Keith incident, so I *know* you can do my kind of work without losing your shit or blabbing about it."

"So tell me, are you recruiting me for an extended period?"

"Well, I mean I'm not going to be drawing up any contracts, but if things go as well as the first time, then yes, I would like you to continue accompanying me."

"How many of these things, these exits, do you do? I mean, how often?"

"It used to be only once every month or two, but demand has increased significantly since word got out, so now we're looking at twice a month – at least for the next several months."

"Pretty soon they'll be nobody left in any of your groups."

"Don't worry, there is plenty of cancer and AIDS going around to keep each group well stocked."

"Wow, that sounded awful."

"I don't deny that. It *is* awful. That's why my services are so vital. So, are you in?"

"I'm willing to give it a go, but if I find once every two weeks is too much for me, you might have to do some of these on your own. Is that okay with you?"

"Sure. I'll consider you flex-time."

"That works."

"Aren't you curious about payment?"

"Oh, I figured this was more of an unpaid internship."

"Hell no. I'm openly opposed to slavery. That said, there aren't exactly any standard salary ranges for a position like this, seeing as how there *are* no positions like this. But what do you say to 25% of whatever a client pays me?"

"Whatever you think is fair."

I handed Zoe an envelope I had placed on the coffee table at the beginning of our chat.

"You tell *me* if it's fair," I said. "That's your take for the greenhouse job."

Zoe reached into the envelope and pulled out a fat wad of $100 bills.

"Holy fuck!" she shouted, trying to count the cash with trembling hands.

"I think you left a few bills in the envelope," I said. "In case you're struggling with the addition, you're holding $10,000."

"Shut up! How can that be?"

"It just is. Sometimes. Like I told you before, some clients insist on paying a huge sum of money. Pete happened to be one of those clients. Don't expect that much every time, or even ever again. You'll typically take away anywhere from $0 to $2,500 per exit – sometimes more. But it's really best you try not to think about the money. Once you start viewing clients in terms of dollar signs, you're no longer qualified to do this work."

Zoe tried to wipe the smile off her face as she clutched a year's worth of rent.

"I'm sorry," she said. "You're right. In fact, I don't think I can accept this."

"Yes, you can. I've already been over the money thing with you. You earned it."

"But $10,000?"

"What you did in there with Pete, you're worth every penny."

"How do you figure?"

"I don't have to – Pete figured it for us."

Zoe shook her head in disbelief, teetering between laughter and tears. It looked as if she might either do a jig or set the cash on fire.

"I realize it takes a while to get comfortable with the financial rewards involved," I said. "Just be careful with what you do with the money, with how 'visible' it is to family, friends and institutions. Don't go on any wild spending sprees, and keep it out of the bank."

"I'll do my best."

"*Better* than your best."

That's when it really dawned on me: I'd gone into business with my girlfriend – a dangerous venture for any couple to undertake, let alone a couple whose business' specialty is punishable by up to 25 years in prison, per transaction. When most pairs break up, the biggest concern each party has is what the other will tell friends about their sexual performance. If Zoe and I were ever to split in a less than amicable fashion, angry gossip could end up opening a closet full of corpses.

Perhaps I *did* need to draw up some contracts.

CHAPTER 21

Zoe showed no signs of a sophomore slump during our second exit outing, which occurred nearly one month to the day of her debut. It took place in the home of Oscar Fuentes, whose HIV had skipped a few grades to graduate early as full-blown AIDS.

Any doubts I might have had about Zoe's resolve and durability were extinguished while watching her expertly handle an overtly emotional Oscar without getting too tangled up in his catharsis. Even I had to fight back tears when Oscar, choking up, told us how he had never forgiven himself for keeping his homosexuality a secret from his devoutly Catholic and long since deceased parents. At one point I thought we might have to postpone the event due to his seemingly inconsolable state, but then Zoe made a miraculous save.

"Would you like me to sing to you, Oscar?"

Oscar stopped crying, removed his hands from his face to look at Zoe, and nodded.

All I could think was, *What do you sing to a man on his suicide deathbed, and how do either of you get through it?*

Zoe hummed a few notes of Paul Simon's "Graceland" and soon broke softly into song. I was pleasantly stunned by the purity and control of her voice, and felt ashamed I had never bothered to ask this woman who made her living through music to sing for me.

Oscar, too, was entranced. Midway through the song, I looked at him and motioned to the plastic bag, careful not to look like I was pressuring him. He smiled, looked at Zoe, then back at me before nodding.

Zoe continued singing while I got Oscar hooked up. Not once did she flub a lyric or let go of his hand. And although Oscar, now hooded, again nodded assertively when I asked if he was ready for me to release the helium, I couldn't help wondering if Zoe's voice – like a siren of the sea's – was hypnotizing him, clouding his judgment, drawing him helplessly toward the rocks.

Then I reminded myself that the rocks were exactly what Oscar wanted, what he needed. He'd been eagerly awaiting this for weeks, checking in with me at every meeting to see if there had been a cancellation that moved him up in the schedule. Now, finally, he was headed straight for his target. I figured far be it from me to question how he chose to soften the collision.

Zoe continued her song, and as Oscar closed his eyes and leaned back against the mahogany headboard in his bedroom, it was clear that Zoe was singing him out of danger, not into it.

That was the end of the beginning. Zoe had only two assists under her belt, but had already shed her rookie status. Probationary period over. She knew her way around a suicide scene – provided it wasn't her own.

Over the next couple of months we continued to work beautifully in unison. I never once had to tell Zoe to move out of the way or to come closer or to speak or to sing or to be quiet. She knew exactly where she needed to sit or stand, what needed to be said or not said, sung or not sung. She was totally in tune with each client and with me. While I still ran the show, it was her warmth and grace that stole it. She was the Vanna White to my Pat Sajak, yet she did so much more than merely look astonishing and spin letters.

Those two months were among the happiest in my life. They certainly marked the golden age of Zoe and my relationship. Things had been going well between us before, but teaming up to end the lives of others really took us to the next level. Not to suggest there was anything perverse about it. It wasn't like facilitating exits turned us on. We weren't hopping into clients' beds or closets for a quickie the second after delivering our services. We didn't get a sexual thrill – or any actual thrill for that matter – out of ending others' pain together. Rather, we experienced a far more profound connection, a shared energy, the kind of ionic bond couples always hope to achieve and sustain through a yoga retreat but never quite get there.

Arriving at and leaving clients' homes as a couple served as a form of camouflage – a benefit I had not anticipated prior to teaming up with Zoe. When I first decided to take her on as my assistant, I feared an extra person meant extra risk. I was, after all, placing a second perpetrator on public display. However, what I soon discovered was that having Zoe by my side actually made entrances and escapes less risky than when I worked alone. Together we were more forgettable. Neighbors, doormen and children playing in streets tend to pay less attention to a couple holding hands than they do to a lone male stranger lurking about.

When it comes to administering suicides, there is safety in numbers.

Of course, not everybody was in the dark about what Zoe and I were up to. Word had gotten out in the inner circle that I had taken on a female assistant. I had no problem with this, as it saved me from having to ask clients for permission to bring a plus-one to their party. They were aware I wouldn't be working alone even before our initial consultation took place, though I'd always remind them just in case.

What they didn't know going in was who exactly my assistant was. Some were curious and would ask me innocuous questions like what her name was and how I knew her, but nobody really pried. They didn't have the time or energy. Even if they did, few would have felt compelled to give me the third degree. I had developed a solid reputation. Dozens of people had trusted me enough to put their death in my hands, and dozens more were right behind them, thus no candidate was about to question my methods. I could have started conducting exits naked, claiming it ensured optimum results, and folks would have been fine with it.

That's not to say a few rumors didn't spread after news got out I had a partner. This wasn't surprising, or even upsetting. I couldn't expect the exit insiders to overcome their innate human tendency to deduce and concoct in the absence of facts. As long as they kept said deductions and concoctions within the circle, it was all well and good with me. I could tell the rumors served as no small source of entertainment for my poor followers, so I did little to quash them.

The rumor that received the most airtime was that I had hired an assistant because I, myself, was dying of an undisclosed disease and wanted to ensure the business lived on after my passing. As for who my assistant was, plenty of fruit grew on the grapevine. Depending on who was telling it and what you believed, my assistant was my sister, my mother, my wife, my girlfriend (*we have a winner!*), an oncology nurse, a med student. I wouldn't have been surprised if there had been a rumor floating around that my assistant was *all* of these things. Chemo and radiation treatments can really end up altering a story.

Nobody ever asked me to confirm or deny the rumors, not even the handful of confidants who took it upon themselves to inform me of the rumors as they circulated. Whenever I heard one, I would simply say, "Hmm," or, "Interesting," – thus leaving things open for interpretation and keeping my assistant shrouded in mystery.

The only people to whom Zoe's identity was accurately revealed were our clients on their exit day. These individuals got to see what she looked like and learn – if they bothered to ask – a little of her backstory. Some were delighted to find out we were romantically involved, others admitted to being intrigued by reports that my assistant was my mother, or a rebellious healthcare professional pushing the envelope.

Rumors were dispelled and confirmed as hands were held and the hood assembled. That is how each client came to know who Zoe was. The myth momentarily illuminated, then placed back in the shadows as the gas rolled in.

One of our clients, Anthony (brain cancer), died three weeks before his scheduled appointment. It was the first incident of *exitus interruptus* since Harve's "untimely" death several months earlier. I must say, Anthony's passing was a little easier to live with. I was upset over not being able to accommodate him in time, but I also knew I couldn't keep bumping clients ahead of others who were just as bad off or worse. Considering how crowded my schedule was, I knew it was only a matter of time before I lost another client to natural causes. Volume was increasing substantially, thus a small percentage of acceptable failure had to be built into the system.

When another client, Mitchell, lost his battle with lung cancer 10 days later – one month before his scheduled departure – I chalked it up to a streak of bad luck. Then, remembering I didn't believe in luck, I started thinking about modifying the system, coming up with a way to prioritize all clients based on the severity of their condition. The very idea of implementing such a change made my temples throb. First-come first-serve had worked so well up to that point. It certainly made things easier for me. But I knew I couldn't let personal convenience supersede client suffering.

Less than three weeks later, Deirdre died unexpectedly. Well, not *exactly* unexpectedly, seeing as how she had late-stage mesothelioma. But certainly ahead of schedule, from my perspective. Initially, Deirdre's death sealed my decision to overhaul the scheduling process, but then the Hardy Boy inside me started evaluating the facts.

Three individuals in the same terminal disease support group had died within a month of one another. This had never happened before without my assistance. While it wasn't out of the realm of possibility that three group members could die of their actual diseases in such rapid succession, the fact that each had reserved an exit but died weeks before it raised red flags high into the air. Add to this the fact that Anthony, Mitchell and Deirdre had all reportedly been found dead in their respective homes – no hospitals or hospices or doctors involved, no ambulances or relatives rushing to an emergency room.

I had good reason to suspect a copycat was on the prowl.

Every couple has its Achilles' heel. For some, it's jealousy. For others, it's financial issues. Or communication problems. Or sexual dysfunction. Or one partner secretly assisting suicides behind the other's back.

I didn't want to believe Zoe could cheat on me like that – sneaking around with our clients after all I had done for her, after all I had risked to bring her into the business. I felt betrayed, though could appreciate the karma. My own secretive exit missions had come full circle; I had spent months lying to Zoe, running around town luring every Tom, Dick and Harry into oblivion, and now it was Zoe's turn to explore behind my back.

If she was guilty, she certainly didn't tip her hand. The incredulity she had expressed upon hearing about each of the three premature deaths was just as genuine as mine was. I paid particularly close attention to her reaction when I told her of Deirdre's passing – the one that really roused my suspicion – but nothing Zoe did or said showed that she was anything but nonplussed by the unfortunate string of early dismissals. Still, who else could it have been?

I couldn't accuse her, I decided, until I gathered more evidence. I was able to collect the exact date and relative time of each conspicuous death through obituary searches and casual conversations with fellow group members. I discovered that both Anthony and Deirdre had died on afternoons when I was working at Jubilee. However, Mitchell, it turns out, died mid-morning on a Sunday – when Zoe and I were out having brunch together. Unless Zoe had trained an apprentice of her own to take care of business while we were sipping mimosas, she couldn't have been at all involved in Mitchell's demise. This single solid alibi, however, didn't clear her of the other two deaths. It was entirely plausible she had put the hood to Anthony and Deirdre, and that Mitchell just happened to die from his horrible illness in between.

I silently cursed Mitchell. Why couldn't he have just been a good boy and died on a weekday afternoon when I was working? It would have strengthened my accusation immeasurably.

What I couldn't figure out was, if my accusation was indeed on the mark, how Zoe could have contacted Anthony and Deirdre – or they her – without me knowing. Zoe had in no way been involved in the scheduling process (other than letting me know what days and times were best for her), nor had she ever been to any group meetings. It seemed slightly less unlikely that Anthony and Deirdre, through some nifty detective work and sly maneuvering of their own, had identified and approached Zoe. Perhaps, after growing impatient while waiting for their seat at the exit table, they had decided to go after the only other person they were aware of who had some bona fide hood experience. But being that covert and furtive requires no small amount of energy – something people with evil cells feasting on functional ones don't have a surplus of.

Despite the gaping holes I was able to poke in each of my own theories, I was unable to let go of the idea that Zoe had gone rogue in our already anarchic game.

And what if she *had*? How would I confront her? Would it mean the end of us as business partners? Bedfellows? Both? Would she accept a punishment, a suspension of sorts, or would she – a woman who perhaps already felt she'd outgrown our team – merely scoff at me if I tried to hand down sanctions?

I felt the acid in my stomach rise above the danger mark as I pondered how ugly things might get. Additional double-crossings. Desperate self-preservation. Sabotage. I even envisioned a contract killer lurking somewhere in the midst.

I couldn't stand the thought of Zoe and me transforming into warring factions so quickly after having achieved such an enviable level of synchronicity. We wouldn't be the only casualties if a civil war were to break out. Scores of innocent civilians, who relied so heavily on us to emancipate them, would pay the heaviest price. Additional days, weeks and months in their decimated vessels.

It was all far too Shakespearean for me to bear. It had been a long time since I had last catastrophized, and I was clearly out of shape. Despite the shield of invincibility and judicial exemption I had managed to forge through dozens of exits, fending off all this imagined entropy was proving an arduous task.

Fortunately order was restored, at least to some extent, a few days later when a woman named Beatrice winked at me at a cancer meeting, and then followed it up with a quiet conversation in the wings during the break.

"I don't think it's right, what's going on," whispered Beatrice, who'd been attending meetings with her husband – a Stage IIIer – for a couple of months.

So this is it.

A part of me knew it was only a matter of time before word leaked to somebody who wasn't down with what I'd been doing.

I could feel the universe unraveling.

"What do you mean?" I asked, wishing I had borrowed Zoe's poker face.

"These people doing it on their own," said Beatrice, this time actually confusing me.

"I'm sorry, I don't follow."

"So you *don't* know. I thought maybe you did, and just didn't mind."

"Know *what?* Didn't mind *what?*"

"People are getting reckless. They're taking things into their own hands, using somebody untrained."

"Are you referring to what happened to Anthony, Mitchell and Deirdre?"

"Yes. And soon there will be others, I'm afraid. I wish they'd just try to be more patient. Wait their turn with you. They don't really know what the hell they're doing. Something is bound to go wrong."

Now that I knew Beatrice was on my team, I could get off my tiptoes.

"I knew something was amiss after hearing about Deirdre passing. So, do you have any idea who is trying to fill my shoes?"

"It's not a single individual. Deirdre used her husband, and I believe Anthony got an old friend to do it. Mitchell I'm not sure. Some say his cousin, others say his brother in-law. Things are getting out of hand. Now that more and more people are hearing about what you do, how effective and painless it is, they're rushing into it."

Being quickly disabused of big ideas never felt so good. I came into the conversation with Beatrice convinced my girlfriend had gone deep cover behind my back. And after Beatrice's opening remark, it appeared I'd met the woman who would put me away. Over the span of less than a minute, however, I'd discovered I'd been way off base on both counts.

Mr. Magoo was back, blindly averting disaster. Every misstep into the abyss somehow ended with a safe landing on solid ground.

Sort of. There was still the matter of well-meaning novices posing as exit experts. I understood how things had come to this, but these people were contaminating the art form and placing more than just themselves and their loved ones at serious risk. I had to act fast, to retake the reins before more hacks took a crack at the hood. I could see this desperate practice degrading into something worse, and shuddered at the grotesque thought of people trying to commit suicide completely on their own.

CHAPTER 22

It was a simple case of demand exceeding supply – an enviable scenario for a typical business, but not so much for an exit provider.

I was already working at maximum capacity. Trying to increase productivity would almost certainly have come at the expense of quality, and quite possibly at the expense of personal sanity. I wasn't willing to risk it. The only way I could complete more than an exit every two weeks was if there were two of me.

And then I realized that wouldn't be so hard to arrange.

I'd already assumed, albeit incorrectly, that Zoe had secretly served a handful of clients. I'd already pictured her pulling off multiple successful exits on her own. I never would have jumped to such conclusions or had such visions had I thought Zoe lacked the necessary skills needed to make her a suspect. I had trained her to be only an assistant, but she had learned plenty about how to work the hood through keen observation on the job.

Now that our client-base was in danger of turning into a bunch of do-it-yourselfers, I felt I had little choice but to offer Zoe a promotion. A big one.

When I returned home from the group meeting and my illuminating conversation with Beatrice, I found Zoe lying on the sofa reading my copy of *The Portable Nietzsche*. I was happy to see it in her hands, not just because it was among my favorite philosophy tomes, but because I knew it would make the transition into the conversation we were about to have a little easier than if she had been flipping through an issue of *Vogue* or *Cosmo*.

"Hi there," she said, in a more jovial tone than one might expect from somebody who'd just perused an excerpt from *The Antichrist*.

"Some light reading this evening, I see."

"Yeah. I needed something to take the edge off after watching a couple of *Friends* reruns."

"Nice. Well, if Nietzsche isn't helping you to relax, there's some exit business I'd like to discuss that might."

"Should I make some popcorn?" Zoe asked, trying unsuccessfully to keep a straight face.

"Not necessary. Listen, I found out something very interesting at the meeting tonight, something about the three would-be clients of ours who recently passed away."

"Do tell," said Zoe, sitting up quickly, eager to hear the news. I watched her reaction closely, as if for a brief moment I had forgotten she was innocent of any involvement.

"It turns out none of them died naturally. They all employed my – *our* – method."

"Oh my god! So the families and everybody know it was suicide? That's going to really –"

"No, no. They each used somebody close to them to do it, and to clean up afterward. Just like with us, only *not* with us."

"Oh shit. This isn't good. Did they do a decent job? I

mean, does anybody suspect anything?"

"Not that I know of, but we can't have this type of thing continue, or eventually somebody's going to fuck up, and things could get real messy for our clients, their friends and family, and us."

"I don't understand, though – why would your clients put a poor friend or family member through all that, all the emotional drama of an exit, instead of just using you?"

"Lack of time. Lack of patience. My – *our* – schedule is packed and people are getting tired of waiting. They already know what method we use and a little about it... I guess they've done some research to find out how exactly to do it. Though I'm sure it isn't pretty."

"So what does this mean? What can you do about it? It's not like you can force clients to wait until you are ready for them."

"I know, but I – *we* – can try to do more."

"You mean try to do more exits, more often? No way. You are already in somewhat over your head."

"I may be, but WE are not."

Zoe squinted her eyes and scratched her cheek.

"I don't follow," she said, though I could tell she had an inkling of what I was on about.

"How would you feel about administering a few exits on your own?" I asked.

"What?" Zoe replied, her eyebrows reaching for the top of her forehead.

"I would never ask if I didn't think you could do it, and if I didn't deem it necessary."

"Eli, I appreciate what you're trying to do, but I don't think I'm ready for that."

"I'm not talking about you going solo immediately, like tomorrow morning or anything. I'll give you all the additional training you need, not that you need very much. You're already close to being ready."

"This is crazy. It's not what I signed up for."

"I realize that. I never signed up for it either, to be honest. It just sort of happened, and you've seen how important it is that it did. You've seen how valuable our service is to these people."

"Yes, what you do –"

"*We*. What *we* do."

"Fine. What *we* do *is* important, but I don't know if I want to commit to it in the way that you have. What you're asking of me is huge."

"Don't you think I know that? But I've seen how you are in the exit room. Your poise and compassion and strength. It's something to behold. A thing of beauty, really. You say you don't know if you're ready to commit, but I'd say you already have. I see it in your eyes, in your actions, every time we work together."

"Exactly, every time we work *together*. I'm able to what I do so well because I know you are there leading the way."

"Let me tell you something, there have been times where I've felt it was the other way around."

"Okay, then you agree we are best as a *team*."

"Yes, and in an ideal world we'd continue to work in tandem, but circumstances have changed. What I'm proposing is the best plan I can think of – and a highly feasible one, at that – to deal with the new challenges that have emerged."

"And if I say no?"

"Don't say no."

"Eli, if I say no?"

"If you say no, I will have to respect your decision. You and I would continue working as a team and hoping against hope that things don't get out of hand, that our clients don't get out of control and bring this whole thing down."

"Lay on guilt much?"

"You asked, and I gave a frank answer. Listen, I wish I didn't have to ask what I'm asking. You have to know that. You have to know how much I enjoy working with you, having you by my side, by the clients' side. You have to know you make each exit a little better, that you make me a better exit man. But now I – and more importantly, our clients – really need you to help me expand the operation."

"So, what would we be talking about here? Each of us doing one every other week?"

"Yeah, something like that. Staggering our weeks for maximum coverage, and to keep from having people die too close together. I don't want two people exiting on the same day or a day apart."

"If we're staggering weeks, that means if one of us has an exit scheduled, the other one will be free, so why not just do an exit a week *together*."

"By splitting up, it gives each of us a much-needed break between jobs, and reduces the risk of either of us screwing up, getting caught. If both of us did one every week, it would most certainly cause burnout, and sloppiness would ensue. Splitting up and staggering will enable us to be there for twice as many clients as before without killing ourselves."

"Speak for yourself. I don't know how doing an exit on my own is going to affect me."

"I understand your apprehension, but I'm not going to

send you in there cold. I'll make sure you have everything you need and know exactly what you're doing. And if, after you give it a shot, you find you can't take it, it's okay. At least you will have tried. That's all I ask."

Zoe stood up from the sofa, let out a big sigh, and walked slowly across the room into the kitchen. I heard the refrigerator door open, followed by glass clinking and a drawer opening. Zoe returned moments later holding two bottles of beer in one hand and a bottle opener in the other. She sat back down on the sofa, opened both bottles and handed me one before raising hers in front of her with an extended arm.

"Here's to my graduation, I guess," she said, motioning for me to consummate the toast with a clink.

I would have much preferred a whiskey, but I wasn't going to let that spoil the moment.

"To an apt pupil, one destined for greatness," I said as we tapped bottles.

I smiled and took a sip of my beer, celebrating my persuasiveness while simultaneously doing my best to repress the dread.

It's no small leap from exit apprentice to exit master. I knew that. Holding a hand and offering soothing words, though invaluable, can't compare to applying the hood and turning the nozzle. The priest who's brought in to perform the last rites for a death row inmate never asks if he can pull the switch.

I also realized asking my girlfriend to step in and help me

handle the spike in suicide demand was not the most romantic gesture, especially with our six-month dating anniversary right around the corner. It would have been one thing if she had been itching to take the reins, if for weeks or months she had been clamoring for a chance to work the hood on her own, but that wasn't the case at all. She was perfectly content serving as my assistant.

I remembered how adamant she had been about accompanying me on the job, and how excited she was when I invited her to join me for Pete's exit. Now that I was giving her a shot at the big time, however, all I sensed from her was apprehension. I was asking my best batboy to play centerfield and hit cleanup. It was evident she questioned her abilities, and naturally this caused me to question my decision. I mean, what was I thinking? We had a good thing going – not just as an exit team, but in our overall relationship. It had developed in such a classic manner: Boy meets suicidal, homicidal girl; boy gets suicidal, homicidal girl; boy helps suicidal, homicidal girl become less suicidal and homicidal; boy lets girl assist him with suicides.

Why couldn't I just leave well enough alone? Most men would have been more than happy with how things had progressed, but I had to go and risk ruining everything by trying to turn her into me, into what I was.

And it's a good thing I did.

Just as she had during initial training months earlier, Zoe quickly absorbed everything I taught her. The physical and chemical properties of helium. Oxygen displacement. Hood construction and break down. Exit bag attachment. Gas release and gauge monitoring. Confirming the client's suicide request at the exit site. Reconfirming said request. Proper pulse checking and double-checking. Fingerprint and DNA evidence elimination tactics. Parking considerations. Proper storage of supplies.

Training focused mostly on the technical and practical aspects of the job; Zoe already had a solid grasp on the "soft" skills. Me teaching her how to communicate with clients and ensure their comfort would have been like me showing Mariano Rivera how to throw a slider.

None of the apprehension and self-doubt exhibited by Zoe when I initially proposed my plan to have us divide and conquer was present during the advanced training period, which took place over five nights at my condo. She was eager to learn the ins and outs of administering an exit, to emulate everything she had seen me do on the job.

Not only did Zoe pay close attention to my instruction and ask pertinent questions throughout training, she offered viable solutions to a couple of problems she foresaw – issues that hadn't even dawned on me. Issues like how a woman of her petite stature would lug a 25-lb duffle bag to clients' homes without drawing unwanted attention or rupturing something. I had always been the one to tote supplies, and had barely managed to avoid a back injury or hernia myself. Zoe solved the overweight duffle bag problem by suggesting I start stocking some small tanks for her at Jubilee. I had always ordered medium- and large-sized ones, since small tanks can inflate only about 50 balloons. Most clients want *at least* that many, and you have to account for the five to ten percent of balloons that pop while being inflated even by an expert like me.

A few dozen balloons-worth of helium may make for a lackluster celebration, but it's more than enough for a stellar suicide – provided the client isn't the size of an NFL lineman. So, the next day I ordered five small tanks – enough for Zoe's first two months in the field.

Once Zoe was all trained up, once I had imparted to her all my exit knowledge and experience, it was time to talk about the money. As ready as she was for her new job from a skills standpoint, she wasn't prepared for the raise she was about to receive. To her credit, she had never stopped to ask – or apparently even think about – what her elevated role meant in terms of dollar signs.

I let her know what it meant while we were lying in my bed following our final training session.

"We are going to split all the earnings from our combined exits. So I hope you are prepared to conceal a lot more money than before."

"Split the earnings? No way. This is your operation. I'm just an employee, certainly not a full partner."

"This isn't up for discussion. You'll now be assuming as much risk as I assume, performing the same tasks as I perform. You deserve equal payment."

"I don't know if I can handle that much money."

"Let's keep things in perspective. I mean, we're hardly talking lottery kind of money here. It ain't Mega Millions."

"Eli, I clear about thirty-five grand as a music teacher in a year... in a *good* year. Now you're telling me you're going to give me, what, that much money or more every couple months? That *is* lottery kind of money, to me anyway."

"I'm not *giving* you anything – you'll be earning every penny."

"Whatever. It's a ton of cash, and I don't know how comfortable I am with it."

"You'll learn how to become comfortable with it. You could always anonymously donate a chunk to a foundation that provides musical instruments and classes and whatnot to economically disadvantaged kids."

Zoe's frown and knitted brow slowly gave way to a smile.

"Actually, I like that idea, Eli. I like it a lot."

"And I like that you like it. It's important you aren't in this solely for the moolah. As I've said before, once you start to get greedy, it's time to take yourself out of the game. Once you start to swear under your breath whenever a client offers little payment or none at all, you're done. Now, it doesn't mean you're a monster if your eyes light up a little at the sound of a twenty grand offer – that's only human. But if you find yourself viewing each client as a revenue source rather than a suffering man or woman who trusts you with their final breath, it's time for *you* to exit."

"I agree, but does a greedy person ever really think they're being greedy? Greed is too easy for one to rationalize. If I start to covet the money, there are all sorts of things my mind can do to convince myself I'm still a good person doing the right thing."

"Perhaps, but I'll be around to keep an eye on you, and I'll organize an intervention if I catch you making plans to buy an island."

Zoe fell asleep a few minutes later, too exhausted from all the training to continue her half-hearted protest of my payment plan. I, on the other hand, was wide awake, entranced by the supine silhouette beside me. This woman with whom I'd shared everything but hardly knew. This lovely creature now proficient in my deadly art. This dangerous angel. This beautiful executioner.

CHAPTER 23

I sat in my parked Pathfinder reading a paperback copy of *The Fall*, pausing every few sentences to check the rearview mirror. I had purposely picked a book I'd read several times before. I knew my mind would be focused on other things, unable to fully absorb any new narrative. Not even Camus could compete with the story unfolding five houses down.

A few minutes later the distant image of a woman wearing a large knapsack appeared in the rearview. Objects may be more deadly than they appear.

I placed my book on the dashboard and turned the key in the ignition, all the while watching the woman grow bigger in the mirror, trying to see if her face would give me an early read on the result. I wasn't able to detect any telling expression, nothing that said mission accomplished or aborted or obliterated. Whatever had happened five houses down, the woman knew how to keep her cool.

While I'm sure she was walking at a normal pace, my memory has her moving in slow motion. A dark heroine passing dramatically through a movie scene. The director distorting the speed. Remove the special effects and the nostalgia and what we really have is a woman with a backpack too big for her body, looking more like a schoolgirl than a suicide specialist.

When she reached my blind spot, I leaned across the passenger seat to open the door.

Welcome to the club, my dear.

Zoe contorted her torso and arms to remove the 15-lb backpack and placed it on the floor of the passenger seat before climbing into the car. To give her more legroom, I reached over and, at an awkward angle, lifted the backpack and heaved it into the back seat, lucky not to strain an oblique muscle in the process.

I had offered to chauffer Zoe to her debut, concerned that her pre-exit jitters and post-exit emotions might adversely affect her driving. We couldn't have her inaugural show as a soloist missed or marred due to a head-on collision. Zoe was responsible for only one body being sent to the morgue that evening, and it wasn't her own or that of some unknown motorist.

"So?" I said as Zoe reached for the seatbelt, her poker face still on. She looked at me and took a deep breath before releasing a wide-eyed sigh.

"Let me just get my bearings," she said, rubbing her cheeks with her hands. "Wow. Just wow."

"Pretty intense, huh?"

"Intense? Intense doesn't quite cover it."

"Did everything go according to plan?" I asked as I pulled away from the curb.

"For the most part. I mean, yes, the most important parts. No apparent witnesses, no problem putting the hood together, and no problem with using it to proper effect. It's just, I hadn't expected there to be so much laughing."

"Laughing? Who was laughing, you or the client?"

"Mostly her, but, you know, it was infectious."

"What the hell was so funny?"

"She asked me to read excerpts from her favorite play – *Waiting for Godot.*"

"Mrs. Bradstreet is… was a fan of Beckett? I *knew* I liked her for a reason. Damn it!"

"What are you angry about?" asked Zoe.

"Cancer has enough people to choose from – can't it spare the few who still know how to read?"

"How very elitist of you."

"I'm just saying."

"Anyway, back to Mrs. Bradstreet. Laughing together with her like that… it was wonderful. We really bonded, but that of course made my job a little more difficult. I had to fight back the tears when it came time to let her go."

"You okay?"

"Yeah. I got through it fine. But next time, maybe try to set me up with somebody less delightful and interesting."

"You've got Mr. Geigel in two weeks. He used to be the editor of a quarterly newsletter for model train enthusiasts."

"Thank God."

Zoe sat back in her seat and gazed out the windshield.

"So tell me, how does it *feel?*" I asked.

"I told you, I'm fine."

"No, I mean, how does it feel? Are you invigorated? Anxious? Remorseful?"

"More than anything, I'm relieved."

"Were you worried something was going to go horribly wrong?"

"No. I mean, I guess that's always in the back of your

mind, but I wasn't really worried about messing up. I'm relieved because I'm *not* remorseful, or anything like that. I'm relieved because, because—"

"Because Mrs. Bradstreet is relieved?" I asked.

Zoe looked at me and nodded.

"Yes, yes, that's it," she said. "There's something very empowering about being able to offer such relief. As much as she was laughing, there was such pain and sadness behind her eyes. I never once second-guessed why I was there, what I was sent to do. What she *wanted* me to do."

I felt like a father who had just watched his kid get his first little league hit. A homerun off a nasty fastball pitcher twice his size. Mixed in with the immense sense of pride, however, was a sexual charge that blew the father-son analogy to bits. There's nothing more arousing than a beautiful girl who knows how to handle a suicide. Helium and humanity make quite the aphrodisiac.

As badly as I wanted Zoe at that moment, there was just enough blood flowing to my brain for me to realize the risk of pulling over and succumbing to base urges. Not that getting caught thrashing about in the backseat of a parked vehicle would instantly rouse suspicion of involvement in a nearby assisted suicide. Still, you can't leave anything to chance in these situations. Helping me to resist taking Zoe right then and there was the way she angrily slapped my hands away as they reached across the passenger seat for the buttons of her blouse.

Over the next month and a half, Zoe and I successfully set free six clients between the two of us. That's the same number of clients I had released during my entire first *year* as an exit man. Here we had an exponential increase in production, one that I knew couldn't possibly be sustained over the long haul.

Not that Zoe showed any signs of slipping. Each subsequent exit outshone the one preceding it. I stopped chauffeuring her after her third – partly because she had fully bloomed and no longer needed me, and partly because she was tired of fighting off my sexual advances in the car. She made me stay behind and told me I would just have to wait until she got home before making any amorous moves. But by that time the scent of the exit was usually so diluted it did little to incite me. Nevertheless, it was exciting to see my protégé performing so admirably in the field.

It was actually *my* performance that wasn't quite up to par during this period. At least that was how I felt; my clients, however likely didn't notice any glitches or hiccups. Not having Zoe by my side on the job meant no "couple cover" whenever entering and leaving client's houses, apartment buildings or condo complexes. I had started to grow accustomed to the comfort level that being a pair in the field afforded, not to mention Zoe's special touch during the actual exit process. This is not to say I botched or butchered anything after going back to working the hood without Zoe in the room, but I did sense a slight dip in the temperature each time I turned the nozzle.

Such dips were more than tolerable when considering the overall impact our increased efficiency was having on our clients' quality of (ending) life. The queue for our services was slashed in half. With waiting periods dramatically reduced, do-it-yourself exit incidents dropped off completely. Everything was going according to plan. Granted, Zoe and I were walking a tightrope, but we were too inside the experience, and elevated by it, to look down.

Plus we both enjoyed having livelier things to chat about during meals together. With us working independently now, we'd spend dinners filling each other in on our latest release, keeping one another up to date on any new hood tricks or tactics we had successfully employed, captivating one another with dramatic accounts of client courage, close calls, and last words. Breakfasts and lunches were often peppered with "Oh, I forgot to tell you about" type anecdotes – intriguing additions and addendums to recent exits. It beat the hell out of chewing our food in all too comfortable silence or making insipid comments on how well the chicken had been prepared. Splitting up the euthanasia duo gave us stories, fostered curiosity. It added wonder to ward off the homeostasis hovering over our relationship. You'd be surprised how quickly the thrill of carrying out mercy killings as a couple can wear off.

One of the biggest challenges of Zoe's and my "divide and conquer" era was making sure the increased helium usage went undetected at Jubilee. It was tricky enough keeping Carl in the dark *before* Zoe and I had switched into overdrive.

Now that we were taking on twice as many clients, concealing the gas embezzlement had become a rather daunting task, even with me being in charge of inventory control.

Not that I was panicking over the possibility of Carl noticing a missing tank or two. It's not like we worked in a nuclear missile production plant where items unaccounted for were cause for serious alarm. If questioned, I could always just confess to Carl that I'd been bending the rules and "borrowing" tanks for assorted celebrations of personal friends and family members. I would slap myself on the wrist in his presence and promise to pay back what was owed. If Carl insisted on raising a fuss, I'd simply fire him for insubordination.

There was little to worry about – a few missing tanks would be completely explainable. Less so, however, was a receipt that I found for a few *extra* ones.

After awakening one night and failing to fall back to sleep, I got out of bed, walked into the living room and turned on my computer. When I went to check my email, I saw that Zoe had forgotten to log out of her email account. She had done this a few times before, but in each instance, being the honorable man I am, I clicked "log out" without hesitation – after quickly scanning the list of senders and subject lines, of course. I never once opened a single message or exchange.

This time, however, the name of one sender caught my attention and begged me to investigate. The email was from "Party Down Express." The subject line read "Thank you for your order."

I clicked on it and read:

Dear Zoe,

Thank you for your express delivery order. Your item(s) should arrive within two business days at the address you provided. (See below for a summary of your order.)

Sincerely,
Party Down Express

ORDER SUMMARY
3 disposable helium tanks (110 cubic ft. each) = $240.00
Express shipping = $20.00
Tax = $13.08
TOTAL = $273.08

Shipping to:
Zoe Blake
17 Cardinal Lane
Blackport, OR 97997

After staring at the screen and scratching my head for several seconds, mouth agape, I went back and searched Zoe's inbox more extensively. I found another order confirmation from Party Down Express dated three weeks earlier. This one was for just a single tank. I again returned to the inbox and typed "Party Down" in the search box, but uncovered no additional entries.

I reread the two order confirmation emails, trying to arrive at some logical explanation. I had provided Zoe with all the helium she needed for her next several exits, and couldn't fathom why she would secretly order – and pay top-dollar

for — extra tanks. All the anxiety I had endured months earlier when I first suspected Zoe had gone rogue on me came
flooding back.

But if she was, in fact, doing extra hood work on the side,
who were her clients? Not a single support group member on
the schedule had died prior to their appointment in over six
weeks, and it had already been confirmed that each of those
other clients had used a family member or close friend to va-
cate the premises. Was Zoe going out on her own and actively lining up customers? Had she started frequenting support
groups for the terminally ill that I didn't know about?

Whatever she was up to, it hadn't been going on for long
and appeared to be ramping up.

CHAPTER 24

When you suspect somebody dear to you of devious behavior, the easiest way to get to the bottom of things is through direct interrogation. However, direct interrogation takes all the fun out of things. It leaves little room for sketchy detective work and absurd inferences. If you ask somebody point blank what they are up to after stumbling upon peculiar evidence against them, you ruin the intrigue, shatter the mystique, deprive yourself of weeks or even months of the kind of excitement that comes with trying to subtly uncover what the fuck is going on.

When Zoe first found my bag full of exit supplies a few months earlier, she opted to immediately confront me. That was her prerogative and I don't fault her for her actions. However, had I been in her shoes, I would have taken at least a day or two to try to dig up the truth on my own, to perhaps even endeavor to catch me in the act rather than extract a confession via hostile questioning. I guess she and I were just different that way.

Sure, I was eager to find out why Zoe had taken to stockpiling her private supply of suicide gas and keeping it from me, but I wasn't about to do something as predictable and unimaginative as asking her.

My strategy was simple and featured a two-pronged approach: 1) Keep a close eye on her daily activity without her noticing; and 2) develop several far-fetched hypotheses with little evidence to support them.

The latter activity was easier, as it could all be done in my head and involved no stealth movement or spying. Hypothesizing, when done with a closed mouth, is very safe. It was just me thinking. Just me examining what few facts were available and then extrapolating. I could partake in such activities with no risk of infuriating or alienating Zoe enough for her to leave me or withhold sex.

My most plausible hypothesis – the one positing that Zoe was lining up her own set of clients and administering exits on her own – has already been touched upon and will be addressed again later.

A second theory of mine was far less damning, but also less likely. This scenario had Zoe ordering helium from an outside source to protect me. It had her worried about botching a job, about the police somehow picking up on a tank and linking it to Jubilee. She certainly had enough money now to fund her own gas supply, and it was satisfying to think she cared enough about me to inspire such noble actions, but I wasn't at all prepared to bank on this one.

The only other possible explanation was that Zoe was planning to create and lead a cult, one where human sacrifices would factor in prominently and be carried out humanely. I should point out that this hypothesis was born at the bottom of a bottle of Buffalo Trace, and was thus the least sturdy of the three.

Keeping a watchful eye on Zoe without being too invasive

or seeming too possessive entailed me doing such things as:

- Carefully checking the helium level of tanks before and after her scheduled exits.
- Calling her more often than usual to say hi while I was at work, then listening for any audible clues in her phone voice or the background (e.g., nervousness, impatience, tribal chanting).
- Asking her to tell me all about her day during dinner, then later asking questions about earlier described activities and searching for incongruities in her answers (e.g., "What was the name again of that bratty piano student you taught today?"; "Where'd you say you went to lunch?"; "So Mary's was the only suicide you facilitated today, right?")
- Calling her to bed while she was busy checking email, then talking to her about Jubilee to lull her to sleep so I could sneak out and take a peek at her messages.
- Following her from a safe distance when she left the house.

I uncovered nothing during three weeks of secret investigation. Zoe was either completely innocent or a solid rock. Either she wasn't at all involved in any extracurricular suicide activities or was but had received advanced training from some intelligence agency specializing in covert missions. Naturally I hoped the former was the case, though couldn't help but experience arousal over the notion of the latter. Spy ninja suicide assassins are incredibly sexy.

I had nothing to go on other than the helium tank order

confirmation emails I had stumbled upon. If I wanted to get to the bottom of the baffling evidence, it looked as if I'd have to confront Zoe directly.

That's just what I decided I would do during my lunch break the following day. I'd drive to her house (she had several music students lined up that day and thus she would be home), tell her what I knew, and ask her to explain.

That was the plan. The next day, however, while en route to her house, I saw Zoe in her ancient Volvo peel out at an intersection and turn left onto a road leading away from her piano lessons.

Maybe she had a feminine emergency requiring her to dash out to a pharmacy or convenience store before her next student arrived.

Perhaps one of her students had sprained a finger or wrist mid-lesson while attempting a tricky concerto and needed to be rushed to the hospital.

Or, it could well have been that Zoe had lied about having lessons that day and was late for an extra-curricular exit.

Zoe's left turn was a right turn for me. When my light turned green a few seconds after Zoe's arrow had directed her across the intersection, I followed. Two cars separated us. When one of them turned onto another street a few moments later, I decelerated to remain a safe distance behind Zoe. She'd be able to identify my filthy black Pathfinder in an instant if I got too close. That said, I knew that if she was, indeed, late for an appointment with a client, she wasn't likely to be paying too close attention to the types of vehicles around her – provided none of them resembled a squad car.

We passed a CVS, a Walgreens and a 7-11, thus eliminating Explanation #1 from the running. And as far as I could tell, Zoe wasn't carrying a passenger, unless he or she was lying down in the back seat. I doubted any injury suffered while playing piano would require one to assume a supine position, so Explanation #2 was out.

About a mile after my pursuit had begun, the Volvo turned right into the parking lot of Sal's Lounge – a bar I'd driven by a hundred times but had never entered. I drove past Sal's and pulled into the parking lot next door, outside a fried chicken joint. My spot afforded me a view of Sal's lone portal, ensuring I wouldn't miss Zoe on her way out.

Drinking in the middle of a workday. As far as I knew, this was not something Zoe did routinely. Then again, those who knew her much better than I did probably didn't know about her euthanasia habit. People always say there aren't enough surprises in the world. I strongly disagree. There are *too many* – we just aren't prepared to see them.

I sat somewhat slumped down in my seat and watched as Zoe got out of her car. She was wearing a tight white T-shirt and even tighter blue jeans that ended just above where her black heels began. This was not the outfit of a woman who had just taught someone Chopin.

As much as I wanted to see what Zoe was up to and who, if anybody, she was meeting, I knew there was no way to walk into the bar unnoticed. Nobody walks into a weekday dive bar unnoticed. The second the door creaks open, every ruined face in the place quickly turns to see if God has been kind enough to send them someone to screw, or if the demons were just at play again, trying to get another fight going. The only folks who don't take notice when you walk into a weekday dive bar are the resident legends passed out or dead beside their scotch. And the bartender.

I considered walking over to Sal's to catch a glimpse of Zoe through a window, but that would have required the building to have actually *had* a window. Not even the door was penetrable by light. Zoe had either had a very rough day, was meeting a very rough client, or was moonlighting as a bottom-tier prostitute.

I felt anxious. Not just because I was bamboozled by Zoe's actions, but because I knew I was loitering. I could gracefully end the lives of multiple human beings any given month but wasn't able to withstand the angst of parking outside a fast-food establishment from which I hadn't made a purchase. To settle my nerves and ease my conscience, I stepped out of the Pathfinder, hurried into the restaurant and ordered a three-piece meal.

I quickly returned to my stakeout spot and devoured the first two pieces of chicken, the grease dripping from my chin, my eyes glued to Sal's door. As I got started on the drumstick, Zoe emerged from the bar with a short, thin man with dark hair who looked to be in his early forties. He was wearing a green polo shirt with khaki chinos and brown topsiders. Most concerning of all was that he didn't appear to be dying of any deadly disease. I would have much preferred Zoe to be sneaking in a few extra exits than to be cheating on me with a middle-aged insurance salesman.

Zoe laughed and made subtle flirtatious gestures – twirling her hair, touching the man's shoulder – as the two walked toward her car. I nearly honked my horn to break up the action, but caught myself in time, opting instead just to quietly bite my forearm until I tasted blood.

Zoe and the man stood by her car and chatted for a few moments before he started to lean in. I gasped and covered my eyes with my both hands, leaving just enough space between my fingers to catch Zoe in the act. But there was no act to catch. Zoe raised her hand to gently reject the man's advances. Actually, it seemed less a rejection and more a "be patient" type of maneuver – followed by a smile on both their faces. Unsatisfactory. In my opinion, a hard slap to the face and a knee to the groin had been in order. I wanted to see fillings fly. Knees buckle. Eyes roll back.

The two exchanged a few more words before the man pointed over to another car in the parking lot. A silver Honda Pilot. Of course. Everything about this man screamed avid player of public golf courses, so why should his automobile have been any different. This guy had to meet my mother. Zoe nodded and got into her car as the man started walking toward his.

Drive off now, Zoe. Drive off and go home and later tell me how you met an old friend or a former co-worker or a second cousin for a drink. Drive off and tonight at dinner describe how this poor sad friend/colleague/cousin made a desperate move on you and how you had to let him down easy so as to not shatter his already brittle psyche. Drive off and... why aren't you driving off?

Zoe sat in her car and waited while the man climbed into the silver Pilot, started the engine, backed out of his space and pulled up beside her. Windows were rolled down. Words were exchanged. And my girlfriend followed a stranger out of the parking lot of a decaying lounge, practically touching his rear bumper as he eased out onto the street.

Let's add a Pathfinder to the procession. Make way for the parade.

I slid down in my seat and hoped Zoe wouldn't recognize my vehicle as she passed the fried chicken restaurant. Seconds later I popped back up, turned the key in the ignition, and continued my pursuit.

Just as before, I remained a safe distance behind — allowing a few cars to come between us, but careful not to lose sight of Zoe's tail lights and turn signals. I had no idea where this civilized chase would lead me. Just kept following, hurt and nervous, but undeniably enthralled.

A left turn a few minutes down the street cost me my buffer, as the two cars separating me from Zoe's Volvo continued straight on. I dropped back 80-100 feet to remain anonymous in its rear view, begging for another car or two to quickly file in. Duplicating a few more of Zoe's turns without any cars or trucks blocking for me would likely catch her eye. All I could hope was that her mind was too focused on philandering for her to take notice of a madman on her tail.

At the risk of losing the Volvo and the Pilot, I pulled over and let two cars behind me pass me up before pulling back out behind them. The maneuver likely elicited some worry in the family minivan in front of me, but I was willing to live with causing a soccer mom some momentary discomfort in order to lower my profile.

The Pilot and the Volvo, now a good 300 feet ahead of me, turned right into a residential subdivision, which was marked by a giant faux stone entrance sign that read "Harbor Meadows." I made the same turn several seconds later and saw that my friends had made another quick right and were in the process of parking on the curb outside a gray brick split-level house on the corner. Worried Zoe might step out of her car and see me, I made a left where they had turned right and slowly drove up the street, all the while watching them carefully through my rearview mirror to ensure they had, indeed, reached their final destination.

I continued down the street, which looped around to the left, and, when I was completely out of sight, I pulled over to the curb and stopped. I waited there until I was sure that enough time had passed for Zoe and the mystery man to enter the house, at which point I did a three-point turn and headed back in their direction.

The party had moved inside. I parked along the curb about 100 feet before the intersection where the man's house occupied a corner. What I was *doing* there, I wasn't sure. All I knew was I had made quite the effort to get there and didn't want Zoe to spot me now that I was finally in position. Of course, her not noticing me in position wouldn't mean much if I ended up succumbing to primal, possessive urges and burst through the door or a window to beat the man so badly it would raise his handicap by 30 or 40 strokes.

I sat and stewed in my parked car. I tried to convince myself there was no way Zoe would ever be with a man like the one she had accompanied inside, but I was in a dark place and couldn't remove from my imagination the image of her tearing off his pleated pants and mounting him while he eased back in his vinyl Barcalounger, the scores and stats of SportsCenter softly playing in the background.

What could she possibly see in this bourgeois oaf? With me, there was witty discourse and intrigue and excitement and suicide. What more could a woman want? Let's not forget I had saved her life. This guy could only save her money on life insurance.

I was torn. Sitting idly by made me feel like a coward, though storming in and trouncing the man seemed like a bad idea – not only because I was generally opposed to violence, but also because there was always the chance that the man would trounce *me*. I hadn't been in a fight since Mikey Bitner had called me a dirty Jew in second grade, and while I did manage to land a couple of pinches (that's not a typo) during that melee, Mikey ultimately emerged victorious after practically taking my left eye out with a Lincoln Log.

There's nothing worse than fighting to defend your honor and losing, and then having to go sit in the corner. Except for perhaps *not* fighting to defend your honor and instead getting nabbed by a neighborhood watch group. I could tell by the pristine lawns and the potted flowers in window boxes outside every humble house on the street, this was not the type of neighborhood that took kindly to unfamiliar men parked in unfamiliar vehicles. I had already seen the curtains move once in the house I had parked in front of, and wondered how many more eyes were on me, how long might it be before a patrol car rolled up.

Before I broke through any doors to give or take any beatings, before any peon policemen were called in to run me out, Zoe came out of the house alone. She had been inside only 10 minutes and her hair and clothes seemed to be kempt, giving me hope that no carnal knowledge had been gained. I watched her walk down the driveway and get into her Volvo. But instead of hearing the rev or her engine moments later, I saw her trunk pop open.

Zoe stepped out, walked to the back of the car, reached into the trunk with both hands and pulled out a very familiar backpack. Either it doubled as her overnight bag, thought I, or things were about to get very interesting. Exits are far less cliché than affairs.

I wasn't sure which one I was rooting for. Certainly I didn't want my girlfriend sleeping with another man, but I also didn't want her engaging in adulterated euthanasia. I had been under the impression we were exclusive, that when it came to suicide, we agreed to keep to the official list and not see other people.

I couldn't win. Whatever Zoe was headed back into the house to do, it amounted to infidelity. Rarely do two things as disparate as sex and assisted suicide share such a common denominator.

Zoe struggled to strap on the backpack, bending her knees and twisting her torso awkwardly to get the package in its proper dorsal position. The backpack's apparent heftiness pointed more to suicide than to a sleepover. A helium tank weighs much more than toiletries and a change of clothes. To avoid jumping to conclusions, however, I considered the possibility that Zoe was secretly working as a daytime dominatrix, toting around a backpack filled with handcuffs and chains. But remembering how upset she had become when I once tried to introduce a minor sadomasochistic element into our own bedroom, I realized the dominatrix hunch had few teeth.

After shutting the trunk, Zoe lugged the backpack up the

driveway and turned onto the short walkway leading to the front door of the house. Before entering she, turned around and scanned the area. Seeing this, I quickly ducked down in my seat. I was less concerned that she might recognize the vehicle (I was parked too far away for her to notice any distinguishing dirt or dents), and more concerned she might see the silhouette of a person witnessing whatever she was up to. I stayed down for a good 20 or 30 seconds before inching my eyeballs back up to window-level, and breathed a sigh of relief upon discovering she was no longer outside. Not that there was very much to be relieved about. She was about to cheat on me – either by screwing another man or releasing him.

Zoe discretely ordering helium online, coupled with having seen her just haul a suspiciously bulky backpack inside, had me betting that an exit – not a sex act – was about to unfold. I then shuddered over the possibility of *both* taking place, but quickly dismissed it. I had neither the physical nor the emotional constitution to cope with the idea of my girlfriend being turned on by the terminally ill, or, worse, being a necrophiliac.

Assuming the man was, indeed, a euthanasia client Zoe had chosen to work with on the side – as most (or at least half) of the evidence suggested – why did he look so healthy? And why had the two of them been flirting with one another outside of Sal's?

I was confounded. Suddenly unable to think straight. An internal voice was shouting, *What kind of man sits and waits outside a house where his woman is doing misdeeds with another man?* I gripped the steering wheel with both hands and shook it violently, furious with myself for having been so passive throughout the pursuit, for having behaved like a private investigator merely observing events when I should have been acting like a double-crossed man demanding answers. Assaulting my steering column wasn't providing any clues, but it was better than complete inertia. The anger and jealousy and uncertainty were taking over. Finally.

I punched my dashboard with all the force I could muster, hard enough to knock the radio from FM to AM. As good as it felt beating the daylights out of my Pathfinder, I was still left very much in the dark.

There was only one way to remedy that.

I jumped out of the car and slammed the door.

Fuck you, suspicious neighbors. Fuck you, crime watch committee. Fuck you, Mr. Pleated Pants – though my apologies if you're dying. And most of all, fuck you...

...Zoe came out of the house and saw me marching across the quiet intersection toward her. I froze. Like a teenager getting caught sneaking out of his bedroom window. I was standing at the edge the intersection near the driveway, my right leg literally suspended in mid-step. Zoe, in contrast, never stopped moving. She was as in a hurry as she was shocked to see me.

"Eli! What the HELL?" she whisper-shouted as she walked toward her Volvo. "Get in your car and meet me at home. Your place." She shooed me in the direction of my Pathfinder. "Go on, goddamnit, go. We have to get out of here."

CHAPTER 25

"Carl, I'm going to be a bit late coming back from lunch. Can you hold down the fort?"

"Sure. Is everything okay? You sound a bit shaken."

"I'm fine. Just some girl trouble."

"Ah. Good luck with that. Don't worry about me – I can take care of things over here. Pretty slow today."

"Thanks. I'll see you later."

"Oh, just one thing, Eli... Eli, you still there?"

"Yes, what is it?"

"We seem to be short a couple of helium tanks."

You picked a fine time to start paying attention, Carl. Keep it up and you'll be out of a job.

"Yeah, I know. Don't worry about that. I'm on it."

I laid my cell phone on the center console and accelerated to catch up to Zoe. I wasn't fully convinced she was driving to my place as she had said, so I thought it wise to stay close. All it takes is one affair and/or unapproved assisted suicide to erode the trust in an otherwise healthy relationship. I hated that we were turning into *that* couple.

But Zoe didn't try to lose me or make any questionable turns. She went straight to my condo complex, where we parked in adjacent spaces and didn't say a word to one another until I had closed the door to unit 106.

"What were you doing there, Eli?" Zoe asked. "Why were you following me?"

"Yeah, I don't think we're going to start this conversation with *me* explaining *my* actions," I replied. "But I appreciate you asking." Admittedly, sarcasm probably wasn't the best way to begin.

"No, seriously," said Zoe, shaking her head and almost smiling. "What were you doing? *There?*"

"Okay, I'll go first, but then it's all you. I wasn't following you... or hadn't *planned* to, anyway. I wanted to swing by your place on my lunch break to talk to you about something. Then I saw you in your car at the light at Gossamer St. and was curious about where you were going."

"So instead of just calling me and telling me where you were and asking me what I was up to, you decided to follow me?"

"That's right. I thought I'd just wait until you arrived at a store or a bank or something and then surprise you. But when I saw you pull into Sal's, I decided to sit back and observe."

"And what did you think I was up to? That I was a closet alcoholic? That I was meeting another man, cheating on you?"

"I entertained each of those theories, but neither really made sense or stuck. Of course, when I saw you come out of the bar with that guy, the latter started to seem a lot more plausible. But I had, er, I *have* another theory."

"Yeah, and what's that?"

"First of all, drop the tone. I've done nothing wrong."

"Yes, you did, you fucking followed me!"

"Are you kidding me? Like you wouldn't have done exactly the same thing if you had been in my place. You're just frazzled because I accidentally caught you doing something you didn't want me to know about."

"And what's that? What did you 'catch' me doing, Eli? You think I'd cheat on you with a guy like that? You don't have a fucking clue what's going on."

"I have a pretty good idea."

"No, you don't."

"Well, I know you've been ordering helium tanks online."

Zoe, who had inhaled in preparation for her next retort even before I had finished my sentence, looked away and exhaled without a word. A few seconds after deflating, she turned back to face me.

"So you're spying on my *Internet* activity, too?" she said in an oddly calm tone.

"No. You left your email open on my computer a couple of weeks ago, and when I went to close the browser window, I noticed a message from Party Down Express in your inbox."

"And you opened it?"

"Yes, I did. I thought it very odd you'd be doing business with a direct competitor of my family's business. I felt compelled to check it out."

"And why didn't you ask me about it then?"

"I don't know. I guess I wanted to figure things out on my own, avoid the confrontation in case I was way off base."

"Well, we're having a confrontation now, Eli."

"True, but I no longer think I'm off base."

"You don't, huh? Think you've 'solved the case'?"

"Look, I wasn't hoping to catch you doing something wrong or bad. I was hoping there was some logical explanation to all this, something that you'd emerge from clean."

Zoe chuckled.

"What the hell's so funny?" I asked.

"You. You're talking as if you know what's going on, but you still don't. You couldn't."

"Zoe, I'm not clueless."

"Okay. Then tell me exactly what it is I'm involved in."

"I never said I was 100% certain, but, I, um, it would seem–"

"Since you're afraid to tell me straight out what you think I've been up to, how about I tell you what *I* think you think I've been up to?"

"I'm not afraid, I'm just–"

"You think I'm assisting suicides in secret," said Zoe with a smirk. "Isn't that right?"

"Isn't it?"

"Let me ask you, did the man you saw me leave Sal's with *look* like he was dying?"

"No, he didn't. That's why I was a little confused. But then when I saw you come out of his house the first time and get your–"

"I know what you saw and what you assumed, Eli. And I even understand why you'd make such an assumption. But you've got it wrong."

"Good – I *want* to have it wrong."

"Don't be so sure."

"Well, you're not fucking or euthanizing men behind my back. I look at that as favorable news."

"That's true, I'm neither fucking nor euthanizing men behind your back."

"Okay then, so let's have it. What *are* you doing?"

"I'm executing them."

Executing them.

Plural.

The way she said it was like genocide.

Executing. Them.

I'd better call Carl again and tell him I might not make it in after all.

Zoe appeared even more stunned than I was, as if hearing herself say what she'd been up to out loud made it real for the first time.

"*Still* glad to have been wrong about me?" she asked. Her eyes screamed "Take that!" along with a touch of "Holy shit what have I done?"

"What do you mean, 'executing'?" I asked, still in disbelief that such a conversation was happening.

Zoe sat down on the sofa and buried her face in her hands. Small convulsions ensued and I braced myself for a big cry. Instead came laughter.

"Zoe, what the hell is going on?"

She looked up at me and started laughing even harder.

"Is this your idea of a joke?" I asked. "Are you fucking with me?"

Zoe fought through the laughter to speak.

"No, no... it's not a joke... and I'm not laughing... at you. It's just... everything that has happened, that's been happening..." she paused and the laughter ceased. "It's just so FUCKING HILARIOUS."

Zoe put her face back in her hands. This time she cried.

She was unraveling. We're talking King George III or William Blake kind of crazy. I'd seen it before in my life. It was hard to say whether I attracted women with loose bolts or if I was the one holding the wrench.

I wasn't about to let the descending madness impede my interrogation.

"What happened back at that house, Zoe? What have you gotten yourself into?"

Zoe regained her composure and looked up.

"I guess you could say I've taken the whole exit thing to the next level."

"You care to elaborate?"

"I didn't think the hood should be reserved only for those who are begging to die. There are others not dying but who *deserve* death."

"And who are these *others*? Who was that man you met at Sal's?"

"It doesn't matter who he was. What matters is what he had done."

"Okay, what did he do?

"The same thing Keith did to me."

"What? That guy... *raped* you?"

"No, not *me*."

"Who then?"

"That's irrelevant."

"How can that be irrelevant?"

Zoe gritted her teeth and balled each of her hands into a fist.

"It's irrelevant because it doesn't matter *who* he raped. What matters is *that* he raped."

"But whom? Someone you know?"

"You're missing the point! That guy – and the others – are the fucking scum of the earth, so I'm wiping them from it."

"Holy shit, Zoe. How many of 'them' have you, um, gotten rid of?"

"That guy you saw me with today, he was the third."

Between teaching Liszt and administering suicides, where DO you find the time?

"Three? You've *killed* three men?"

"Four if you count Keith. And I'm not done yet."

Jack the Ripper had his prostitutes. John Wayne Gacy had his teenage boys. Zoe had her sex offenders.

My girlfriend. The vigilante serial killer.

I made a mental note to further postpone introducing her to my mother.

"I don't understan... I mean, how do you... where do you–"

"I'm happy to answer all of your fragments, Eli, but first I need you to calm down."

When an un-medicated bipolar assassin tells you to calm down, it's best to obey. Never mind that she keeps a toothbrush in your bathroom and underwear in one of your drawers.

I took several deep breaths before asking Zoe to enlighten me.

"First off, how do you select your victims?"

"I prefer to call them 'targets' – 'victim' is too sympathetic for these fuckers."

"Fair enough. So, how do you choose them?"

"There's a whole list of them on the Oregon Sex Offender Inquiry System – available online to the public. All you have to do is type in "Blackport" or another nearby city, and then some additional information like age range, weight range, et cetera. If your search is too general, like if you only type in a city name, the system will tell you your query returned too many results and will ask you to narrow your search. Me, I've been searching for 21 to 50 year-old males who weigh less than 180 pounds, as I don't want to kill some senile old man who doesn't really even know what he's doing, nor do I want to come up against some giant monster of a guy."

"So you do these searches and up pop a bunch of names and addresses?"

"Yup, and much, much more. Each entry also includes a color photo of the bastard, what he's been convicted of, who his typical victims are, his modus operandi, and what conditions and restrictions apply to him. For example, the guy you saw me with today, he is – or was – 34, weighed 165, has served time for first-degree rape and also was convicted of two other counts of attempted sexual abuse. He prefers adolescent females and young boys, and gains access to his victims by establishing a false sense of trust and authority. Oh, and among his conditions and restrictions, he is prohibited from frequenting any place where minors regularly congregate as well as bars or taverns. And he must attend sex offender treatment on a weekly basis. I guess he's going to miss his next appointment."

"You said he couldn't enter any bars or taverns, but you guys went to Sal's."

"Places like Sal's don't exactly have bouncers or bartenders who check for that kind of shit."

"Goddamn," I said, shaking my head. "That website really serves these guys up on a platter to pissed off or paranoid citizens."

"What, you feel *sorry* for them?"

"No, no, I'm just saying. I'm glad they don't have a system like that for euthanasia purveyors."

"Well, the site very clearly states that its purpose is to provide users with information only to protect themselves or a child who may be at risk – NOT to punish the offender. It says that you'll go to jail for using the system to discriminate against, harass or injure a registered sex offender. But I've killed three of them with no consequences thus far, so I guess the disclaimer doesn't really have teeth."

"Knock on wood. I mean, not a lot of time has passed since you started committing these cr... I mean, since you started taking action. The cops could very well be just a clue or two away from catching on."

"Ha! Like I'm worried about the Blackport police. They never found anything tying me to Keith's death, and I wasn't even *trying* to conceal anything when I took *him* out. With these other raping motherfuckers, I have a system, a set of precautions to keep me invisible throughout the hunt. And, of course, I have the helium, which, as you well know, doesn't leave any gaping wounds or traceable bullets behind. The cops are lost puppies."

I was familiar with such delusional thoughts. The powerful sense of invincibility you experience once you go so far over the law you can no longer see it. Once you feel it can no longer see you.

Zoe was a chip off the old block. If she hadn't already made several mistakes in her newest line of work, she soon would, even if she didn't believe it. I only hoped she, like me, had some Mr. Magoo in her.

"Tell me more about how you stay 'invisible,'" I said. "Walk me through one of your hunts, from target selection to target elimination."

"Not right now, Eli. I'm exhausted. I need to rest a little and then get back to my place for a lesson at three." She lay down on the sofa and curled into the fetal position.

"I don't care," I said. "This conversation doesn't just end at, 'Yeah, I kill rapists but I'm careful.' You'll have plenty of time to rest tonight. Right now you're going to tell me everything."

I wasn't sure what to be more concerned about – the fact that my girlfriend was murdering dangerous men, or that she thought it appropriate to take a nap in the middle of confessing it.

"Fine," Zoe whined while sitting back up and clutching a throw pillow, her knees tucked into her chest. "But I'm too tired to run through everything all at once. Just ask me whatever you need to know and I'll answer you… at least until I pass out."

I took a moment to organize the mess of questions in my head.

"Okay, so I get how you use the online system to find these guys, but how do you decide whom to go after, and how do you contact them without leaving some sort of trail?"

"Some of the guys listed have, like, just one attempted sexual abuse charge against them and nothing else. I leave them alone. For now. I look for the sons of bitches with 'Rape

1' and 'Rape 2' listed among their crimes. 'Rape 3' will get you shortlisted, but won't boost you to the top. I also look for anybody with sexual abuse charges and whose victims are children. Those lovely men fit right in with the hardcore rapists. I haven't seen anybody with multiple rape charges yet – they're all probably still incarcerated. Lucky for them."

"What if two guys have pretty much identical charges – say a 'Rape 1' and a sexual abuse with similar victim types – do you just do eeny meeny miney moe?"

"I look at their photo and decide which one looks more despicable. Then I choose the *other* one. It's the guy who looks less dangerous and demented you *really* have to watch out for. Like that guy today. He looked like he worked at Best Buy, right? Anyway, it doesn't matter – all the guys who 'come in second,' I'll get them, too."

"And how do you approach these men?"

"Well, naturally I don't want to leave any phone or email trails, so I just go to their home. I know it sounds dangerous, but not really, not the way I do it. I knock on their door or ring their bell, and when they open the door, I act confused for a second and then politely apologize for having the wrong house and for disturbing them.' But all the while I'm apologizing, I'm twirling my hair in my fingers and batting my eyelashes, looking like a silly little woman who's lost but who likes what she sees."

"Are you nuts? These guys could really hurt you."

"No. Most have recently gotten out of prison or have strict probationary restrictions, and while they are horny, they aren't about to do something stupid and get sent back to the slammer. Yes, they light up at my subtle flirtation, but they don't dare try to drag me inside."

"Maybe not YET. Jesus Zoe, some of these guys are truly sick. They can't control themselves."

"I'm not saying I don't bring protection. All the while I'm twirling and batting and flirting, I've got one hand in my pocket holding a small canister of mace. Just in case. Also, in my purse I carry a Swiss Army knife with one of the blades already out."

"I don't like this."

"My approach doesn't need your approval. It works."

I wasn't prepared to argue. Yet.

"What comes after the 'Oops, I'm sorry' and the flirting?"

"These guys invariably try to be helpful. 'Who are you looking for, darling?' or 'What's the house number? Maybe I can get you where you're going.' I make up a name, tell them I must have written the address down wrong, say how stupid I feel. Anything to keep the conversation going. I tell them how nice they are being about it all, how I, myself, hate it when somebody I don't know comes to my door. And of course I keep sticking my chest and ass out. They say 'No bother at all' or 'Don't worry about it' and start to get excited that I haven't walked away yet. I initiate more small talk, then start to get bold with something like, 'Well, I do feel dumb for getting the house wrong, but I'm kind of glad I did.' These guys aren't used to a pretty girl giving them any such attention. They get all nervous and awkward, so I help them out with, 'I hope you don't think me too forward, but would you maybe want to meet up for a drink sometime?' I try to look past the drooling at this point. After they nod their head or manage to eke out a 'Yes,' I say, 'How about tomorrow?' and tell them where to meet me."

"Sal's."

"That was just today. I've used another dive bar and a dingy restaurant, too. Got to switch it up. I don't want to become too familiar with the staff at any of these places."

"Good thinking," I said, then wondered why I was commending an element of my girlfriend's murder strategy.

"So anyway, I tell these guys I don't like to give out my name or phone number, how I think it's more exciting to just meet up. You should see their expression. They're each putty in my hands at this point. What they don't know is they're already dead."

Zoe was no longer sleepy. Painting a picture for me had woken her right up. Gotten her blood pumping. And mine.

"What I don't get," I said, sitting down next to her on the sofa, "is how you subdue them enough to be able to work the helium in. What do you do, conk them over the head with something when you get to their place?"

"Nope, I take a page right out of Keith's playbook," she responded, a devilish grin forming on her face. "I slip them a roofie at the bar or restaurant."

"Doesn't that risk them crashing their car while you're following them to their house?"

"It's always a possibility, but that's why I whisper, 'Let's get out of here,' pretty much immediately after drugging them. They may start to feel a little sluggish behind the wheel, but they manage to make it to their destination. There have been no car crashes, thus far at least."

"Man, you are taking some real chances."

"Oh, and picking off fellow support group members one by one *isn't* taking chances? You know better than most, Eli, that you have to take chances to accomplish anything worth accomplishing."

"Yeah, I guess I just don't... I'm sorry, but I'm just not sure if what you're accomplishing is... warranted."

"What the hell does that mean?"

"I mean, do these guys all really *deserve* to die?"

Zoe bit her lower lip and shook her head. I readied myself in case I had to block a slap or a punch to the face.

"Do they deserve to die?" she said through her teeth. "I guess *you've* never been raped, Eli."

"What happened to you is awful, and you're right, I can't imagine what it must feel like to go through something like that. All I'm saying is you don't know the whole story behind each of these other cases, what these men may be doing to try to change their lives and make up for their horrendous deeds."

"I don't *need* to know the whole story. These men were all convicted of first or second degree rape, with no appeals. It's not like they were innocently walking down the street, accidentally tripped, and somehow had their dick pop out of their pants and penetrate a girl or boy they landed on."

"What if you found out one of the men you've killed had, say, I don't know, started taking medication that stabilized him, and that he had profoundly apologized to and been forgiven by his victim or victims? Maybe he even started volunteering at a church or a shelter or something."

"I'd say too bad he hadn't started taking that medication *before* he brutally violated any innocent people."

"That's it? So then you're all for capital punishment of anyone and everyone who commits a violent crime? Just kill'em all?"

"I had always taken the same liberal stance you're taking now, Eli. That was *before* I got raped. Should the government be putting to death every single rapist and violent criminal out there? Probably not. But if a person or someone they love ever ends up a rape victim, and that person decides to put their life on the line to get revenge, I say more power to them."

"But you *weren't* the victim of any of these men you're snuffing out, and neither was anyone you love."

"And now I don't have to worry about any of us *becoming* one."

"So is it vengeance, or a preemptive strike?"

"Call it whatever the hell you want. All I know is it feels right... just like your *exits* feel right."

"So then, tell me, where does it stop?"

"I don't know – when I get it all out of my system. Where does it stop with *you*?"

CHAPTER 26

When you start dating a woman on the heels of her shooting her ex-fiancé, you have no real right to act incredulous if she later goes on a killing spree.

Especially when you, yourself, taught her how to use the weapon.

While I wasn't at all pleased about the way Zoe had decided to express her fury over having been raped, it was good to see that her murders had yet to interfere with her suicide work. She hadn't botched any exits or even stumbled slightly with a client since starting her vigilante ways nearly two months earlier.

Still, I knew it was only a matter of time before a slip-up in either arena would send the ceiling crashing down on both of us. Whether she got caught seeking vengeance or administering mercy, it wouldn't take long before all eyes would be on me, the boyfriend who, it just so happened, had a day job with direct and regular access to the lethal gas in question. Even if Zoe ended up not uttering a word to implicate me, the tangible and intangible evidence had me pegged at least as an accomplice.

Perhaps the most emotionally taxing aspect of all this was

knowing that Zoe and I were likely on the outs. It's very difficult to sustain a romantic relationship when one of the partners starts committing homicide. Up to that point, I had seen us growing as a team who specialized in a noble and humane form of killing, but apparently she felt the need to commit more severe crimes. We clearly wanted different things.

I didn't know what to do next. A break-up would be exceedingly complicated. And there was no couple's therapy for what we were dealing with.

As confounded as I was, I couldn't help being a little impressed by her bold attempt to single handedly wipe our corner of Northeast Oregon clean of sex offenders. If Zoe had been a heroine in a movie I was watching rather than my girlfriend in a life I was living, I would have been rooting for her all the way. She made a damn sexy underground superhero, and I'm sure the film would have portrayed her targets in a way that made me forget they might have been deserving of forgiveness and a second chance.

Had this been the cinema, I'd have been digging into a vat of popcorn and shouting at the screen, "Get'em, Rape Girl – send those bastards straight to hell with your helium kiss!" I might even have bought the special director's cut DVD when it came out.

But I wasn't buying *this*. *This* didn't end with me just getting up out of a theater seat and going home to masturbate to a dark celluloid dream. This was me pushed through the screen, forced to pick up all the pieces of debris that our heroine had left in her wake.

Perhaps I'd have felt differently had Zoe worn a custom-fitted Lycra onesie that hugged her contours whenever going after the bad guys. But as things stood, I wasn't at all down with her mission.

We had it out several times over the next couple of days, with neither of us budging from our respective position. Whenever I'd toss up that I was worried about her and that she was jeopardizing our entire operation, she'd counter with how I was being selfish, how I was only worried about myself and my clients. Whenever I'd point out that some of the men she was targeting may be working hard to rehabilitate and may have families, she'd lambast me for portraying such monsters as victims. I tried to convince her that soon enough she'd get killed or caught. She accused me of being a control freak intent on keeping her under my thumb. I accused her of being delusional. She threw a plate at my head.

Hey, all couples fight.

I guess I just wasn't comfortable ending a relationship with a woman so quick to fling stoneware, and so adept at murder.

Eventually we came to a compromise on the whole hunting down sex offenders thing. Realizing there was no way Zoe would quit cold turkey, I insisted she at least cut down. No more than one rapist every two months. She agreed. I also instituted a "don't ask, don't tell" policy – to keep me from prying and to keep Zoe from reminding me she was mental. In addition, I told Zoe that as long as she continued doing what she was doing, I would no longer supply her with helium, and asked her to return the last tank I had given her. If and when she got caught taking out one of her personal targets, I didn't want any subsequent police searches turning up a tank tied to Jubilee and me. Zoe initially protested this last condition, but eventually signed off on it.

Once the parameters were set and we were on the same

page, things went relatively smoothly – as smoothly as things *can* go when you're trying to curb your girlfriend's homicide habit so that her suicide work doesn't suffer. From what I could tell, Zoe was holding to her side of the bargain. She seemed to always be where she was supposed to be over the next few weeks, and didn't show up with any scratches or bruises or black eyes – the kinds of injuries I envisioned a registered sex offender inflicting on a woman alone in a room with him. I noted no suspicious behavior, not secretive sneaking, no contradictory statements or stories when she reviewed her day for me during dinner. The two exits she administered during this period went well, at least by her account. I couldn't check with the clients directly.

But cracks soon started to appear. Zoe began exhibiting a shorter temper. She snapped at me one night for having boiled rather than steamed the string beans. Gave me an earful for the way I folded her laundry. Elbowed me in the ribs when I tried to initiate sex. (Granted, I shouldn't have tried to initiate sex the same night I botched the string beans and the laundry.) When she wasn't irritated, she was distracted, disassociated. I asked her on several occasions if something was bothering her, if she needed to talk, but she'd just shake her head and continue staring at the TV or her laptop or the carpet.

Some nights she'd go to bed late and wake up numerous times before angrily giving up and getting out of bed for good before dawn. Other nights she'd retire early and sleep in until noon, occasionally calling students to cancel lessons. I couldn't tell if her rapidly fluctuating temperament was due to my having imposed rules on her deadly little initiative and slowing production, or if the strain from the initiative itself was wreaking havoc on her hypothalamus. I wasn't sure if she had struck again since we had come to our agreement. She'd been given the green light to gas one target every two months, and with about five weeks having passed since our big talk, it was entirely possible she'd already used her token. I couldn't ask. She couldn't tell.

Zoe started staying at her house a few nights a week, explaining that it was easier for work. She didn't indicate what *kind* of work. Though I was a little hurt by her decision, I felt some space would be good for both of us. She'd feel less supervised and smothered, and I'd suffer fewer internal injuries.

Sure enough, Zoe's spirits quickly lifted. The trouble was, I didn't like why – or what I *assumed* to be the reason. I may have agreed to look the other way while she got her kill on, but promising to sit idly by is much easier than the actual sitting. A part of me had hoped that having found out about her secret slayings and expressing my disapproval would cause her to cease carrying them out. Unfortunately, external validation had little hold on her.

I couldn't prove that Zoe's suddenly elevated mood was due to her just having dispatched a bad guy, for I didn't know if she, in fact, had. But that didn't stop me from believing it. I was like a jealous husband, convinced that some other man – albeit it a dead one – was responsible for my wife's new smile.

But it didn't take long for Zoe's glow to dim. Within days she returned to her irascible, distracted state. Though it was no joy to experience her agitation and figurative absence, I preferred it to exuberance fueled by what was surely a mounting body count.

I couldn't ask. She couldn't tell. But I could step in and say something if her lack of presence ever negatively affected a company-approved exit.

Unfortunately, I soon got my chance.

"Where is your hat?" I asked Zoe one evening after she'd returned to my place from the home of a client named Alice Newhook (liver cancer).

"What are you talking about?" she asked, annoyed by my brash greeting.

"Your *hat* – the one you always wear and tuck your hair up into whenever doing hood work – where is it?"

"Oh, that. I guess I must have taken it off and left it in the car. What's the big deal?"

"The big deal is that I found the hat in question on my dresser... while you were *out*."

"If you already knew where my hat was, then why did you ask me about it?"

"The bigger question, Zoe, is what, if anything, did you wear on your head during the job in place of the hat you left here?"

Zoe glared at me and shook her head, trapped between contempt and panic. "Don't worry about it," she muttered.

"Don't worry about it because you wore a different hat? Or don't worry about it because you just realized you fucked up and don't want to have to think about it?"

"What the fuck, Eli? You're really enjoying this, aren't you?" She gritted her teeth.

"Yes, I'm really enjoying that you may very well have left strands of red hair all over the house and next to the body of the person you just euthanized. I'm really enjoying that your lack of focus – no doubt caused by the lovely work you are doing on the side – may land both our asses in prison!"

"Will you relax! Do you really think there's going to be a

homicide investigation of a 77 year-old woman with terminal cancer found dead in her bed with no evidence of forced entry or a struggle?"

"No, I don't think there will be, but I do think there *could* be. That's why we always, always, ALWAYS cover our tracks. It's impossible to be too safe. Just assume that every exit scene will be analyzed by a crack CSI team."

"That's ridiculous."

"No, what's ridiculous is going in for an exit without being completely prepared and totally focused. It's not even just about us getting away with the exit, it's about doing the kind of quality job our clients *deserve*."

"Enough with the lecturing already. I get it. I slipped up. It won't happen again, okay? Satisfied?"

"I'm not even close to satisfied. You need to get your fucking head back in the game. The way you've been acting lately, I don't know how comfortable I am sending you to another client."

"Fine! It's not like I begged you for the job! You're the one who needed help, and I stepped in."

"Yeah, and you've sure seemed to enjoy it – so much so, you decided to start doing a little extra work on the side."

"That's what this is really about. You just can't stand me being independent, having a little power."

"No, I can't stand you being a murderer!"

"A murderer? Fuck you – I'm a hero! What you do is nice and all, comforting the dying, but I'm helping to rid the world of evil."

"Oh, then why stop at local sex offenders? Why not go after terrorists? Despots? Corporate tyrants. Better yet, reality TV producers?"

Zoe inflated her lungs for an explosive retort, but then let all the air out and tried to hide a smile. It was difficult to tell whether my sarcasm had disarmed her or put some ambitious plans in her head. Was she entertained by my suggestion, or entertaining it?

Then she started to cry and I realized it was neither.

Moments earlier I wanted nothing more than to knock some sense into her; now all I wanted was to tell her everything was going to be okay. But I couldn't lie.

"Let it out," I said as I stepped closer and stroked her hair. "I can't imagine the amount of pressure you're feeling. You've got quite the complex schedule."

Zoe pushed my hand away. "It's not that," she said, still crying. "It's that I just now saw how you see me – as some psychotic freak. The way you speak to me, the way you mock me, I can see you think I'm out of my mind. It makes me feel kind of worthless."

From hero to worthless in 30 seconds. A sharp and sudden plummet. I wanted her to come to her senses, not shatter against the rocks.

"That's not my intention," I said. "You're hardly worthless – you're fascinating. I just think you've let things get a little out of hand."

"I don't think I can stop," Zoe responded. She started crying even harder than before.

"Yes you can. I know there's a lot of fury driving you to do what you're doing, but you can overcome it."

"I can't! You just don't understand."

"Then let me find someone who can help you."

Zoe paused to regain her composure. "What are you talking about?" she asked. "It's not like I can go to a shrink about this."

"Why not?"

"Because they don't keep secrets about dead bodies."

"You don't have to tell them the specifics, just tell them what happened to you, without mentioning Keith of course, and that you're now experiencing uncontrollable rage."

"You want to know what that will likely get me? Committed to an institution and plugged with tranquilizers. Especially with my history of 'mood disorders.' I'd be better off dead."

"Zoe, we have money. I'm sure we can find a renowned psychiatr... specialist who doesn't rely on putting patients away and turning them into zombies."

"Have you ever seen a shrink, Eli?"

"No, but—"

"You don't know how the mental health system works. I've been in and out of clinics most of my life, dealing with doctors and therapists who only care about sticking you with a nice clean definition from their DSM-IV and drugging you accordingly."

"C'mon, there have to be some progressive practitioners who do things differently."

"What do you think, Eli? I'm going to find someone who, with the help of some role-playing and Valerian root, will get me to come to grips with my past so that I can stop killing rapists and concentrate more on killing cancer patients? Everything is so far beyond fucked up right now, let's stop trying to pretend it's fixable."

She had a point. But at least she acknowledged there was something wrong with whacking past sex offenders. The first step is admitting you have a problem.

"So what do you suggest?" I asked. "How would you like

to proceed?"

Zoe flashed a look of surprise. "That's the first time you've asked me that. You've been so busy giving directives."

"Okay, and your answer?"

"I have no fucking idea."

Zoe decided she'd try to kick her killing habit, without the benefit of psychoactive substances or psychiatric sessions. She'd recently read about a serial killer who lost his lust for blood and found lasting calm by switching to a vegetarian diet while in prison. She told me how the convict in question reportedly transformed from lion to lamb after just a few weeks on a strictly plant-based diet, and that he didn't even fight back when a fellow inmate stabbed him to death with a fork in the dining hall. I promised Zoe I'd start stocking my place with spinach and beans, and to not attack her with any utensils.

Eliminating meat and dairy made Zoe's skin glow like never before, but did little to bring her inner peace. Maybe she needed bars on the windows and doors to experience the full effect. While she wasn't as angry or as volatile as before, I could tell she was being eaten up inside. She was quiet and withdrawn. Each time I asked if everything was okay, she'd just nod and let out a long, slow sigh. Thinking she might have been suffering from some kind of carnivore withdrawal, I secretly added beef broth to a soup I'd made for us for one evening, but it didn't help. Nor did the ground chuck I snuck into our soy burgers the next night.

This wasn't the meat she was missing.

A few days later Zoe told me she was going to stay at her place for a couple nights. I knew, or I assumed I knew, what that meant. But I had to let her go. I had to give her the benefit of the doubt. Issuing a mandate for her to stay put and keep her hands where I could see them would only push her further away. I couldn't afford to irk or to alienate her, not with her next scheduled exit coming up in two days. Rodney Davis (colorectal cancer). Aside from the incident of the forgotten hat, Zoe had yet to let me, or any of our clients, down. I didn't know for sure if she had plans to hunt again. All I knew was that she'd be there for Mr. Davis.

Two days later, all I knew was that all I *thought* I knew was wrong.

"Hello, may I please speak to Eli?" said the weak voice coming through my phone.

"May I ask who's calling?"

"Eli? This is Rodney Davis. Um, I think there might have been a mix-up."

I'll say. You should be deceased by now.

"What? You mean… she never even… just hang tight Mr. Davis. I'll be over in a few minutes. You're at 1616 Seneca, right?"

"Yes, but I don't understand what hap–"

"I can't tell you how sorry I am about this, Mr. Davis. One thing before I head over, are you expecting any visitors this afternoon?"

"No, just your associate."

"I'll be filling in. Be there in ten."

Oh, Zoe, you've done it now!

It was bad enough that a dead man's last call on official record would be to me. Now I had to do a suicide while distracted by fantasies of killing my girlfriend.

Two calls I made to Zoe while speeding to Mr. Davis' house went unanswered. I'd have to deal with her later. I was in full recovery mode and had to focus. Fuming over Zoe's no-show and wondering where the hell she was and what the hell she was doing wouldn't accomplish anything – except perhaps increase the chances of Mr. Davis' exit becoming even more of a disaster.

Poor Mr. Davis. There's nothing worse than desperately wanting to leave a party but not being able to find your ride.

I tried to picture him, lying prone on his sofa or bed, trying to find a position that didn't aggravate his symptoms, staring at a spot on a pillow to distract him from the fact that he had been stood up on his date with death. There's nothing you can do to set this right. "I'll make it up to you" doesn't cut it here.

When I arrived at his house, Mr. Davis came to the door in a much more jovial mood than I had anticipated.

"That was fast," he said, holding a glass of water. "Hope you didn't run any red lights on my account."

This man had just been severely dishonored, dismissed, forced to wait to receive something he was paying $10,000 for, and yet he was concerned about being a bother. I would have hugged the man if I hadn't feared it would cause irreparable internal bleeding.

"Mr. Davis, words cannot express how deeply sorry I am for this unacceptable mistake. I hope you–"

"Let me stop you there. Truth is, you did me a favor."

"How do you mean, sir?"

"I mean I've changed my mind. I would have called you back to tell you and save you the trip, but I just decided a couple of minutes ago, and figured you'd be here soon enough. Besides, you shouldn't use the phone while driving."

"Mr. Davis–"

"Please, call me Rodney."

"Rodney, I can understand if my associate's no-show has destroyed your trust and confidence in our services, but I assure you our methods are extremely safe and completely painless. We've never had an incident."

"No, no, it's not that. Her not showing up, I've taken it as a sign. With all due respect for what you do, I now see it's not how the universe wants me to go out. I'm gonna stick it out a little longer, suffering and all. Who knows, maybe by some miracle I'll even beat this thing."

Not the "m" word. The very notion of miracles defies everything I do.

"I respect your decision, Mr. D– ...Rodney. I just need to know you're absolutely sure it's what you want."

"I'm sure, thank you. And I'm sorry to have taken up your time on all this. I realize you have a very busy schedule."

"Please. You have no reason to apologize. I'm just glad you figured out what you wanted before it was too late."

"I'd still like to pay you for your trouble."

"Absolutely not. I won't hear of it."

"Don't you know you shouldn't argue with a dying man?"

"I don't know a lot of things, Rodney."

I took a few minutes to convince Mr. Davis I wouldn't budge on the money issue. Afterward, I shook his icy hand and bid him farewell.

As I walked to my Pathfinder, I felt a sense of both relief

and defeat. The relief came from not having to perform an exit while distracted, and from knowing I wouldn't have to worry about anyone finding my phone number listed among a corpse's recent calls. The defeat, well, that came from having lost a client. Sure, I'd lost clients before – Harve, who'd run out of time; others, who'd run out of patience – but this one was different. This one was still breathing.

Sitting in my car, the anger returned. Zoe. Still not answering her phone.

While Mr. Davis may have seen her forgetfulness as saving his life, I knew all it had done was ruin his death.

CHAPTER 27

I can put up with a lot in a relationship. I'm a broad-minded man, one who realizes that sometimes a girl has to do things like shoot her ex or jump off a bridge or carry out a vendetta on low, lawless men. But one thing I cannot abide is tardiness. Worse, absenteeism.

Where before I had convinced myself Zoe would soon stop making rapists dead and recommit to a good clean life of music teaching and euthanasia, I now realized she'd gone too far over to the dark side for any real rehabilitation to occur. Blowing off somebody's suicide? There's no coming back from that.

As soon as I pulled onto Zoe's street I could see her Volvo parked in her driveway. Either she was home or had somehow found time to add grand theft auto to her rap sheet. I parked out on the street, cut the engine, and took several deep breaths to calm myself. I didn't want my popping in to escalate into a crime of passion.

I pressed the doorbell and rapped on the door. No response. This was to be expected. You don't ditch on an exit and then openly receive visitors. I rang and knocked again, to no avail.

I then remembered she kept an extra key inside a fake rock on the ground near the walkway. I'd never seen it, but she had told me about it late one night while we were watching an old movie in which the hero hoisted a boulder that was obviously made out of papier-mâché. The faux rock containing Zoe's house key wasn't quite as easy to spot, but after crouching down and inspecting the various stones in the vicinity, I finally came upon one that was trying a little too hard to fit in. There's such a thing as too good a disguise. I picked up the relatively lightweight imposter, which was made out of some kind of polymer, and found a seam. Moments later the key was in the door and I was in the house.

"Zoe, it's me" I called out. "I'm sorry to barge in, but we obviously have a lot to talk about."

Silence.

I walked through the living room, where her baby grand stood alone, and made my way toward her bedroom. I passed the guest bedroom, the door to which was wide open providing a clear view of an empty bed.

The door to Zoe's bedroom was slightly ajar. "Zoe?" I said softly, listening for groans or the shuffling of sheets – the sounds of a waking woman – but I heard nothing. I peeked through the crack in the door and caught a glimpse of a perfectly made up bed. Perhaps she was sitting in the chair she kept in the corner of her room, patiently waiting for me to enter. Or perhaps she was standing behind the door clutching an iron candlestick holder.

"I'm coming in."

I pushed open the door and stepped into the room. No sign of Zoe anywhere. A peek under the bed and into the walk-in closet revealed nothing but shoes and clothes.

I left the bedroom and did a quick once-over of the house, making sure I hadn't overlooked Zoe napping on the futon in the living room in the process. I looked out back to see if maybe she had decided to rest al fresco in a lawn chair, but I saw only birds and squirrels.

The bathroom. It was the only place I hadn't checked. Not the best hiding place, but she might not have been hiding. It was entirely possible I had entered the house while she was in the middle of doing some very personal business, which may have left her too embarrassed to speak up when I called out her name.

There was a sensitive way to handle this.

I walked back down the hallway to the bedrooms and stood a good five feet from the closed door of the bathroom.

"Zoe? Are you in there?"

I took a couple steps closer. "I just want to talk."

Not a sound.

One more step closer. I was now standing right outside the bathroom door.

That's when I smelled the metal.

The faint scent of copper and iron rust. Along with something almost sweet.

Probably just old pipes mixing with an air freshener.

Until I grabbed the doorknob and found that it was locked.

"Zoe! Zoe!" I shouted as I rattled the doorknob. "Are you in there? Please say something!"

I took two steps back, lowered my right shoulder and slammed the side of my body against the door, which contorted, but didn't open. Ample structural damage had been done, however, as there was now a centimeter or so of space in several places where the injured door was supposed to cleave to the jamb. I shuddered upon not hearing a single word or shout of protest from Zoe after the loud ramming. Something. Anything. A single, "What the fuck?" A simple, "Are you out of your mind?" Some sign of...

I reared back and again flung my right shoulder, arm, hip and thigh against the door. This time it flew open, the back of it ricocheting off some linen shelves that sent the door back toward its original closed position. I stuck my foot out to stop it, then pushed it back open to bring the nightmare behind it into full view.

A small screw or nail – shrapnel from the busted open door lock – was spinning on the floor between the toilet and the bathtub. It spun as if it would never stop. That's not the first thing I saw or the last thing I remember about the scene. It's just where my mind chooses to rest whenever I go back to visit.

Zoe was lying motionless in the bathtub, soaking in red Easter egg dye, wearing a bra and panties. Her eyes were closed. The same could not be said about either of her wrists.

On the edge of the tub sat a razor blade lined with blood. Some of it had trickled down the white porcelain to a light green bath rug.

I think I screamed out her name before kneeling down and placing my ear to her chest. It's hard to say for sure. I do recall futilely checking her carotid for a pulse, thinking that laying my finger on her neck and focusing all of my energy on the spot might miraculously jolt her back to life.

Ten minutes. It might have been twenty. Or maybe an hour. It doesn't matter how long I actually sat with my back slumped against the outside of the tub staring at the chrome faucet of the sink in front of me. It didn't change anything. Occasionally I'd turn my head and torso slowly to look behind me, half expecting to find the tub empty and dry and white. That wouldn't have been any less absurd than what I'd already seen.

They say you can change the world by changing your mind. That we create our own reality. That reality is entirely subjective and thus can be altered by our thoughts. But no matter how many times I looked away or closed my eyes and tried to rewrite the scene, Zoe's face remained as white and as cold and as quiet as when I had I broken open the door.

After asking myself "Why?" over and over while lying on the bathroom floor, the question soon changed to "Why *this* way?" Why would a woman with the skills and immediate access to the equipment needed to exit cleanly and neatly opt to cut through skin and veins instead? After pondering this for a few minutes, I had the answer: She wanted to protect *me*.

Zoe knew that if anybody besides me had found her body and saw her hooked up to the hood, I'd become the prime suspect. Maybe not for murder, but certainly for aiding and abetting. Only an investigation team with a serious collective mental deficiency would fail to make the Jubilee-helium tank connection. And even if Zoe had used one of the tanks she had purchased online, she knew I'd have a lot of questions to answer.

Those who say suicide is an entirely selfish act don't know what the fuck they're talking about.

But now I was back to my original question.

Why?

Though deep down, I knew the answer.

As jarring and as tragic and as heartbreaking as it was,

looking back I can't pretend that finding Zoe lying in the tub was the shock of the century. Not after what she had been through, what she had become involved in. Not with her trying to process everything with a bipolar mind and no lithium to weather the storm. And not with a boyfriend who knew all of this, but who didn't do nearly enough to rescue her. A boyfriend who was more concerned with saving strangers.

As I sat there looking at an alabaster angel bathing in a crimson sea, I realized that, while I may have kept Zoe from jumping from the bridge that one day, I played no small hand in pushing her over the edge in the end.

There'd be plenty of time for guilt and self-pity after I finished with the business at hand.

But I couldn't remember – *who do you call when you find someone dead?* I was pretty sure it was 911, but dialing that particular trio of numerals didn't seem appropriate unless there was danger to be averted or an injury or illness to be immediately treated. I had always associated 911 with speeding ambulances and fire trucks, blaring sirens, paramedics moving like light to keep a perfect stranger's heart pumping. Twisted metal. Shattered glass. Black streaks staining macadam and highway dividers. Jaws of life. Defibrillators. Poison treatment kits. But what use were speed and noise and heroics now? Why shatter the afternoon sun and disrupt traffic by sending teams of highly trained men and women away from their cozy posts to save nobody? Why ruin the serenity and the stillness that had descended?

As reluctant as I was about ushering in the emergency vehicles, I knew I had to make the call. But not until I recovered a few things.

I found Zoe's car keys on a small table by the front door. I grabbed them and walked out to the driveway, where I popped the trunk of the Volvo and found three helium tanks – one from Jubilee, one from Zoe's online supplier – and Zoe's backpack, which contained another Party Down tank and the rest of the hood supplies. I took my keys out of my pocket, aimed them at the Pathfinder and pressed the unlock button on the key remote. After transferring the tanks and backpack to my car, I returned to the Volvo to search the inside for any additional paraphernalia that investigators might find interesting. The car was clean. Nothing but a couple of empty water bottles and a discarded paper bag from a local café.

I went back inside and searched the house for anything else that would raise eyebrows aside from the drained body in the bathtub, but I found nothing. I thought about taking Zoe's laptop and phone so that the police couldn't check her recent "activity," but then realized they wouldn't need her actual apparatus to do that. All they'd have to do is get with her Internet and cellular providers. Big Brother is very much alive and well in the Digital Age.

Her exit earnings. I remembered Zoe telling me she wrapped all her cash in foil and kept it duct-taped to the underside of her piano. I checked, and sure enough I found four or five aluminum bricks stuck to the belly of the majestic instrument. As I carefully peeled them from the wood, I couldn't help but feel I was stealing rather than protecting, even though keeping the money for myself never entered my mind. I decided that, in a few days, some non-profit organization dedicated to providing musical instruments and lessons to underprivileged children would receive an anonymous envelope or two stuffed with tens, twenties, fifties and hundreds.

I put the bricks of cash into a brown paper grocery bag I

found in the kitchen, carried the stash to my car, and hid it in the luggage well. Confident I'd covered Zoe's and my tracks as best I could, I walked back into the house and pulled my cell phone from my pocket to report the end of the world.

"She is... she was my girlfriend. I came over to the house to take her out for a surprise dinner and found her in the tub."

The detective, a tall and burly black man in his mid-forties, scribbled in his note pad while we stood in Zoe's living room. The paramedics had moments earlier moved through with a stretcher and an empty body bag en route to the bathroom.

"Had she been suffering any serious depression or been under any serious stress?" asked the detective.

"Not really. Not recently, at least."

"What do you mean, 'not recently'?"

"I just mean she's had some bouts of depression in the past, but who hasn't?"

"Was she on any medication?"

"I know she had once been prescribed lithium for bipolar disorder – but she stopped taking it regularly years ago."

My responses were far too coherent and concise given the situation. I should have been crying my eyes out. I reached deep inside for tears, but failed to produce any. The adrenalin must have been blocking my ducts. Talking to a cop will do that, especially when you're concealing the fact you're a mass murderer – albeit it a socially conscious one.

"Do you live here, too?" the detective asked.

"No. I have a place closer to downtown. Zoe usually stayed with me. Mostly she just worked here – she is… was a music teacher."

I thought of her poor students who, after hearing the news, would spend the rest of their lives wondering if their pitiful scale-playing was what prompted their instructor to slash her wrists.

"Yeah, I know she's a music teacher," the detective said. "She and I met about a year ago – when she was called in for questioning after her ex-fiancé turned up dead of a gunshot wound. Were you two together back then?"

"No. I actually met Zoe a little bit after that. His murder really messed her up for a while."

"I know. She'd call us on occasion to find out if we'd made any progress on the case. Always sounded shaken up."

Excellent performance, Zoe. Hopefully my acting can measure up.

"The person who killed Keith, is he still on the loose?"

"Unfortunately, yes. The case is still open, but we've pretty much exhausted all our leads." The Detective didn't take his eyes off me as he bent to scratch his knee. "Let me ask you," he said pointing in the direction of the bathroom, "do you think *this* had anything to do with her never fully getting over Keith Carlson's murder?"

"Oh, I don't know. I wouldn't think so. Like I said, she'd been doing okay lately. But who knows, maybe she was scarred much more deeply than she let on." I lowered my head and placed my hand over my eyes to show the detective how upset I *should* have been.

"How did the two of you meet?" he asked.

"With all due respect, Detective, how is that relevant

here? I'm sorry, but my girlfriend is lying dead in the other room – I'm not quite up for a trip down memory lane."

"I know this is difficult. I'm just trying to create the clearest picture possible. It's not my intention to upset you."

"It's too late for me not to be upset."

"I understand, and I'm indeed sorry for your loss. Tell you what, let me just get your contact information. That way if I have any other questions for you, I can just get in touch after you've had some time to cope with all this."

"Thank you. I'd appreciate that. I'm not trying to be uncooperative, it's just –"

"No need to explain."

He took down my name, address and phone number before extending his hand.

"Again, sorry for your loss, Mr. Edelmann. You are free to go, unless you prefer to stick around."

"I think I'll go, if it's all the same. I already said my goodbyes before you all arrived, and I'd rather not see her being brought out in that bag."

"Of course, sir. Are you okay to drive? Do you need us to call somebody or drop you anywhere?"

"I'll be okay, thank you." I turned to leave, then stopped and turned back around. "Just one thing, Detective. Who's going to notify her family, her mother and her sister? I never met them and have no real way of getting in contact."

"We'll take care of that, don't worry. You just get home safely and try to get some rest. I'll get in touch with you again if necessary."

Sounds good. Maybe over donuts you can ask me if I know anything about my dead girlfriend's suspected killing spree.

After shaking the detective's hand, I made my way toward the door and walked out into the shards of the evening. I wondered if any neighbors had noticed me hanging around the house for nearly an hour before the police and paramedics arrived. I wondered if anyone had seen me empty Zoe's trunk. If so, I wondered if they'd bother to take time away from their TV and their laptop and their tablet and their smartphone to share what they'd seen.

I climbed into my Pathfinder and tried to fathom how I'd lost the most dangerous and divine woman I'd ever known. I was alone again. Before Zoe, such a statement would bring relief, uttered as a slow yet joyful sentiment. A welcomed melancholy following a forced romance. But now alone meant alone. Without. Without the woman I might have loved.

Gone not only were fragments of my heart, but also the backbone of the exit team. The deaths of dozens of people hung in the balance. People who'd been patiently awaiting the release I'd promised. I couldn't possibly handle the schedule on my own. In fact, I couldn't even handle my usual share. Until I was certain I was off the police's radar with regard to Zoe's death, I'd have to suspend operations.

Imagine the only cardio-thoracic surgeon of his kind telling leagues of eager patients he was taking a break, that they'd have to wait a couple months for the new ticker they thought they were getting, and desperately needed, in a week or two. It was actually worse than that. A surgeon didn't have to worry about patients trying to perform operations on their own, nor about reporting him to the authorities out of anger over his sabbatical.

CHAPTER 28

How I got from Zoe's home back to mine without plowing into any vehicles, pedestrians or trees is beyond me. Of course, I'm merely *assuming* my dazed and confused drive across town occurred without any accidents or casualties. For all I know I could have run over some dog or cat or child – something too small to jolt me out of my daydreams or change the trajectory of the Pathfinder. But for now let's give me the benefit of the doubt and just say I did not unknowingly commit and get away with a hit and run. I've dodged enough charges as it is.

Traffic lights and lane lines and road signs just don't captivate the mind like dead lovers and lost clients and evidence trails do. All I could think while blindly maneuvering two tons of steel through the city was, *Zoe's dead Zoe's dead Zoe's dead how can the police NOT uncover something what with her recent serial slayings of men who have something very obvious in common so common all the cops would have to do is do a search on who's been searching the sex offender site unless Zoe was smart enough to do her searches from a public computer like the ones at the library but if not it's only a matter of time before an investigation ensues if one hasn't already begun hey maybe the detective was already on to something when he talked to me at the house Zoe's dead Zoe's dead Zoe's dead but there's still the matter of them figuring out the helium piece of the puzzle they'd have to exhume some dead men and do an autopsy and still likely wouldn't find any traces of our noble gas in his system but they're also going to be going through all her online activity including those Party Down purchases and surely they'll wonder why helium why helium what do people do with it besides inflate balloons "Has she celebrated any birthdays or thrown any parties recently Mr. Edelmann and if so why didn't she just use tanks from YOUR shop seeing as how you're her boyfriend and all?" not sure how I'll field that one though I could always concoct something about how I had suspected her of having an affair and this whole helium thing seems to confirm it goddamn it she threw a party for the guy and everything man that hurts I might want to consider taking acting lessons and Googling "how to beat a polygraph" I guess you could call it karma for when I told Zoe how she could outsmart one with ease in case she had to take one after shooting Keith that seems so long ago everything was just starting well not everything but everything with us and now Zoe's dead Zoe's dead she's fucking dead and now the police will be keeping an eye on me so I can't very well continue going to group meetings and even worse my clients will have to stay alive longer than they should ever have had to or force a friend or loved one to fill in for me I really can't blame them for that but it's a goddamn shame that I won't be able to be there for them and do my job it's very difficult going back to being a man when you know something about what it's like to be a god.*

I remained inside my head for the next few days. It wouldn't be accurate to say I was hiding, as my body, from what I can gather, did make several public appearances. A receipt I found in my jeans and a bottle I found by my bed show that I purchased some whiskey at one point. The fact I didn't starve to death or even lose weight leads me to believe I went to a restaurant or grocery store, as well. I'm told I also popped in to Jubilee to check on business and to finally explain – falsely, of course – the missing helium tanks to Carl. I was sent home and told not to worry about it.

I recollect remnants of some phone calls, too, the most notable of which came from Zoe's sister, who explained that the body was being transported to Denver for burial, and that their mother had requested I stay away and not attend any of the services.

"I'm sorry, Eli, but my mother doesn't want to have to bear the added burden of being kind to you."

I also got a call from my mother, who still had no idea the girl I'd been dating was dead. Mom just wanted to know if I could come for dinner that Sunday. "You seem a little out of it, Eli," she said at one point during the call.

"It's been a tough week, Mom. I'll explain when I see you Sunday."

I wanted to tell her what had happened to Zoe right then and there over the phone. I wanted her to rush over to my place and make me some hot cocoa and hold me while I wailed and screamed. But it's very difficult going back to being a boy when you know something about what it's like to be a god.

Besides, I didn't deserve to be consoled.

It had been four days since Zoe's death and I hadn't been contacted by the detective, or by any other member of the force, for that matter. Perhaps, through a conversation with one of Zoe's past doctors or pharmacists, the police had chalked her suicide up to a simple chemical imbalance. No need to dig deeper when a serotonin shortage is involved. Surely they were still investigating the mysterious case of the three dead sex offenders, but maybe Zoe had effectively covered all her tracks, and thus mine as well.

I returned to work, much to the relief of Carl, who had covered every shift during my absence and even managed to accrue some decent sales numbers. As my first order of business back at Jubilee I raised Carl's pay by $2 an hour, not only in appreciation for his coming through in a pinch, but also for having dropped the little matter of the missing helium tanks. The way things were going, I doubted the police would ever be questioning Carl about me. Nevertheless, I considered the extra $50-$75 per week I was now paying him to be a kind of insurance, even though it was entirely possible that Carl had completely forgotten all about the inventory issue. There's nothing wrong with a little subliminal greasing of the palm. A karmic bribe of sorts.

Work served as a welcomed distraction, a way to erase Zoe from my mind for a few minutes here and there. Burying myself in cartons and customers and complaints kept me from bloody bathtubs and imagined arrests. But there's only so much hiding you can do when you've got a bunch of people expecting you to subtract them in the very near future. It was early April and, according to the schedule, we – I mean I – had seven exits to administer by the end of May. Seven clients counting on me to sweep them off their feet. Seven people who were about to be severely disappointed.

The same week I returned to Jubilee I had plans to attend a meeting of each support group to start shutting down production. Telling individuals you won't be able to help them die is a lot more difficult than promoting your services in the first place.

The initial meeting took place the evening of my first day back in the shop. There were three members of this particular group I had to speak to urgently. I cornered the first one, Garrett Kirby (pancreatic cancer), on his way to the restroom 10 minutes before kickoff.

"I have some very unfortunate news," I said to the man I was set to dispatch in three days.

"In my condition, how bad can the news be?" Garrett said, his smirk outdueling his concern.

"I no longer will be able to 'assist' you."

"What? Why not?"

"There's been a... an incident. And I believe the police may now be keeping an eye on me."

"Did somebody tell on you?"

"No, nothing like that."

"Then what is it?"

"It's rather complicated. I can't really go into detail on the incident right now... just know that my hands are tied."

"Well, what about your partner. I know you have an associate who works with you – can she maybe help me?"

"I'm afraid *she* was the incident."

"She got caught?"

"No, she died."

"Jesus! I'm so sorry. Wow. Weren't you two, like, together?"

"Is that what you've heard?"

"Yeah, there's been some talk."

"I guess there's no harm in sharing now. Yes, she was my girlfriend."

"Oh my god! I'm SO sorry. Damn. Was she sick?"

"No. She… she killed herself."

"Christ! That's horrible! When?"

"A few days ago."

"Are you okay?"

"Not yet, but I'll get there."

"If you don't mind me asking, why are the police watching *you*? Do they… suspect you had something to do with her–"

"No, no. It's not that. She slit her wrists, an obvious suicide. But I must lay low now, as it's quite possible the police or her family might discover some things about her… about us… that could be suspicious."

"Shit. So, is this just a temporary thing, or do you think you're done?" Garrett asked.

"I don't know, man. Things have gotten a little out of control. The risk factor seems to have gone way up, you know?"

"Sure, sure. I understand." He was lying through his teeth for my benefit. It's difficult to empathize with anyone when you have less than six months to live.

As Garrett started to walk away, looking like a kid who'd been forced to return a found puppy to its rightful owner, I realized I was making a huge mistake. I wasn't ready to call it quits, to take off my cape, to relinquish my power. You don't get into the exit game to play it safe. You don't come that far and make that much of an impact on the lives and deaths of others only to toss in the towel at the first real sign of trouble. And what life would I be returning to if hung up the helium tank? I had a dead girlfriend, a dead-end day job, and a drinking problem that would only get worse if I didn't have the hood to get me high.

Thou giveth and thou taketh away. But thou can always

choose to giveth back again.

"Garrett, wait," I said as I caught up with him. "You're going to think I'm nuts, but I want you to forget everything I just said. You can count on me to be there for you on Friday, as scheduled."

"Wha? Really? What about all the–"

"Don't worry about all that. I have a tendency to be a little overdramatic."

"Overdramatic? Your girlfriend just killed herself and possibly left a trail to your euthanasia ring. I don't think 'over-dramatic' is possible here."

"Listen, I want to do this for you. I'm not going to pull out just because the cops might end up with something that gives them an inkling something's up."

"Are you sure? I don't want to be the reason why you get put away."

"You won't be. So, Friday at ten in the morning, like we originally discussed?"

"I don't know, I just feel–"

"Garrett, if your hesitation has to do with you having fears and second thoughts over the actual *procedure*, then yes, let's definitely call this off. But don't cancel just because of what I told you before. I'm totally ready and willing to help you… if you still want me to."

"I do," said Garrett, fighting to hold back tears. "I'm ready."

"Then I'll see you Friday, my friend."

Garrett put his hand on my shoulder. "Thank you… for sticking it out."

"Please, Garrett, it's hardly a burden. It's my calling."

There's a feeling of tranquility that comes when you allow something to be bigger than you.

I no longer felt I was powerful and important because of the work I was doing – I now saw only the work itself as being powerful and important. I was merely fortunate enough to be in the position to carry it out. This is very different than feeling invincible. This is knowing you are *not* and still pressing forward. Without fear. Without resignation.

This is being willing to die for a cause.

Perhaps "die" is a little strong. This is being willing to wear an orange jumpsuit for a very extended period and have your name reduced to a number. For a cause.

Of course, that doesn't mean you don't take some extra precautions.

Zoe's helium tanks. The ones I had removed from her trunk and brought home. One of them was full, the other had enough for at least one more exit. Between the two I easily had enough for my next four or five clients, thus could go a month or more without drawing any investigator's attention to inventory issues, assuming an investigation was even going on. That would give me time to come up with a plan on how to attain helium discreetly going forward. Perhaps I could hop around to other party suppliers in the region for a while and pay cash for the goods. Then, once I was certain I was in the clear with the police, I could go back to using Jubilee tanks. I'd just have to hope Carl would go back to college or find a better job in the meantime. Otherwise, I'd have little other choice but to keep giving him pay raises.

Even without the helium supply issues, I had a daunting two months ahead of me. I was looking at one exit per week, on my own, with the cops possibly watching. But the good news was I wouldn't have to sustain such a rate over the long haul. Only seven of my upcoming clients had been given dates on the calendar. My plan was to honor my commitment to each of them, despite having since had my exit staff halved, and then cut back to one or two exits a month, or even every two months. Just like the good ol' days.

I said I was *willing* to go to prison for my cause – I didn't say I was *eager*.

Eager is what I was when it came time for Garrett's appointment. You can't get through seven exits in seven weeks until you tackle the first one. Also, I was antsy to get on with the show after the Mr. Davis debacle. Nobody wants to end an illustrious career with a strikeout.

Garrett was what you'd call an ideal client. He was amiable, unwavering in his decision, had a disease that didn't impede his breathing, and lived in a single-family house on acres of private wooded property. No neighbors to speak of – only a wife of 41 years, whom he assured me would be off playing canasta with her lady friends the morning of our meeting. While you can never assume an exit is in the bag, this one was as perfect as they get on paper.

I just hadn't planned on Zoe showing up.

She appeared the moment I opened my duffle bag and started constructing the hood in Garrett's living room. I knew she wasn't real and that Garrett couldn't see her, but hallucinations have a way of rattling you, especially in pressure situations.

"Is everything okay?" Garrett asked after watching me continuously interrupt construction to look over at my dead girlfriend sitting next to him on the edge of the brown leather sofa.

"Hmmm? Oh, yes, everything's fine, Garrett. Just, uh, working a little kink out in my neck. Slept a little funny, is all."

"I have some muscle relaxants I could give you," he responded, pointing in the direction of what I assume was the bathroom. "I won't be needing them anymore."

"No, no, I'm okay, really. Thanks though."

The image of Zoe was so vivid it took everything I had not to talk to her. At one point I even opened my mouth, but was able to stifle the words with a fake yawn. I couldn't have Garrett thinking he was spending his final moments with a schizophrenic. It was bad enough he thought he was spending them with someone in much need of a chiropractor and a nap.

But then I realized Zoe had come not to throw me off my game, but to keep me on it. I remembered how, back when we were a duet, she would soothe clients while I set up. I smiled as I recalled how she, with just a few soft words and glances, and a touch of her hand, could turn a routine exit into a ceremony worthy of the life that was leaving us. She was sitting next to Garrett now, but she had come to comfort me.

"Okay, Garrett, everything is set over here. Whenever you are ready, we can get started."

Garrett looked at me as he inhaled and exhaled deeply. It was as if he was taking advantage of the fact he still could. He reached out to touch the helium tank and ran his finger up the outside of the plastic tubing to the hood.

"So this is it," he said, sounding more victorious than defeated.

"Yes, and I assure you it works beautifully. You will feel no pain, suffer no discomfort. All you need to do is breathe as easily as you can, and within a couple minutes you'll be asleep."

"And you?"

"Me?"

"Yes, what happens to you?"

"I don't think I understand, Garrett."

"I don't know. I guess I want to know what life will look like when I'm gone, and since you're the only one I can ask, I want to know what *your* life will look like."

"Like, where do I see myself?"

"Not like in five years or anything like that. I mean right after I'm gone. What does your day look like?"

"You want to know what I'm doing the rest of the day?"

"Yes. Please. I won't be here in a few minutes, but you will be. It's fascinating and absurd, don't you think?"

"I suppose it is, but I guess I'm a little uncomfortable talking about it. Feels like I'm rubbing it in, you know?"

"Don't be ridiculous – I *want* to talk about it. Here, I'll make it easier for you, a more natural conversation. Hey Eli, what you got going on today?"

"Well… after I get everything packed up and make sure that, um, *this* looks as natural as possible, and after I pay my respects to you, of course, I'll drive home, relax a little, have some lunch. Then I have to get over to the party supply store I manage and work an afternoon shift."

"Okay. Then what?"

"I guess I'll just go home and have some dinner, maybe read a little and go to bed."

Garrett stared at me, expressionless, then nodded a few

times while rubbing his knees.

"Thanks," he said. "It's kind of nice to know I'm not missing too much. All right, let's do this."

Glad I was able to inspire.

After making a mental note to add some more excitement in my life, I reviewed the exit procedure with Garrett and asked if he had any special requests.

"Actually, yes – I'd like very much for you to read from this," he said, handing me a paperback copy of *Finnegans Wake*. "I find the nonsensical language Joyce uses throughout and the lack of any coherent plot to be quite soothing."

"Really? Most readers just scratch their head and toss the book after trying to tackle the first three pages."

"That's because they're trying to understand it. That's the first mistake. We do it with everything."

I just nodded and smiled. There simply wasn't time for deep existential or literary discourse. Canasta games don't last forever; it only seems that way.

"So, is there any particular passage you want to hear?" I asked.

"Nah, just open it up to anywhere."

A minute later Garrett was all hooked up and I began reading from a random page.

"Yes, the viability of vicinals if invisible is invincible. And we are not trespassing on his corns either. Look at all the plotsch! Fluminian! If this was Hannibal's walk it was Hercules' work. And a hungried thousand of the unemancipated slaved the way. …"

Garrett leaned back on the sofa, closed his eyes and folded his hands over his stomach, looking more like a man listening to Motzart than to gibberish. It was obvious he didn't need Zoe by his side to help calm him, but there she was. And after reciting three full pages of a dream language I couldn't pretend to comprehend, I said a final goodbye to both of them.

CHAPTER 29

There's nothing quite like a perfectly executed suicide to get you feeling right again. Sure, I was still grieving over Zoe, but my renewed commitment to my clients helped stop the spiral. Most of the pain and all of the panic and confusion had lifted. Thoughts of the crazed schedule ahead left me feeling Herculean. I was unfazed by the idea of being detained, of being convicted and locked away. There was only one thing at this point that I looked upon with dread.

Dinner with my mother. In three hours.

She still didn't know about Zoe. I would have to tell her that evening. It was not going to be easy explaining why I'd waited over a week to notify her of the tragic death of the girlfriend I'd never bothered to introduce to her. Making matters worse, it was Sunday. The liquor stores were closed. I'd have to bring a bottle from home. It wouldn't be a full one.

On the drive over, fueled by a couple shots of liquor, I tried to come up with a legitimate excuse to give my mother. "I was too despondent to talk" was a viable option and not too far from the truth, but lame nonetheless. Moreover, it was disrespectful. Jewish mothers lived for sharing their children's despondency, and I'd robbed mine of a big opportunity. After mulling over a few other options, ranging from "It kills me to see you cry" to "I misplaced my phone and car keys," I decided I'd go with "I went completely mad." The perfect defense. For proof of my brief bout of insanity, I'd embellish and explain how I'd spent the past several days wandering around Wal-Mart.

When I pulled up to the house where I grew up and saw what was in the driveway, I realized I might need more than just one alibi.

Parked next to my mother's Honda Accord was an Oregon state police squad car.

Perhaps Mom had stolen somebody's tee time. More likely, however, was that the police had come to question her before charging me with whatever crime or crimes they had uncovered. Murder. Manslaughter. Aiding and abetting. Impersonating a terminal disease support group member.

I thought to park down the street and wait until the police left, but just as I pressed the accelerator, the front door of the house swung open and out came two officers.

They were escorting my mother to their car. She was wearing handcuffs.

I quickly swerved into the driveway and parked behind the squad car, startling both officers and prompting one to grab his holster. Not entirely sold on getting shot, I opened my door slowly and stepped out with my hands clearly visible.

"What's going on here, officers? You okay, Mom?"

"It's okay, Eli," she answered quietly. "I'm fine."

"This doesn't look fine."

"Sir, Mrs. Edelmann is under arrest for the murder of Mr. David Edelmann," one of the officers said coldly.

"Murder? David... my FATHER? What are you talking

about? My father died of cancer nearly two years ago!"

"Sir, the suspect has already given us a confession."

"A confession? This is crazy!" I looked at my mother, who was hanging her head. "Mom?"

"Get her in the car," the officer said to his partner before turning back to me. "I'm sorry, but we have to take her to the station for booking."

I stood there, stunned and helpless, as my mother was placed in the back seat.

"Can't I just talk to her for a minute?" I asked.

"I'm afraid not. You can follow us to the station and wait there, but you're not likely going to get a chance to speak to the suspect until after she's transferred to a holding cell over at our homicide unit."

"My mom is going to jail?"

"A holding cell. For now."

"This is insane!"

"Please calm down, sir. Are you okay to follow us? We'd like to have you answer a few questions."

"And I've got a couple of my own."

"So you'll come down?"

"Yes, I'll be right behind you."

Few things are as disturbing as witnessing the arrest of the woman who used to pack your Snoopy lunchbox and cut off your crusts. Not until I was in my car on the way to the station did I fully understand why the officer had asked me if I was okay to follow them.

Words like murder and homicide and holding cell don't mix with mother. And none of them mix with whiskey. Especially on an empty stomach. I was angry I had missed dinner. And angry with myself for being angry about that.

Whatever Mom had cooked, I hoped she had turned off the oven.

While driving behind the dark blue Dodge Charger carrying my handcuffed mother, I couldn't stop thinking there's no golf in prison. Not even a putting green. My mother wouldn't survive one week.

I also thought about how she had done it. Murdered my father. Though I had a pretty good idea.

When we arrived at the station, the officer who had tucked my mother into the squad car quickly escorted her out of the vehicle and up the walkway to the station entrance. This before I'd even cut my engine. It was obvious they didn't want us interacting. The other officer – the one who'd done all the talking earlier – got out of the car and walked over to mine. For the first time I noticed his name badge. Detective Ellison. He motioned for me to lower my window.

"I'll take you inside now," he said.

I got out and followed him into the station, which was surprisingly busy for a Sunday evening. Apparently Blackport wasn't as law-abiding and low-key as I had always assumed. Not that I was impressed. The air was thick with the smell of domestic disturbances and DUIs. So unimaginative.

Walking through the bustling station with Detective Ellison, I searched for my mother, hoping I could at least flash her a quick forgiving smile to carry along with her. No such luck. She had already been removed from public view. Like a criminal.

Detective Ellison brought me to a small, gray room equipped with only a table and two chairs. A large rectangular window looked out to the hallway.

"Please take a seat and wait here," said Detective Ellison. "Either myself or my partner will be with you as soon as we can."

"How soon might that be?"

"Hard to say."

"Fifteen minutes? An hour?"

"Perhaps somewhere in that range."

"Is there any way I could score something to read? A magazine maybe?"

Detective Ellison scowled. "Why don't you worry a little more about your mother and a little less about how you're going to entertain yourself?" he said before leaving the room and shutting the door behind him.

How strange to be in that room not as a prime suspect but rather merely as a possible witness. There I was, somebody who, by the state's definition, had murdered (or been behind the murder of) nearly two dozen people – three in the last three weeks – being asked to help shed light on a single iso-lated homicide perpetrated by someone else. It was like asking Ted Bundy if he'd seen any suspicious activity in and around his neighborhood.

The police may not have had anything solid they could stick to me, but if they were paying attention and taking even mediocre notes, they surely suspected me and my family of first-degree drama and dysfunction. Mom killing my dying dad. Me dating a girl who'd very recently offed herself, and whose ex had been murdered. When enough such incidents accumulate, however unrelated they may be or seem, it becomes exceedingly difficult to continue living quietly in the shadows.

It wasn't long, perhaps 20 minutes, before Detective Ellison returned, startling me when he abruptly opened the door.

"Your mother has given us a complete confession on the record, so we're going to allow you to speak to her before she's taken over to a holding cell. It's not customary, but since she's already come clean and waived her right to counsel, there's no harm in letting you two talk."

"I appreciate it," I said, not yet fully absorbing what I'd been told.

"We'll bring her in momentarily."

I'd soon be walking out of the station with my freedom completely intact. Meanwhile, my mother would be getting prepped for prison. It was too surreal and sorrowful to believe.

As Detective Ellison and his partner escorted my mother into the room, I was relieved to see they'd removed her handcuffs. She looked at me and bit her upper lip to keep from crying, then sat down on the chair across from me. I reached out with both hands and touched her wrists, which were still red and bruised from the shackles.

"We'll give you two five minutes alone," said Detective Ellison.

"Will you be able to hear everything we say?" I asked.

"No. We haven't turned on the speaker or the audio surveillance monitor in this room," he replied.

"Okay. We're grateful for the privacy."

Detective Ellison nodded. He and his partner, whose nameplate I could now see read Palatnik, walked out before shutting the door behind them.

"I'm so sorry to put you through all this, Eli," said my mother, her voice weak and shaking.

"I still don't know what you did exactly," I responded, doing my best not to let on that I, in fact, had a very strong hunch. "What the hell are they talking about you 'murdered' Dad?"

"I know. They make it sound so horrible, but trust me, it wasn't."

"Mom, what did you DO?"

"I did what your father needed me to do."

"You helped him... die? Like, like a mercy killing?"

"Yes. Eli, he just couldn't stand it anymore. He *asked* me to do it."

"What, exactly?"

My mother proceeded to tell me a story that, unbeknownst to her, didn't surprise me. Most of it, anyway. How a conversation between my father and Sgt. Rush had sparked the plan. Why helium was used and how it was administered. How hard it was keeping everything from me. How close she had come to slipping on a hood herself at the height of her grief. And how glad she was that she didn't – how she'd come to not only accept what she'd done, but to feel proud to have been able to end such suffering.

And I had thought we didn't have anything in common.

After feigning shock and offering real empathy, I asked something I truly did not know the answer to. "How did the police find out?"

"One of the ladies I golf with, Jan Rosow, spilled the beans. I told her my secret one afternoon a couple of weeks ago after having had a few too many vodka gimlets in the clubhouse. She, or somebody she blabbed to, must have notified the police. I helped this woman lower her handicap by six strokes, and this is how she repays me!"

"Why did you confess so readily when the cops came for you?" I asked. "It was just your word against Mrs. Rosow's. There was no tangible proof you did anything."

"I can't lie like that, especially to the police. I figured I'd come clean, you know, do the right thing, and hope to get the minimum sentence."

"You wouldn't have had to lie, Mom. You could have just said nothing and waited to lawyer up. That's what 'You have the right to remain silent' means."

"Well excuse me! It's not like I regularly have run-ins with the law and am well versed on what the hell to do in these situations."

"I realize that, but you've watched enough *Law and Order* to know you shut up when the cops come!"

"I still don't really think I did anything wrong!"

"It doesn't matter what you think, Mom. State law sees it as murder. That's what you're going to go to jail for. *Murder!* You still glad you confessed?"

My mother glared at me, snorting through her nose, like she had just hooked three straight shots into a sand trap. Moments later, when her face returned from red to pale, the tears started rolling.

She wasn't crying because she'd been apprehended, or over the prospect of prison, or because she'd been forced to relive the death of her husband repeatedly. She was crying because her beloved son was too busy bombarding her with "should haves" and "could haves" to recognize her extraordinary strength.

Releasing a whole host of strangers and casual acquaintances was one thing. Releasing your husband and half your life was another thing entirely.

I reached across the table with my right hand and stroked my mother's face.

"It's okay, Mom. Everything's going to be all right."

"I'm… so sorry," she barely managed to utter.

"Shhh. You have no reason to be sorry."

Our moment was disrupted by a rap on the interrogation room window. Outside stood Detective Ellison holding up his index finger and mouthing, "One minute."

I nodded and looked back at my mother.

"Listen Mom," I said quietly. "There's no time for me to explain the details now, but I have a plan. After I speak to these guys, they're probably going to want to talk to you again. Don't say anything except that you *didn't* do it, that you gave a false confession. Then tell them you want to talk to your lawyer, and then don't say another word."

"But I already confessed."

"I know, don't worry. You've got to trust me on this. It's your only chance. Just maintain that you didn't do it, lawyer up, then shut up."

"I don't like this, Eli."

"Do you prefer 20 years to life? Please, just do as I say."

"Okay, I'll try."

"Now, about before, I'm sorry I shouted. I'm not angry with you. I'm just very upset with the world that you got caught."

My mother smiled and wiped away the tears streaming down her cheek. "So, you think I did the right thing, Eli?"

I placed my hand softly on hers, leaned across the table

and whispered, "I would have done exactly the same."

Maybe it was the thought of my mother eating the remainder of her meals off a tin tray and never again gripping a nine iron.

Maybe it was knowing one day Mr. Magoo would step out in mid air and find no girder waiting to carry him safely away.

Maybe I was viewing the recent news of a helium shortage (and the associated price hike) as a sign.

Maybe.

But what it mostly came down to was a change in purpose.

I could continue ending many lives, or I could save my mother's.

Detective Ellison, Detective Palatnik and a policewoman I hadn't seen before were waiting for us when we exited the interrogation room. I kissed mother on the cheek, and as she was getting whisked away by the unknown officer, I said loud enough for all to hear, "You'll be a free woman very soon, Mom. I'm going to tell them what *really* happened."

When she and the officer disappeared around a corner, I turned to face a confused Detective Ellison.

"We need to talk," I said. I looked through the window of the interrogation room. "Can we go in there?"

"What did you mean you're going to tell us what *really* happened?"

"Let's go sit down and I'll explain everything. And this time you can record everything."

Detective Ellison opened the door to the room and motioned for me to enter. Detective Palatnik tapped him on the shoulder and asked, "You got this? I've got a ton of reports to catch up on."

"Yeah, I can handle it," Detective Ellison responded before following me into the room.

He sat down at the table. I remained standing.

"You might want to hold off on transferring my mother to the homicide unit," I said as I started to pace the floor.

"I already told you, she gave us a full confession," Detective Ellison responded, looking aggravated. "There's no gray area here."

"What she told you is a lie."

"Listen, Mr. Edelmann, I understand you are upset about all that's happened, but if this is just some desperate ploy to—"

"There's nothing desperate about my ploy, Officer. I'm telling you, with certainty, my mother didn't euthanize my father."

"Then why did she confess that she did?"

"To protect the person who actually carried out the act."

"And who was that?"

"Just give me a minute. I'll get to that."

"But she confessed to a friend before the police were even *involved*. Why would she do that?"

"She was drunk. Did you know that? When she told her friend, she was blitzed on vodka gimlets and didn't really know what the hell she was saying."

"People don't confess to murder when—"

"Euthanasia."

"Fine – people don't confess to *euthanasia* when they're inebriated."

"*Falsely* confess."

"That's even more outlandish."

"Officer, I knew a guy who got drunk off his ass one night and told me and some other friends that he killed a guy back in high school. Turns out it was a total fabrication. Sometimes people like to cause shock, to invent stories when they feel they don't have anything truly interesting to share. Especially when they're intoxicated."

"But in the case of your friend, there was probably no body ever found, right? That was just some idiot telling tales. But your mother, there *was* a body involved – that of her sick *husband* – and everything she confessed to adds up."

"My father *was* euthanized, but my mother didn't do it. Who knows why she told her friend she did. I can't get inside the mind of an inebriated post-menopausal suburban woman."

"Then why didn't she vehemently deny the charges when we came to arrest her? Why didn't she insist she did nothing and that your father had simply died of his advanced cancer? We still would have brought her in for questioning, of course, but she'd have a heck of a lot more of a defense than she does now."

"I'll tell you why – loyalty. She probably knew there'd be an investigation and didn't want the person she's protecting to get dragged into it."

"Then I'll ask you again – who is she protecting?"

"One of your own."

"What, you mean a *cop*?"

"Yes sir."

"Uh, care to give me a *name*?"

"Sgt. William Rush."

"Sgt. *Rush? Medal of Valor* Sgt. Rush? *Award for Divisional Achievement* Sgt. Rush? *Two-time Officer of the Year* Sgt. Rush? I'm supposed to believe that one of the finest and most decorated men who ever worked on our force killed – oh, sorry – *euthanized* your father?"

"No, you're not supposed to believe it. It's unbelievable. But it's also the truth."

"Why in the hell would Sgt. Rush have gotten wrapped up in something like that?"

"He and my father were very good friends."

"So your father asked his friend – a retired *police sergeant* – to kill him?"

"Euthanize."

"Whatever!"

"Well, the thing is, it was actually Sgt. Rush who first mentioned the whole helium thing as an option. A little while after Mrs. Rush died and Sgt. Rush's emphysema started to get worse, he joked to my father about renting one of the helium tanks from his party supply shop and 'checking out.' My father didn't really get the joke, so Sgt. Rush explained how he had read that helium inhalation was the most humane and the cleanest method of suicide. From then on, whenever one of them was feeling down or frustrated, they'd say in jest, 'It's time to bring in the helium.'"

"Okay, but Sgt. Rush joking about such a thing and *actually* helping a friend do it are two very different things."

"When my father's cancer reached Stage IV and showed no signs of slowing down, he truly wanted out. One night while Sgt. Rush was over visiting, my father made the familiar 'It's time to bring in the helium' joke, only Sgt. Rush could tell he wasn't really joking. That's when he offered to help my father."

"I don't buy that Sgt. Rush would knowingly commit a class 1 felony."

"First of all, let's put this in context. I know that what he did is considered 'murder' in the State's eyes, but does Sgt. Rush sound like a murderer to you in this scenario? Secondly, don't forget that Sgt. Rush was quite ill himself, and because of that he probably had less fear of getting caught than another man might have."

"How do you know so much detail about what you allege happened between your father and Sgt. Rush?" Detective Ellison sounded less incredulous than he had moments earlier.

"My mother and I didn't know anything about any of this until a month or so after my father died. Mom invited Sgt. Rush over for dinner one night and the three of us got to talking about Mrs. Rush and about my father and about how much it sucked that two such wonderful people had to die before their time and suffer so much. Alcohol was involved, of course, and my mother got a little over-emotional – even for a woman who'd lost her husband a month earlier – and started bawling and saying how guilty she felt for being out golfing the afternoon my father died and how she'd always wonder how much pain and suffering he endured in that house all alone. So–"

"Why was your mother out golfing if her husband was so sick at home?"

"My father *told* her to go. He'd had a relatively decent few days and said he was feeling particularly good that afternoon. He told my mom not to worry about him, that she deserved some sunshine and fresh air."

"Okay, go on."

"So, as I was saying, my mother was beside herself with grief and guilt after dinner. That's when Sgt. Rush said, 'I have to tell you something that I hope will ease your worries about what happened to David.' He then proceeded to tell us all about the plan, about what he had done for my father, about how he had come to the house with the helium tank and a special hood thingy while my mother was out golfing and gave my father – and I remember this is exactly how Sgt. Rush put it – 'the peaceful ending he wanted and deserved.'"

"How did your mother and you react to that news?"

"At first we were somewhat in shock. Amazed really. I could tell Sgt. Rush was bracing for an angry response from us, but my mother and I, though stunned, were incredibly moved by his account of what happened. I mean, we had some questions and it took a few minutes for everything to sink in, but afterward we felt... lighter. Knowing that my father had died on his own terms and with a close friend by his side, well, it helped us a lot. I know Sgt. Rush was supposed to keep it all a secret, but he did us – especially my mother – a very big favor sharing what he shared. And of course we promised him that his secret was safe with us."

"Until now."

"Yes, and that's on me. My mother, she held true to her word. She'd sooner do time for a 'murder' she didn't commit than give up the man who risked everything for her husband. Me, I just can't sit idly by and let her rot in jail for this. And I know Sgt. Rush wouldn't have either."

Detective Ellison bowed his head and rubbed his temples with one hand as he sighed loudly. "You do realize that since your mother and you knew about what you allege happened and didn't notify the authorities, you both could be charged with being an 'accessory after the fact.'"

"Yes, but I can live with us each doing a few years for something we are actually guilty of. I *cannot* live with my mother doing 10 to 20 or more for something she didn't do."

Detective Ellison rubbed his temples again. "What a god-damn mess," he muttered before standing up from the table. "I'll be back in few minutes. You're going to have to wait here again."

He walked toward the door and turned to me as he opened it. "Can I get you some water or coffee?"

"No thanks, I'm good," I said as I watched him leave. The door locked behind him.

I sat down, having been standing since Detective Ellison and I had entered the room. My legs could no longer support me. I'd expended all my energy on the most elaborate lie I'd ever told. Spun fact into fiction and vice versa, weaving an intricate tapestry of inverted and imagined truths, a tapestry I wished I could see and worried I couldn't duplicate.

I was going to jail, as was my mother. I just didn't yet know on what charges. If the tapestry kept its stitching, we were both looking at accessory after the fact. If the stitching fell apart, I was looking at obstructing justice, my mother at murder. Neither of my crimes would intimidate my fellow inmates, but at least the boys would know I'd had somebody's back. I'd still have to stay alert in the showers, but not as alert as the pedophiles, the wife abusers and the snitches.

I thought about whom I was going to spend my one phone call on. Carl, to tell him to take good care of the shop? My condo leasing office, to find out if subletting was permitted? Or Penelope Grayson, my next scheduled client (bladder cancer), to break the bad news that she'd have to live a little longer?

Other, more inane thoughts and concerns occupied my mind while awaiting Detective Ellison's return. With my mother serving time and my father and Zoe dead, would I ever receive a visitor while incarcerated? Could a mother-son prisoner visit be arranged? Were orange jumpsuits still the standard? Was Nietzsche on the prison's "prohibited reading" list? If given the choice, would I take the top bunk or the bottom? Was I subconsciously thinking euphemistically?

Fortunately before my mind could wander any further astray, Detective Ellison returned, looking exasperated.

"By the way, I'm sorry about your girlfriend," he said as he sat down and resumed rubbing his temples. "We ran you through the system earlier... I saw you were the one who found her. That's rough."

"Thank you," I said, not able to tell if he was simply offering condolences or preparing to complicate matters significantly. Who knew what they had on me at this point.

"Now, back to the matter at hand," he continued. "Let's say I buy your story about—"

"I'm not *selling* any stories."

"How about you let me finish?"

"Sorry."

"If Sgt. Rush was indeed the person who euthanized your father, I still don't get why your mother is willing to go to prison for him. I mean, it's honorable and all, but why protect a dead man? It's not like Sgt. Rush can get in any trouble now."

"My mother feels forever indebted to him for what he did. She also knows what a pillar he was in the community, and I guess she doesn't want his name getting dragged through the mud. She doesn't want his family – his daughter and grand-children – to endure what the media and the general populace will do with this. She knows not everybody will view what he did as being noble. She does. I do. But we're not everybody."

Detective Ellison's temple-rubbing continued. I feared his fingers would eat through the skin on the side of his skull.

"I spoke to our captain about this," he said. "About your mother's arrest and confession, and about your detailed account that contradicts it."

"And?"

"He asked me what I thought about your story. I–"

"It's not a story," I interjected.

"It's best you shut up now, Mr. Edelmann."

"Sorry."

"I told him a man would try anything to save his mother."

"That's true, but what I told you actually happened. I couldn't make that stuff up."

We create our own reality.

"I think you could. You seem like a pretty bright guy, Mr. Edelmann."

"Oh c'mon. If I had that level of imagination, I'd be writing novels or making movies – not managing a measly party supply store. You *have* to know I'm not lying."

"No, I don't have to know you're not lying. I *don't* know you're not lying. However, I also don't know that you *are*. We have a polygraph machine for that."

"Fine, hook me up right now."

You can change the world by changing your mind.

"I didn't say I was going to *use* the polygraph, I just explained why we *have* it."

"Well, I'm ready to take the test if you decide to give it."

"I'm actually going to give you something better."

"What's that?"

"The benefit of the doubt."

This has to be a trick, a ploy to get me to drop my guard.

"What do you mean?" I asked. "What happens now?"

"What happens now is we release you and your mother."

"What, you mean on bail, right?"

"No, there's no bail. All charges are being dropped."

"Even accessory after the fact?"

"Correct."

"That's fantastic! I don't really know what to say."

"Well, there's been a sort of new development that helps your case."

"A new development?"

"I'm not at liberty to elaborate, Mr. Edelmann. Just know that my captain informed me of something pertinent while he and I were talking. So, rest assured, we aren't just releasing you on a lark."

Utter confusion coupled with elation. There needs to be a word for that. What you'd feel if a complete stranger left you $1 million in their will. Or if you fell asleep in a bus station in Newark and woke up on a beach in Bora Bora. Or if you were given a stay of execution with no explanation.

It's what I felt while waiting for my mother to be returned from the homicide unit back to the precinct. It's certainly what my mother felt while being transported. Not until after we got to her house – after I'd spent the entire drive recounting the story I'd told Detective Ellison – did the confusion begin to wear away. Turns out my mother knew a little something about the "new development" Detective Ellison had mentioned.

"Sgt. Rush told your father something that your father swore he'd never tell anybody," my mother said while we sipped some of the whiskey I had brought for our Sunday dinner. "But your father told me a few days before he died."

"And what was that?" I asked.

"What I did for your father, Sgt. Rush had already done for Mrs. Rush. After her cancer became untreatable."

"You mean he… with helium?"

"Yes. It's how he knew it worked so well. It's why he came to your father when he himself got sick."

"Wow. Mrs. Rush. That must have been extremely difficult for him."

My mother made a face like a trick-or-treater who'd gotten skipped in the candy line.

"Oh, I'm sorry, Mom. I got so caught up in the story I told the police I almost forgot that it was you who… assisted Dad."

"It's okay. You are right about it being very hard. But I'd do it again."

I felt the same way after MY first time.

"We don't have to talk about it now," I said, eager to uncover the reason behind our sudden release from the precinct just half an hour earlier. "So how does what Sgt. Rush did five years ago relate to the 'new development' today?"

"It seems some of the men he worked with suspected

him of 'assisting' Mrs. Rush, at least that's what he told your father. Sgt. Rush said nobody said anything specific or took any action against him, though. He said he felt he was kind of protected. So today, when the officer who was questioning you went to speak to his captain, I'm thinking the captain knew or had heard something about what Sgt. Rush had done, or *allegedly* done. I bet the captain shared this information with the detective and told him that your seemingly crazy story was entirely plausible."

"So Sgt. Rush saved our asses?"

"My ass especially. All you did was lie to save your mother. I, on the other hand, was facing murder!"

"Actually," I said, "despite my story sort of checking out, they still could have charged us both with 'accessory after the fact' since we, according *to* my story, knew about Sgt. Rush's deed but didn't report it. But I guess they respected us for protecting him, and they weren't about to let his legend become tainted during a trial."

I raised my glass of whiskey in the air. My mother followed suit.

"To Sgt. Rush," I said.

"To Sgt. Rush," said my mother, brushing away a tear, her wrist still visibly bruised from the handcuffs she had worn just a couple hours earlier.

Though we were in the clear with the police, I couldn't afford to let my guard down. Not even with my mother, despite what we had just gone through together, despite knowing she had an exit of her own under her belt. My mother had gotten away with the kindest murder, but I wasn't ready to share with her my underworld. I knew how loose her lips got after a few drinks.

I was relieved when, later on that night, our relationship resumed normal mother-son status. She asking me if I wanted a sandwich. Saying my hair was getting too long. Telling me to take my feet off the coffee table.

And I guess she wouldn't have been fulfilling her motherly duties if she didn't ask her son about his love life.

"How's that girlfriend of yours?"

I decided on the spot there had been enough drama for one day.

"We're no longer together, Mom. She's back in Denver."

"What? When did this happen?"

"Almost two weeks ago."

"You really should keep your mother better informed about what's going on in your life. I mean, what's the point of you living in the same city as me if you never call or visit?"

"You're right, Mom. I'll work on that."

"Good," said my mother, patting my knee with her hand. "So, besides losing a girlfriend I never got to meet, what have you been up to lately?"

"Not much," I replied. "Just trying to keep all my customers happy."

"So business has been steady, huh?"

"Sure has. And it doesn't show any signs of slowing down."

ABOUT THE AUTHOR

Having spent much of his life weaving intricate tales to get out of things like gym class and jury duty, Greg Levin is no stranger to fiction. Greg's debut novel, *Notes on an Orange Burial* was published in November 2011 by Elixirist (now 48fourteen) and has sold over 11 copies to his immediate family. Greg's second book, *The Exit Man*, is already being hailed as one of the top two novels he has ever written.

When not busy writing, Greg enjoys *thinking* about writing, and spending time with his wife and daughter. He also enjoys cooking, traveling and exercising, as well as freestyle rapping for his friends even when they don't do anything to deserve such mistreatment.

Greg was born in Huntington, New York in 1969, and then moved to Harrisburg, Pennsylvania with his family when he was six. He attended the University of New Hampshire and graduated summa cum laude in 1991 with a BA in Communication and a special concentration in Creative Writing.

Greg currently resides in Austin, Texas, where he is one of just 17 people who don't play a musical instrument or write songs. He is currently wanted by Austin authorities for refusing to eat pork ribs or dance the two-step.

greglevin.com

ACKNOWLEDGEMENTS

There simply isn't enough space here to thank everybody who has helped me along my writing and life path. Here's an earnest attempt at a condensed version:

First and foremost, I would like to thank the collie I grew up with – Cinnamon – who has been dead for 30 years but who always truly believed in me. I'd also like to thank my wonderful parents, all the English teachers and writing coaches I've had in my life, my amazing wife, my awesome brothers, my bright and beautiful daughter, and the kid who way back in little league hit me in the head with a fastball that damaged my cerebral cortex just enough to enable me to come up with the kinds of stories I write. Actually, I should probably thank that kid even more than I thank my dead collie. Oh yeah, and I certainly want to thank all my readers – you marvelous, marvelous people.

Special thanks to Deputy Williams of the Travis County Sherriff's Department (Austin, Texas) for taking the time to verify the accuracy and plausibility of some of the scenes depicting police work in this book.

CPSIA information can be obtained at www.ICGtesting.com
Printed in the USA
LVOW10s1519280116

472715LV00018B/1239/P